PRAISE FOR
BROGAN THOMAS

Brogan's writing has such depth, it's impossible not to fall in love with her amazing characters. Her books are fast paced, fun and so emotive. I'm rooting for her main characters with everything in me and Brogan never disappoints.

— HEATHER G HARRIS AUTHOR

Brogan Thomas is brilliant; she is creative with an incredible imagination. Her world-building is phenomenal, packed with all types of supernatural components. The characters are well-developed, definitely appealing, and fascinating.

— GOODREADS REVIEWER

From the moment I opened this book, I fell deeply in love. The author draws you in with splendid visuals, great character development, and a compelling storyline.

— AMAZON REVIEWER

REBEL
UNICORN

REBEL
OF THE
OTHERWORLD

REBEL
UNICORN

1

BROGAN THOMAS

Published by Brogan Thomas
WWW.BROGANTHOMAS.COM

Copyright © 2023 by Brogan Thomas

Ebook ASIN: B0B3XPSR2K
Paperback ISBN: 9781915946003
Hardcover ISBN: 9781915946010

Edited by Victory Editing and proofread by Sam Everard.
Cover design by Luminescence Covers

For my hubby

CHAPTER
ONE

I WIGGLE MY SHOULDERS, and a low moan rumbles in my throat as sweat beads down my spine and soaks into my black combat top. Gross. About now, I could really do with a spell to keep myself cool.

I snort. Yeah, right. Those things are super expensive, and I use them to keep myself alive, not to make myself comfortable. I'd rather be sweaty than broke. I stifle another moan. I'm so not a hot-weather fan. I'd rather add layers to keep warm than wish I could peel the skin off my bones.

Summer is way more irritating. I much prefer winter. I love those perfect English mornings when the sky is bright blue and everything is cold and crisp. The world looks so much prettier with a dusting of ice. For those first few hours in the morning, it covers all the crap and makes even the worst eyesore look magical. Except for that one time when I was a kid and I was homeless. I didn't like winter then. No, that winter was horrendous.

Instead, it's August and the country is going through a heatwave, and tonight is unpleasant and muggy. To add more insult to the mix, what feels like a million of those horrendous biting flies are zipping around me like flying piranhas.

Usually the little monsters don't bite me. I don't make much of a snack—something to do with the awful taste of my hybrid blood—but tonight the little suckers... I moan louder and rub my burning face on my shoulder. They are in good form. I'll give them that.

An old memory skips and shudders to the forefront of my mind. I duck my head and rub my mouth to muffle a laugh. As a kid, I once asked my adoptive grandad if the flies consumed my blood, would I turn them into vampire midges? He laughed for about twenty minutes. I don't know what he found so damn funny. At the time, I thought it was a valid question. If not a horrific thought. *Vampire midges.* I shudder.

Gosh, I miss him. It has been nine years, but it feels like only yesterday since his premature death. *The Reaper takes all the best people first.* Isn't that the truth.

Uncomfortable with both my thoughts and the solid, unyielding ridged roof sheet I'm lying on, I rock from side to side. Being stuck in this prone position is causing my lower back to ache. *It shouldn't be too much longer.* I know from experience that with jobs like this, you must have the patience of a saint.

I drag my arms into a better position, and my left hand trembles. I stuff the annoying limb underneath my chin and

2

do my best to ignore it. It makes me look like a blood junkie. Hand tremors are the first unpleasant reminder; I'm overdue a ration, and seeing my blood donor is... awkward.

"Stand by," I whisper when I catch the distant sound of an approaching vehicle.

The rhythmic squeaking behind me stops.

I don't have to look at the wolf shifter to know my whispered words have gained her attention, and while I still have some foresight to keep most of my awareness on the road and on any unfriendly company within the rapidly approaching car, my eyes, without my permission, are drawn to her.

Forrest.

I do a mental eye roll. She's still hanging upside down on the leftover scaffolding. Hanging by her knees like a manic monkey. Her pale pink hair pools onto the roof, washed almost white by the moonlight. I refrain from shaking my head, and I barely conceal my exasperation, which also contains a splash of amusement and perhaps a smidgen of jealousy.

Such wacky yet endearing behaviour. There is something to be said about being strong enough not to care what other people think, and that shifter has nailed it. She has the ultimate freedom of being unique. Plus it looks like she's having fun hanging up there.

The pink-haired shifter is my sole backup, and I admit I'm lucky to have her. I've heard plenty of rumours about her history—the creatures in our world love to talk—but there is no way I'm asking for her story. If you look beyond her compact, tiny pink packaging, Forrest projects a quiet menace. You just know by gut feeling or sixth sense that aggravating her is a terrible idea. One look in those cold, dead yellow eyes of hers expels that silly notion. Even now, as she hangs upside down like a child, she stares back at me blankly.

She is not right in the head and is more wolf than person.

An unpleasant shiver follows the sweat trickling down my spine, and I give her a respectful nod. I turn my full attention back to the road just as a black car trundles around the corner and into the empty industrial estate. The tyres crunch against the tarmac and grind against the kerb as it pulls up to the nondescript warehouse. A warehouse we are crouched upon.

The front passenger door clicks open, and a big vampire gets out. As he adjusts his cheap suit, the car door thuds closed behind him. He takes in the surrounding area with a narrow-eyed glare. He doesn't even think to look up. I recognise his face. He's a prominent target.

My lips part as each one of my breaths becomes shallow. Adrenaline sloshes through my system, and in response to the spike of the neurotransmitter and hormone, my limbs tingle with the need to move. I love this part of my job. *The hunting.* It must be the vampire side of me that enjoys stalking prey.

Two other men exit the back of the vehicle. I smile. Bingo. My smile fades as my somewhat insistent inner voice cuts through my excitement like a knife. *Come on, Tru. It's not too late for you to go home. You know this isn't your fight.*

I can fight. I scowl and roll my shoulders. I train hard to keep myself and my chosen family safe, but I know from experience there will always be a creature who can and will wipe the floor with me. Like most normal people, I don't enjoy a fist to the face, and even though I can shift to heal, pain is still pain.

Yes, I'm an assassin, but I complete my contracts from a distance using illegal long-range weapons or from the shadows, and unlike the wolf shifter and her fearsome reputation, I'm not one to smash my way through a problem. That's how you get hurt or, worse, get someone you love killed.

The door to the warehouse opens, and the vampires shuffle inside.

I know my apprehension is justified. The once small and simple assassination job I started with this morning has somehow morphed into this clustersuck of epic proportions.

Isn't that the way of things?

This situation is well above my training and pay grade. There are so many professionals better suited to do this than me. I'm not a soldier.

Yeah, Tru, you are not good enough. I once again ignore my nasty thoughts and the screaming gut feeling that insists things are about to go spectacularly wrong. I push away the worry. It's us or nothing, and there are *kids* involved. I can't walk away. I won't.

A tiny click sounds, followed by a tweak of pain in the middle of my forehead, and I signal Forrest to get ready. *Targets confirmed. All targets are a go.* I wince as the soft, lilting voice of Story, my best friend, explodes in my head. The communication spell is an unpleasant scratch against my brain.

Forrest hums a tune under her breath. I frown. Is that...

I tilt my head and hold my breath to listen. "Mission Impossible?" It is. I huff out a silent laugh and then focus on a final weapon check as the humming wolf shifter prowls towards me.

Now at my side, Forrest gives me a nudge. "Tru." She wiggles her right hand in front of my face. An impressive set of six-inch claws tips her fingers.

"Wow," I whisper with a nod of appreciation. I press my hands against my thighs to stop myself from touching them. I can't remember seeing anyone else do a partial shift in real life. It's a powerful thing. You've got to be at least six hundred years old to be strong enough to do it.

No way is she that old. No, she is like me.

Forrest is as powerful as the whispers say. No wonder she scares the crap out of everyone. Good for her.

The wolf stares down at my pinned hands as if to say "Go on then. I've shown you mine; you show me yours."

I smile ruefully and shake my head.

"What? I thought you were badass. Aren't you a super-strong hybrid or something?"

Oh, I am.

"Can't you shift your hands?" Her voice is shockingly rough, like the kind of rough where instead of water every morning after she brushes her teeth, she gargles with glass. It's not the voice of a girl who is barely over five foot with pale pink hair.

"Me? No." I scoff. I wave my arm in the air and loosely ball my hand into a fist. "Hooves," I explain. I grin and wiggle my fingers. "Not as useful as your claws. It would be... you know, weird."

"Oh yeah. I forgot about the unicorn thing." She slaps her forehead. "Awkward."

I pull out my phone.

"Cool. That is so cool. Unicorns are my favourite creature. I have these epic fluffy unicorn pyjamas..." Forrest is kind of oblivious to the fact that I can still hear her as she continues to mumble about claws, hooves, and unicorns.

I side-eye her as she waffles. Apart from the planning stage and a few grunted words, Forrest never said anything during the time we've been waiting. She has made zero small talk, and we have been waiting for hours. So this transformation from a slightly unhinged but consummate professional to a unicorn fan is jarring.

Her dead eyes sparkle, and her hands flop around animatedly as she whispers. She then lifts her top and flashes me her unicorn sports bra.

I blink a few times, nod, and hand her one of the military-grade sleeping spells we are going to use to render the baddies inert.

Still nodding, I *slowly* back away.

Forrest is still talking.

I glance down at the phone to double-check the footage of the cameras inside the building. A few hours ago, when I realised this wasn't a single assassination but a rescue mission, I launched hundreds of microscopic flying surveillance cameras into the warehouse.

All the baddies are chatting with the new vampires. I stuff the phone back into my pocket and move to the gap in the roof where a transparent roof sheet used to be.

With precision, I lower myself onto one of the steel roof beams and drop into a crouch.

It says a lot about me. That I'm more willing to face a warehouse full of killers than deal with the excited, unicorn-loving wolf shifter. I ready the first sleeping grenade.

"What...? Tru? Tru? Where did you go...?"

There's a moment of silence. I stare up at the gap in the roof and shake my head.

"Ha, wow, that's what that feels like," Forrest mutters.

It's showtime.

CHAPTER
TWO

I CROUCH like a spider and creep across the dark red steel beam. I've got to trust my senses, balance, and my peripheral vision to spot any movement or danger from below.

Slowly, slowly, Tru.

My steps are whisper quiet. The hammering of my pulse and the steady whoosh of my breathing is all I hear from this far up. Most of my focus remains on the beam so I can avoid the scratched-up parts of the steel. I'm mindful not to sprinkle the creatures below with patches of crumbly rust.

Heck, as if I want them to look up. A silly mistake like that would be awkward and dangerous. Ooh, and heavens forbid if I fall.

Without incident, I make it to roughly the centre of the building, and I suck in a relieved breath. A strange taste tickles the back of my throat. I frown as I prod one of my fangs with my tongue. They ache. My throat burns.

Something isn't right... my instincts are screaming at me. It's then I recognise the overwhelming smell. I glance down.

I blink.

Time stands still. *I feel dizzy.* The world tilts dangerously, and my heart feels like it has dropped through my body and onto the floor below.

"What the hell?" I rasp.

The creatures...

I blink. I swallow. Gosh, my mouth is so dry. I drag my eyes away from the scene below and stare at the military-grade spell in my numb hand. The sleeping grenade feels alien and heavy. *The baddies should be going nighty-night now.* Instead... I swallow. They are nothing but colourful inkblots on the concrete floor.

Ink. Blots.

Creatures have different colours of blood. For instance, demon blood is green, angel gold, and fae blood has various shades of blue. The wild educational thought rattles about in my head. Dimly, I acknowledge my brain is sensibly trying to disassociate. *I'd like to go home now. Run.* I shake my head and force my eyes to drop back to the ground below, and I macabrely trace the coloured patterns—it's like someone has spilt paint. No, spilt bits of people. Bits of henchmen are all over the warehouse floor.

Putrid colourful sludge. People goo.

Oh crap. Bile rushes up my throat, and I gag. I cover my mouth with the back of my hand. I swallow a few times. I don't want to throw up.

Yeah, Tru, let's not add to the colours. Add to the mess.

I fight the urge to close my eyes to pretend this isn't happening. A small squeak of inappropriate, horrified— bordering on manic—laughter bubbles out of my mouth. Crikey, I need to get a grip. I'm an assassin, and I see dead people all the time.

No, it's not that they're dead. It's the manner in which they were killed. That's what is freaking me out. This is on another level. This is nasty. Scary. My body sways, and a delicate hand firmly takes hold of my elbow.

Forrest. She steadies me.

"Shit," she grumbles. She lets go of me as soon as I am steady, and her pretty face scrunches up. Her expression is full of disgust as she takes in the mess below. Compared to me, the older shifter is cool as a cucumber.

"Yeah." Shit indeed. "What a mess."

Forrest puts the unneeded sleeping grenade away, and I attempt to do the same and find my coordination is messed up. It takes me three tries to unarm the sleeping grenade and put it back in the right pocket.

We could have died.

Forrest waves her mobile at me with a still-clawed hand. "Should I ring for backup?" Her yellow gaze is disconcerting, and I don't like the excitement shining in their depths.

The nutty wolf is having way too much fun.

Backup. "Ah." I clear my throat. *No. Hell no.* She means her mate. She thinks calling in her mate would be helpful. "Nooo, no, no, no, thank you." I shake my head.

Forrest narrows her eyes, tilts her head to the left and half smiles. *Creepy.*

"So that's a no then?"

"It's hell no." Calling him in would be like using a

flamethrower when all you need is a single match. Epic overkill. "We need to see what we're dealing with before we call anybody in to help. After all, the spell"—I wave to the floor—"didn't activate itself." I pull out the phone. "The cameras will give us an unprecedented view of what the heck happened."

Forrest shrugs and slumps onto the beam with a clatter of weapons. I flop down beside her. It's a good thing I do as my poor hand is shaking—let's pretend it's from shock and not from hunger. I brace my elbow on my thigh to steady it.

We silently watch the footage, and everything is fine until seconds before I enter the building, and then it happens. One moment over a dozen creatures are alive and well, standing around in small groups, talking, and in the next second, *poof,* they are all gone. And I literally mean *poof.* They are no longer in existence. There is a blast wave of power, and then droplets of blood mist the air and rain down to pool on the floor of the old warehouse.

We could have died.

"That was a hell of a spell. I didn't hear or feel a thing."

"No, neither did I. I didn't see the perpetrator either." *I wonder if I'll still get paid. Dead is still dead, right?* The cynical, analytical side of me pipes up.

I aim my next thoughts at the communication spell and Story. *There were so many outstanding kill orders for these targets from different agencies we could probably get paid double.* I've never been in this situation where someone else has done the killing. But the micro-cameras are top of the range. They have inbuilt DNA profiling. We have evidence aplenty, and my gut tells me no one else will claim the hits.

Please, will you send the kill confirmations with the footage to the Assassins Guild?

Will do, Story answers.

Now I need to locate the caster. I stab at the phone as I double-check the footage and nibble on my bottom lip.

"Hungry?" Forrest raises a pale pink eyebrow and shoots me a poorly veiled smirk. She doesn't miss a trick. She then nods to the congealing blood splattered on the floor below. "Yum."

"Ew." I do a dramatic, full-body shudder. Is she serious, or was that a well-timed vampire joke? "No, not particularly. Thanks," I mumble back.

Bloody wolf. Her silly question does the trick though, and my worry and horror fade to a manageable level for a heartbeat or two. My elbow comes out, and I playfully nudge her.

She grins and nudges me back.

Forrest is joking, but it's incredible how many well-educated people would imagine I'd want to lick the floor. *That floor.* Gross.

Blood. I barely repress another shudder; blood is nature's way of messing with me. Being the hybrid that I am, I'm all out of whack.

Chaos. That's what happens when two incompatible races are squished together—that's why, before me, being a hybrid was an automatic death sentence. Add in the finicky digestive system from my unicorn side. I'm a vegetarian. Combine that with an apex blood predator, and there you have it—*me,* an evolutionary joke of epic proportions.

One that really shouldn't have survived conception.

I drink from a donor. A donor who is my former

guardian and the love of my life. My stomach flips, and I huff out a sad-sounding sigh.

Our relationship is... complicated.

And as the years trickle past, I drink from him less and less. I can't bear the thought of taking blood from anyone other than him. So even though it makes me sick, I stick to synthesised bottled blood. It is gross, but I can just about keep the awful stuff down.

Meh, it is what it is.

Nowadays, any vampire worth their salt would be out of their damn mind to drink the real stuff from an unknown source. Even fair-trade blood is no longer donor-friendly, what with the increase in prices and the awful illegal blood trade springing up out of the woodwork. Eighty per cent of my time is spent dealing with those monsters. What with protected humans and little kids being kidnapped—

My heart misses a beat.

Oh no.

"The children," I whisper. My leg stings as my hand flops down weightlessly, and the corner of the phone digs into my thigh. I stare at Forrest in horror, and she looks back at me with wide yellow eyes. "The bloody children. With the vaporisation of the creatures"—and selfishly thinking about the money—"I forgot about the kids." Heart pounding, I snatch up the phone and once again frantically search the footage for the kids.

I know when things went down, I didn't see them. I've got to presume for my sanity that they are safe. *Please be safe.* I frantically double-triple-check the footage. Knowing through our communication spell Story is doing the same.

Nothing.

My eyes flick around the building, and I point to a covered area just out of sight. "Perhaps over there. There must be a room that's airtight as the cameras—"

Without saying a word, Forrest pushes off the beam, and like she's in a film, she drops the twelve metres to the floor.

CHAPTER
THREE

A squeak of surprise leaves my lips. I lean forward as far as I dare and watch as her falling form shimmers as if she is about to shift, but she does not. It was only a few microseconds of distortion, and I convince myself it must be my wonky vision as it makes little sense.

Legs bent, Forrest lands whisper-softly on the only clean patch of concrete.

"—the cameras can't penetrate that room." I finish lamely.

Uh-oh.

"Forrest, what about the creature who blew everyone up? The one who did the horrific vaporising spell. We need a plan!" I yell as the wolf disappears behind a thick metal girder. I wince and rub my forehead as my voice echoes around the warehouse.

Yay! Nice one, Tru. Yelling like a banshee is so going to help. What the heck happened to you being sneaky?

I rub my mouth and mumble, "Shit, shit, shit," into my palm. I wait to see if anything happens. Straining my ears for any sound, I count to twenty in my head, and my eyes flick about, searching for any movement. Where the hell is she? Where did she go? Pixies only know what trouble she's going to find.

Story, are you getting all this? We will need to film everything for when this goes pear-shaped.

Yes, and I'm making copies. Ava is helping.

Ava is a seriously talented tech witch. To have her on this is a massive relief. We met her and her human friend Emma when I was around nineteen. Her magic is technomancy, and it is so unique. Ava combines magic with technology. We have a you-scratch-my-back-I'll-scratch-yours business relationship. The witch handles the technology, and I handle the killing.

Thank you.

You need to get out of there. Story's singsong voice drops to a concerned whisper. *I have a bad feeling.*

I draw in a shaky breath. *Me too.* I swallow down a lump of dread that has been building in my throat. *But you know I can't.* I know Story wants to grumble, to lecture me, but she doesn't. Her silence is telling but appreciated.

My entire body twitches with the need to do something, and I chew on my lip. I can't just sit here like a proper numpty. I need to get down there. What the hell am I thinking? I should have bloody jumped down when Forrest did. But I'm not about to jump twelve metres from the roof like the wolf. I have the equipment. But it will take me forever to abseil.

"Ah, screw it."

With a growl and a buzz of concentrated shifter magic that flutters across the skin of my back, my wings snap out.

Sweat runs down my face, the heavy white feathers not helping with the heat. I adjust and tug at my combat top as it is biting into my neck. Years ago, I drank a priceless clothing-retention spell. The spell was worth its exorbitant cost. It allows me to shift without damaging my clothes. Male shifters don't seem to mind their body parts swinging in the wind. No way did I want to fight with my boobs hanging out. Now even when I shift into a full unicorn, my clothes and weapons shift with me, and when I turn back, they are miraculously intact.

Witch magic is seriously and scarily impressive.

When no one appears and the warehouse remains silent, I push myself off the beam. My body jolts as my wings catch the air, and I glide to the floor.

I land on the same clear spot of concrete as Forrest. As my feet touch down close to all the icky blood, I hold my breath. If I can't smell the blood and *stuff* around me, it's okay. Even if I know the disgusting scent will seep into my clothes and pores. Everything is fine.

I leap to another dryish spot, and my left heel slaps into a puddle of bluish goo. Right, that's it. When I get home, I'm so burning these clothes. I'm going to burn everything, including my beloved Doc Martens boots. This entire warehouse is gross.

"Forrest," I whisper yell. *Where the heck did she go?* I'm

all for saving kids, but there are ways to do this kind of thing that doesn't put us at risk.

Forrest peeks from around the corner, and I sigh in relief. "What the…" She points at my wings with a face of thunder. "You! You said you couldn't do a partial shift. What the heck is this?" She flaps her hands about as she angry whispers, "Where did those wings come from?" Forrest settles her clawed hands on her narrow hips. "You're a unicorn vampire hybrid. Since when did those creatures have wings? Huh? Huh?"

Oh yeah, the wings. My donor's blood has interesting side effects. But sensibly, I keep that information to myself. Only a handful of people know about them. It's not something I advertise. My wings flutter, and I bounce from foot to foot and scratch the back of my head.

"I never said I couldn't partially shift; I said I didn't have claws—"

Forrest cuts me off with a middle finger.

Nice.

"Why does everyone have wings?" she grumbles and petulantly stamps her foot. "I want wings."

My lips twitch. With a tingle of magic, I allow the contentious appendages to disappear before the angry wolf rips them from my back.

Forrest growls and thumbs behind her. "The door to the back area was locked. I opened it. Are we going to split up, or do you want to search together?"

"Together?"

Forrest grunts and stomps away.

Favourite short sword in hand and with a grin—she is a fucking delight—I follow her down the dark narrow hallway. With each step I take, I rotate the blade to warm up my wrist. At the end of the corridor, we come to a room.

Like I thought, the doorframe has the remnants of a magical seal, a seal that Forrest must have broken.

Hold. Story's loud voice crackles inside my head. I wince and tap the wall to get Forrest's attention. The wolf shifter pauses, and her yellow eyes narrow as I signal for her to wait. I tap my forehead. She nods. *The missing children have been recovered. They were spat out of a portal at the Sanctuary*—a fancy pocket realm—*around the same time as the vaporising spell hit. They are all accounted for and physically safe.*

Physically safe, but not mentally, I bet. Poor kids.

I hate this bloody horrible world that makes childhood non-existent. So-called immortality. It's a joke. You'd think children would have all the time in the world to mature 'cause if you technically live forever, being a child should be extended, right? Wrong. It's never the case. Living gets harder and harder each year and even more dangerous.

That's why I do what I do. It's not just for the money. If I can scrape some evil from this world, perhaps some poor innocent sod will have the chance to live.

Thank you. I then relay the information to Forrest.

Her head rolls back, and she huffs out a relieved breath. "Thank goodness."

"Yeah." I swap my sword into my left hand and continue with the small rotations. Unfortunately for us, we still have to clear the building.

Huh. I guess my gut feeling was wrong. No crying kids and add in the mushed-up and vaporised killers. It should be just a building check. This job is not so bad after all.

Without waiting for a countdown, Forrest kicks the door in. We spring through, me slightly behind. With practised speed, I move away from the door and scan the interior for any threats. The blood ring has converted the rundown office area into some freaky, temporary prison. As I clear the area on the left, I automatically expect Forrest to do the same to the right. But she doesn't.

Something is wrong. Is it a spell? Have we walked into a trap?

The seconds tick as Forrest remains frozen at the door with a look of blind terror stamped across her face. She eyes the scattered empty cages as if they are going to swallow her whole. Her pale face has gone a sickly white. I catch the small whine as it stutters from her lips. As I watch, she shakes her head and snaps out of it.

"Not your cage, not your concern," she mutters, followed by an audible gulp. "I don't like this job."

"Me neither." It's my turn to approach and offer reassurance. I gently squeeze her arm. "Hey." I cough to clear my throat. "I've got this. I can do this room. Do you want to check out the rest of the building?"

Blank, cold eyes move from the cages to stare back at me, and it feels like I'm face-to-face with a predator.

I awkwardly pat her shoulder. Ah, have I overstepped? I wince and drop my hand. Perhaps pointing out her issue is not the smartest thing to do.

I get a flash of teeth through a pale, sickly smile. With no further conversation needed, Forrest nods and backs out of the room. The door clicks closed behind her.

Okey-dokey. I blow out a breath and get back to work. Spreading out my senses, I start again with the clearing.

It is impossible not to jump to conclusions about what must have happened here. Thankfully, it is empty of life, but there is evidence aplenty. *Important stuff.* It's not my job to gather evidence, but you never know when something will come in handy. I know the micro-cameras will film everything. So I use the tip of the sword to flip a few pages of the paperwork scattered around.

Once the Hunters Guild takes over the site, I will never see this stuff again. Thank goodness.

I wrinkle my nose at the smell. I gag a little as my feet stick to the residual goo on the thin blue carpet. I'm glad I am not an empath or psychic. This room makes me want to bathe in bleach.

The communication spell clicks, and without saying anything, Story excitedly hums. Most of the time, we keep our conversations to the minimum as the invasive spell plays havoc with my head.

What's up? I roll my eyes. *I know you're dying to say something.*

Story lets out an excited squeal that makes me wince. I rub my temple.

You know the posh house in Bay Horse, the one you have been drooling over for the past six months?

The house with twenty-eight acres of organic grass? The land that makes my unicorn heart sing. *The property we can't afford?* It is a beautiful old farmhouse that has put buyers off as it needs such a tremendous amount of work. Renovation work that I can do myself with a bit of help from trade professionals. Yes, the farm is perfect if not for the hefty price tag. Where is she going with this?

The Assassins Guild has already transferred the money

for the vaporised minions. We have enough money to put an offer on the house.

Wait... What? Are you sure? Of course she's sure. This is Story. *Okay, well, if you're not too tired when we have finished here, do you mind calling them to put in an offer?*

Story lets out another squeal. *We jumping?*

We are so jumping. Knowing my friend is doing the exact same thing and not caring that this is all on camera, I bounce up and down with glee and mentally join in with Story's squeals of delight. *Jumping, jumping, jumping.*

Life is so hard, and yes, we celebrate every win like we are five.

Doing it here might be inappropriate, but we never wait. Our lives are too complicated, too dangerous. So we have learned over the years to take our joy when we can get it.

Otherwise—my eyes unwillingly drift to the tiny cages —like many others, we will run out of time.

When we have finished our silly manic celebration, and I'm slightly out of breath, I put my game face back on and head for the door. Out the corner of my eye, I catch a shimmer of something that makes the tiny hairs on the back of my neck rise. When I look at the area directly, I can't see anything wrong. It's only when I turn my head that I see it, a flicker in my peripheral vision. A change of texture in the air.

Huh. The remains of the portal? No, that's not it. I creep forwards. A Don't See Me Now spell? Or an exceptionally strong Look Away spell? I shrug. Perhaps.

Watching out for any concealed traps, I carefully, as if I'm going through a minefield, head towards the empty, dusty area of the room. I move closer until I feel the slightest change in air pressure and magic whispers against my sweaty skin. I pause.

Ever so slowly, my hand drifts to the small pocket of my combats, and I pull out something that should break the spell. It's a small green vial. I give it a shake, and the contents goop against the glass. I toss the potion at the magical shimmer and hold my breath. The vial shatters, and the little shards of glass disintegrate on impact. I wait. *Nothing.* I huff. It hasn't worked. At least I'm not seeing things and know for sure magic is there. Disappointed, I search another pocket for something else. I peek down—

Boom.

With a violent whoosh, the spell in front of me disintegrates. The sudden vacuum of power throws me off my feet onto the sticky floor. The impact jars my joints, and my knees—badly—break my fall.

I end up on my side. My heavy multicoloured hair tumbles over my head and covers my eyes. *Crikey. I've lost my hat.* The spell has ripped it from my head. *I've also lost my sword.*

I am then hit with a rotten egg smell. Sulphur.

Uh-oh.

The scent fades... or I've gone nose blind. I groan and shove the mass of tangled hair away from my face. Millimetres in front of my nose, I see the ominous glowing lines of a chalk circle.

CHAPTER FOUR

THE CIRCLE GLOWS WHITE, and all sound vanishes; with each breath I take, little specks of chalk dust dance in its light. *Gosh, that was a close call.* I almost smushed my nose against the glowing lines. Hand on the grotty floor, I push up, and on my bottom, like a lame crab, I rapidly shuffle back. As I move, I spot the strange twisting markings that mar the circle's neatly curved lines.

The language is Hellish.

Hellish? *It's a demon trap, and this one has been activated.* As soon as that thought enters my head, my eyes snap to the centre of the circle.

Ah, bloody hell. There's a creature inside.

Sitting in the centre of the roughly eight-foot circle is a demon. Considering someone trapped him and he is a prisoner, the demon's posture is deceptively relaxed.

Chin resting on his knee, one leg bent and the other

neatly folded underneath his upper thigh. Pale blue skin. Lots of naked blue skin. His face is chiselled, with high cheekbones, full lips, and heavy dark blue brows. With no discernible iris, pupil, or white sclera, his overly large eyes are an endless black.

I think he's deceptively relaxed as the tail next to his bent leg is flicking forwards and back, agitated like a cat. A sure sign he's not so unaffected as he pretends, and I don't blame him. Nobody wants to be trapped inside a demon-killing circle, as that's what this thing is. It's some funky dangerous magic, magic I have never seen and only heard whispers of.

Who would trap a demon? *You'd have to be out of your damn mind.* The trap renders a demon powerless, making them easy to kill. But if they get out... it's no longer fun and games. It is, after all, just a chalk circle.

Intently we watch each other. Derision on his handsome face. No doubt fear and shock plastered on mine.

"Good morning," he says pleasantly. The sound of his voice is deeply refined, and... bloody hell, he is so utterly beautiful. The demon moves ever so slightly, and the muscles in his abdomen ripple.

Wow. My eyes home in on the movement, and I blink a few times. I need to stop staring. I'm being incredibly rude.

What is shocking is that I find him attractive. It has been a very long time, nine years to be exact, since I have found another man so captivating. I pluck at the delicate bracelet on my wrist. I'm not blind. I see them all the time. But my brain, body, soul—I roll my eyes—whatever... is only *his*. My blood donor.

Even if a man is drop-dead gorgeous, my only response

has been "Congratulations on your face," not this... this visceral reaction.

It freaks me the heck out.

Why him? Why now? It must be some funky demon power. Yes! Phew, that explains it. Magic. *He's in a demon trap. He shouldn't have any power.*

Uh-oh.

I need to act like this is a regular daily occurrence. Like I see demons all the time. *Be cool.* I scramble to my feet. "Hello," I respond in an equally pleasant tone—if we both ignore the undignified squeak at the end. I cringe.

For something to do, I wipe my hands on my combats. *Okay, look, you need to see beyond his beauty. This is a bloody demon. A creature that you wouldn't want to meet at night.* I rub the back of my neck. Yep, the tiny hairs are standing up in bloody fright. Who am I kidding? This is a creature that you won't want to meet even in full daylight.

I know about demons, and I know enough to drop my eyes. *So if that's the case, Tru, stop bloody ogling him!* My eyes snap to the floor, and I inspect the circle. The power coming off that thing is immense. "It looks like you're in a bit of a pickle," I mumble as I drift around the circle's edge.

I do my best to ignore the intent way the demon watches me.

Theoretically, I know about demons. Like angels they aren't from our world. They came from another realm using the ancient ley line system of portals. To these powerful creatures, our realm is unappealing, and our inhabitants are merely barbarians. Ordinary people have little to no contact with them, and then there are all the treaties in place.

Only the elite are allowed on Earth.

So to find a demon, a higher-level demon, imprisoned in a shitty warehouse in Lancashire? It is unbelievable, and it also makes little sense. It would be more believable to have... I don't know, an entire theme park stuffed in the room's corner.

This is nuts.

And then there is still the mystery of whoever wielded the magic. A person powerful and merciful enough to portal the stolen children to safety and to unleash a spell that, within seconds, vaporises more than a dozen creatures. Leaving the only sign of their existence as puddles on the floor.

A demon could do all that.

I swallow. Is he a victim? Unless those were his spells. And he was the one who activated the demon trap. A convenient "Look, I was powerless for the entire time. It wasn't me."

Story? I wait for a beat. The annoying, grating feeling of the communication spell is gone, and I have a horrible, sinking feeling I'm alone in my head. *Story?* I say. I call out a few more times just to be sure, without success.

Crikey, that isn't good.

I would have loved the input of my best friend as she's the voice of reason. I bet if I also pull out the phone and check the camera feed, there will be no recording of this encounter either. *I don't like this.* I swallow again. My mouth is dry, and my tongue is trying its best to stick to the roof of my mouth. There's also no damn air in this horrible room. I tug at my collar.

This is bad. Bad, bad, bad.

Gosh, I want to scurry off home. What the hell—pun intended—am I going to do?

It's not like I'm going to leave him. That would be a really, really stupid thing to do. To run off with a wave and a "bye-bye, demon" and then wait for him to get out of the circle and hunt me down. Eat me. Yeah, I'm not willing to play demon hide-and-seek.

But letting him out, there's no guarantee this guy will not eat my face right off as soon as he steps over that chalk line.

Sucks to be me.

Nah. I think I've answered my own question by saying that the demons on Earth are elite. This handsome devil didn't just sneak in. He couldn't, right? Which means he has permission to be here. I'm back to the outlandish victim theory, and that narrative doesn't sit right with me.

The demon has been silently observing me this entire time. I can feel the heat of a blush as it spreads across my cheeks. I clear my throat. "Do you know how I can get you out of this trap, and if I do, do I have your word that you won't try any funny business?" *Funny business? Really?* At least I sound better than my initial hello.

"You are perfectly safe with me, Tru. Just break the circle."

My stomach flips, and my eyes widen to the point they might roll out of my head. *He knows my name!* That isn't good. I continue to eye the glowing chalk lines.

"You know my name. You have me at a disadvantage." I lift my eyes and meet his endless black gaze.

"Doesn't everyone know your names, Tru Dennison?

The rebel leader, the unicorn-and-vampire hybrid, my shadow, the angel's plaything."

I wince.

"The abomination and, my personal favourite, the secret assassin."

"Yeah, well, few people know about that, the assassin thing. It wouldn't be much of a secret now, would it?" I grumble. Except for my chosen family, Ava, and my boss, I rarely work with others. Forrest tonight was an exception.

Who is the one in the trap, Tru?

I shiver.

Ah well. Like my grandad used to say, in for a penny, in for a pound. *Screw it.* I scuff the glowing chalk with my boot.

CHAPTER
FIVE

THE INFLUX of power makes the demon tilt his head back and groan. His bones pop and crack as he rises from the floor, unfurling himself like some giant beast. Unending blue skin ripples until he stands there proudly. Heck, he must be over eight foot tall.

Wow, he's ginormous.

Hard, powerful muscle sheaths his massive frame. Pure force in physical form. Unusual for a demon as the ones I have seen on television have been delicate, birdlike. Not this guy. He's something else. A totally different breed. Made to whack creatures' heads off with a sword. And his power? The circle sure curtailed his magic. The power he emits makes my bowels twist.

"I will just get going now. Leave you to it." I flap my hands about in a floppy wave and hastily back away in an awkward shuffle. I don't think it's possible for me to physically turn my back on this guy. Nope, no way.

"Thank you for the rescue, little unicorn."

I snort. I can't help it. I have never been called *little* in my life. I suppose everyone is little to him, bloody big bugger.

"What amazes me is you didn't ask for anything in return."

I pause. "No, of course not—"

"I would like to give you a gift," he says, cutting me off.

I shoot him a wobbly grin. "Oh no, no, no, nooooo, thank you, I'm fine." I wave both my hands this time. The demon steps over the inactive chalk line. My heart misses a beat, and I almost swallow my tongue.

Oh no, I have made a mistake! Retreat. Retreat.

Would it be inappropriate to scream for Forrest? Perhaps I should have got her opinion *before* I let the bloody demon out. Being dazzled by his male beauty hasn't helped my thought process. Not at all. Now I can't seem to move away from him. My feet are magically stuck to the floor.

How bloody rude.

I lift my chin, refusing to cower despite the bite of powerful magic reverberating in the air around us.

"You are so hungry. I feel the discomfort thrumming through you. Does he starve you on purpose?" He tilts his head, and his tail snaps against the carpeted floor.

Dumbfounded, I blink. "No, he doesn't starve me. I'm used to this level of hunger, and I know it won't kill me." *Mind your own damn business, demon,* I mentally huff.

"Would you like a taste?" He bends to my height, tilts

his head to the side, and slyly watches me out the corner of his eye.

"Erm no, no, thank you," I whisper.

Of their own accord, my eyes zero in on a plump, yummy vein. I swallow the spit that floods my mouth, and with my tongue, I force my upper canine teeth back into place. "I haven't... I have never..." I've never taken blood from anyone else apart from my angel and never from the throat. *That would be way too intimate.* What am I thinking? I don't want this monster's blood!

The demon runs a finger sensually across his neck. His short black nail must be sharp, as it barely traces over his skin and a bead of dark green blood bubbles up. He catches the drop and balances it perfectly on the pad of his index finger.

Suddenly I'm starving. The smell of his blood is overwhelming. My mouth is full of fangs. The blood smells delicious. Inside my head, I'm screaming. *What the heck is he doing?* But my body doesn't care. I'm ravenous.

He watches me intently as his bloody finger slowly moves to my face and hovers over my mouth. My eyes widen as he tilts his hand, and the drop of blood rolls, falling in slow motion it splatters against my lips.

With an indignant flare of my nostrils, I clamp my mouth closed. *What the heck is he doing?* Blood is sacred. You don't just spill it willy-nilly. It's nuts he thinks it's okay to bleed all over me. Who does that?

Okay, I know it's just a drop, and I know I'm a vampire and blood is my thing, but that shit is rude. Like walking up to some random human and shoving a carrot in their mouth while saying they looked hungry.

I wish I could move more than just my mouth. I need to wipe it away. My lips tingle. The urge to lick them is almost overwhelming. But I will not give in. I won't.

How dare he do this to me? I don't want his horrible rotten blood. He smirks. Gah, demon or not, the urge to rip his stupidly handsome head off his shoulders is real.

"Very well, pretty vampire, a different gift. It will take but a moment." Define a moment! His massive blue hand takes hold of mine in what could have been a bruising grip but isn't. His skin against mine is nice. Oh no. My heart feels like it is going to burst alienesque out of my chest.

Oi dickhead, get off me.

Well done, Tru. I mentally pat myself on the back. *You've done it this time, rescued a bloody monster.*

He scowls and flicks the bracelet—a gift from my angel blood donor—further down my forearm. I get the impression that if he could get away with it, he'd rip it from my wrist. Then the demon leans forward, his black eyes assessing, and slowly, oh so slowly, my trapped hand ascends to his face.

Uh-oh.

Uh-oh. Is he going to chomp on my hand? I know better than to stick a limb anywhere near a stranger's mouth. I huff out a pained breath. *Been there, done that.*

Is it not too late to fight his magic just enough so I can punch him in the face? I wonder recklessly. *No, Tru, you can't.* Dealing with creatures stronger than you is always a dangerous balancing act. I am dead if I hit him.

I can't help it—I let out an undignified, frightened squeak as the back of my hand meets his lips. Just above my knuckles, he places a kiss. Ew. The demon *kisses* my hand. Only creeps do that. He better not slobber.

His lips are pillowy soft... I huff in frustration. I'm halfway to rolling my eyes while trying not to enjoy his soft lips on my skin. It's horrible. *No, it's not.* My skin is super-sensitive, or maybe it's just his touch that makes it feel that way. How messed up is that? I try to fight the magic just enough to wiggle my hand free... and that is when the pain hits.

The skin against his lips *burns*. I yelp. "What did you do?"

He traces his thumb along the inside of my wrist, shushes me, and gently blows on the... wound? The pain fades.

"A gift. A promise. I will aid you in a time of need. All you need to do is kiss the same spot, and I will find you wherever you are."

"Why? Why would you do that?"

With a last brush of his fingers, he lets go of both my hand and the magic that has frozen me to the floor. I snatch my poor, aching hand closer to inspect it. There is an angry red burn in the perfect shape of his lips.

"You—you scarred my hand." *Bloody demon.* "That's not a very nice gift." I bite my bottom lip.

The demon smiles. "Ah, now that is where you are wrong, Tru. It is the highest of honours to get a demon kiss."

CHAPTER
SIX

A DEMON KISS. What on earth is that? I have absolutely
no idea. I lick my lips, and his smile gets wider, dazzling,
and the demon does this low, throaty kind of chuckle. The
sound rolls over my skin, and I get goosebumps.

He seems suddenly very pleased with himself.

Awkwardly, I drop my eyes to focus on my hand. I guess
it's exactly what it says on the tin. He's a demon, and he
kissed my hand. That's something to worry about later
when I'm far away from this situation and this *monster*.

"Monster? Now that's a little unfair." The demon's
thick blue eyebrows wiggle into a frown, and he puffs his
bottom lip out into the best kind of masculine pout. On
anyone else, his expression would look ridiculous. *Why do I
find him so irresistibly handsome?* It takes me a few seconds
to work out what he said as I'm staring at his mouth, but
when my slow brain filters through his words, it clicks.

Did he... Did I... Did I say that out loud? Nah, I couldn't have, could I? Can this man read minds? I stare back at him in utter confusion. Unless I'm not controlling my expression, I thought I had my resting bitch face down pat.

He would only know what I am thinking if he is, in fact, reading every thought that enters my head. I flinch. *Well crap.*

While I'm silently freaking out, the air around him bubbles and flutters. Fluid stuff seems to leak out of his skin, and then it shifts into fabric. Whoa, that must be the weirdest thing I have ever seen. He's now wearing clothes. A crisp white Henley and black jeans cling to his blue form, highlighting every lump and bump of his muscled torso. His broad shoulders strain the fabric, and the outline of muscle on his chest and arms is plainly visible. Everything about him is overwhelmingly masculine.

Oh! I almost lick my lips when I remember in time his blood is still on my mouth. I was almost too late. The demon burning my hand had completely put me off. I use the bottom of my top to aggressively scrub the trace amount away. Phew, that was a close call. I still cannot believe he put blood on my lips. Then he covers up his faux pas by spelling me without asking.

Gift, my arse.

I'm glad I have only met one demon in the flesh because, bloody hell, I don't know what I'm going to do if I meet another.

Run. Fuck being polite.

The demon grins at my scrubbing antics and, undoubtedly, at my mental voice. *One, two, three, testing, testing.* He smiles so wide he flashes his teeth, and my heart skips another beat.

His face is breathtaking.

Damn it. I scrub harder. I should seriously be concerned, what with those razor-sharp teeth. No square chompers for this monster. I know I have fangs, but those teeth are ridiculous. I'm surprised he doesn't shred his own tongue.

A bead of sweat rolls down the side of my face. Compared to the man standing in front of me, I feel and undoubtedly look like a sweaty mess. I finally cease scrubbing at my mouth and drop my top. I can't wait to have a shower and for this day to end.

The demon moves, and before I can dodge him, he pokes me in the middle of my forehead. *Hecky thump. What now?* From the spot underneath his finger, magic spreads. I slap his hand away and then vigorously, with a scowl, rub my forehead. What has he done now?

His magic tickles across my scalp and cheeks. Coolness spreads. It drips down my throat and pitter-patters like raindrops onto my chest. I shiver as it runs down my back. At first, it is icy cold against my heated skin, but within moments, the icy magic becomes second to the fact that the sticky, gross, overheated feeling is gone. Leaving behind a perfect not-too-hot-nor-too-cold sensation.

The Goldilocks principle. Whoa. Considering I left school at fourteen, I do not know where that little nugget of information came from. My brain is always full of facts, strange, sometimes helpful, but mostly useless drivel. But this time, my brain is right, I feel like a real-life Goldilocks where my body is the porridge and it has found the perfect, just-right temperature.

"So you are always comfortable," the demon says gruffly, his black eyes soft. Kind.

"Erm, thanks," I say while I shuffle my feet and twist my hands. Now I feel kind of bad for slapping his hand away. I am so confused. What is this guy's problem? What does he want?

For magic's sake, I only scuffed a chalk line, and he's throwing free stuff at me. Offering me blood and freaky-hand-kiss magic, and now, when he sees me sweating like a dryad in a sawmill, he taps my forehead and, hey presto, a spell that controls my body temperature.

Nobody gives anything away for free.

Nobody is this helpful, and demons aren't kind. So of course that begs the question: what the hell does this guy want?

"You are very loud." He points to his head. "You practically throw your thoughts at me."

Yep, the demon can read my mind.

Uh-oh.

I do a full-body awkward shrug. What can I say to that? *Sorry!* I scream the apology at him, and he winces. What can I say? There's a lot of stuff going on inside my head. If he doesn't like it, he doesn't have to listen. *You don't have to listen. They are my thoughts.*

It's then my turn to wince as I try my best not to go over every thought since I walked into this room. The jumping. Every little thought I've had about him. The more I try, the more they pop back into my head in punishing, horrifying, glorified, naked detail.

Eff my life and his rippling abs. Now uncomfortable and mortified, I clear my throat. "So why are you helping me?"

"Because I want to."

Ah, right, good to know.

"My name is Kleric. I will see you soon, Tru."

What? Wait, is that it? "You are going?" I watch, dumbfounded, as the demon, *Kleric*, just walks away. He casually strolls across the room, and then he is gone. He vanishes.

My ears pop, and the fake silence disperses. I puff out my cheeks with a relieved breath, happy to be alone. Right? My hand itches to remind me of the gift he left behind. I need to shift to heal. Perhaps my unicorn magic will make it go away? At least I feel refreshed. I shimmy a little. I don't even feel grimy anymore. It's a handy trick and strangely kind.

Gah. Sometimes I hate that side of me, the soft squidgy side. It always gets me into so much trouble. He's a monster. *A monster,* I tell myself.

Story?

Yes, I'm here. You disappeared from everything. Are you okay? she replies. Her voice is several octaves higher than usual.

I'm sorry about that, and yeah, I am okay. There was a spell, a demon trap, oh, and a demon.

A demon? Story squeaks. *Has the demon gone?*

I *uh-huh* in acknowledgement, and my eyes drift back to the door leading to the dark hallway with a frown. I rush to the door and yank it open. The hallway is empty. Where the heck did he go?

All we got from our end was an explosion, and then you

40

were thrown to the floor and the cameras went dead. We couldn't hear from you or see you anymore. Even Ava couldn't find you.

Ah, I had a feeling that would be the case. I will tell you everything when I get home.

Okay.

Have you got the live video back?

Yes.

Once Story confirms that the cameras have thoroughly filmed the chalk circle, I do a strange shuffling dance, moving my feet until all the lines are blurred and indistinguishable. I can't use a Clean Me Now spell as the one I have is so powerful it will clean the entire room and its evidence. That's an excellent way to piss off the Hunters Guild.

The ripped-up carpet makes it obvious that something was here, but that's another person's problem. My gut is telling me it's crucial that I don't let anyone else get hold of the demon trap design.

A quick search of the floor and I find my sword and hat. I scoop both up. Luckily, no harm has been done to my beautiful weapon.

I frown and click my tongue. Mmm. I have such a pleasant taste in my mouth, a taste I can't place. Almost like the best kind of chocolate. How strange. I shake my head and quickly plait my hair—I have no idea where my bobble has gone, so I tuck the heavy plait underneath the hat with the hope it will not unravel. The black cotton of my hat is more pleasant now that my entire head doesn't feel like it's going to burst into flames.

As I'm leaving, I catch sight of another door. I tilt my

head back and, hands on hips, look to the heavens for strength and patience. Not another bloody room. It must have been hidden with the same Don't See Me Now spell that hid the demon. I never noticed it with Mr Huge, Blue, and Muscly taking up my entire focus.

Blade in hand, I press the handle down, and I channel Forrest as I give the door a shove with my boot.

The smell of ozone makes my sensitive nose itch. Inside the room is the heavy magic buzz of an active ward.

The ward, an opaque dome, blocks me from entering as it fills the entire room. Cautiously, I give the ward a poke with my blade and meet no resistance as the tip of my sword disappears. Huh. This ward isn't meant to keep people out. It's more to stop sounds and smells from escaping.

I lay my palm millimetres above the buzzing surface, and the magic nips at my hand. With a swirl, like the parting of clouds, the opaqueness obediently falls away.

For the second time tonight, my mind struggles to make sense of what I'm seeing. Coloured rags. Someone has haphazardly piled lumps of multicoloured clothing and... It is like an optical illusion, one of those ambiguous images.

I tilt my head—

Then I see it. A random shoe. My head snaps back as if I have taken a punch to the face. The shoe is a glossy red, and it is falling off a foot. The rest of the body becomes apparent. It is trapped underneath a dozen other bodies.

Not rags. People.

My rapid breaths fog the dome. They have dumped people inside the ward. Each body left in an undignified heap, as if whoever they were in life didn't matter. Stomach acid burns up my oesophagus. Only lots of swallowing keeps it down. Something deep inside me whimpers and withdraws to rock in a corner, but I can't allow myself to physically follow up on that instinct.

Mother Nature, Story whispers in horror.

I allow my mental voice to be laced with vampire compulsion when I tell her, *Don't look, Story. Please don't look.* She needs no more nightmares. I force myself to look, to count, as I take in the horror. I need to know what I'm dealing with.

I gulp and shove away the guilt that rattles me to the very core. I couldn't have done anything about this. I know that logically. From the state of their remains, these people were long dead before I even knew of this warehouse's existence. This wasn't my fault. No, it was *them*.

In my mind's eye, I see the puddles of blood on the concrete floor, and my top lip twitches with a snarl. I'm then immensely grateful to whoever vaporised those bastards in the main warehouse and to whoever saved those kids from this awful fate.

I need to take down the ward and allow the cameras to get DNA samples of the bodies, but rightly or wrongly, I can't do it. I can't seem to make myself. To do it feels wrong, sacrilegious. So with a heavy heart, I turn away and, reaching for the door, close it behind me with as much care and reverence as I can muster.

I rest my forehead against the doorframe. I just need a moment. My entire body sinks, and my head feels so very heavy. This would be the time any normal person would reconsider a change of career. Any normal person would run as fast as they could to get away from this evil.

But I can't.

Horrible stuff like this motivates me to try harder. This is why I took hold of my adoptive grandad's legacy. He was a fae assassin, and from the time I was six to the age of seventeen, he taught me everything that he knew, and for the past nine years, I have continued to hone my skills. And maybe I'm fooling myself, and all this is for nothing. Maybe when I take out an evil creature, another two slide into their place.

The damn burn on my hand throbs, and the odd sensation gives me the strength to lift my head. I can't fall apart. No. I won't fall apart. I will use the rage I'm feeling to make a difference.

Even if I have to kill them all.

CHAPTER
SEVEN

Heads up, Tru. We have incoming. At the same time as Story's warning, Forrest screams my name. I rush across the room. *I am so sorry. I messed up. What was behind that ward shocked me. I took my eye off the ball.*

Hey, don't worry, I tell her as I fling the door open.

Tru, watch out!

A body lunges at me. With a squeak, I lean back, barely a hair out of the way, as a blade whistles through the air past my face. Little pieces of wooden shrapnel pepper me, and the skin on my face stings as the massive sword crunches into the doorframe.

The troll on the other end of the blade snarls. Our swords sing as they clash, and I get my blade up to block his backswing.

Thank fate for my unicorn strength.

With a grunt and a flick of my wrist, I pull out an iron

dagger with my free hand. As he swings his blade at my neck, I duck under the strike, and my dagger finds a temporary home between his ribs. Surprise flickers across his green face. The massive warrior troll sure didn't expect me to fight back or close the distance between us.

"Ahh, did that tickle?"

I angle the dagger until I get his lung, and there's a horrible gurgling sound that makes me wince. His arm sags, and he drops his sword. With a growl, I dance away, and with a practised jump and an elegant swing, I take his head. His noggin bounces with a wet-sounding splat somewhere behind me, and his headless corpse crashes to the floor.

Without preamble, I jump over his fallen body and into the hall.

In the dark corridor, another troll waits. This guy is wide as he is tall. Great. I groan and barely refrain from rolling my eyes as his eyes flick to the body of his fallen friend, and he opens his mouth and roars. My ears ring, and he backhands me.

With an *oof*, I hit the opposite wall. Damn it to hell. I was watching for his sword. At least my tiredness and hunger have gone, and with adrenaline now gushing through my system and with a wiggle of my jaw, I find, luckily, I don't feel any pain. I can't feel anything at all. Hopefully, my vampire healing will kick in before it starts to sting. It's not safe to shift. Even if it takes just seconds, in a fight, a microsecond can get you killed.

With a shake of my head, I dive back in. I push off the wall and just have enough room to do a spinning jump kick. My boot lands smack-bang in his face. The troll collapses, his face bloody.

I kick him again and again, the toe of my Doc Martens boot hitting his temple. The sweet spot. The troll goes still. Blue blood and drool drip from his open mouth, and as I listen, I realise he's no longer breathing. Good enough. A sharp knife to his throat finishes the job.

I liquid prowl down the corridor to the main warehouse. As I strut, I roll my shoulders and both wrists.

"Morning." The gravelly voice of Forrest greets me. The wolf has shimmied halfway up a steel girder and gives me a cheery wave. "Glad you're still alive." Her friendly words gain me the attention of four more trolls.

Yay. I inwardly sigh when they turn towards me.

The look in their eyes makes me cringe, seeing as I have blue troll blood coating my skin and dripping from my weapons. Predictably, in unison, they bellow a challenge, and as a group, they charge. Ah shit.

"Or maybe not," Forrest mumbles. "Don't worry!" she yells. "I rang for backup."

Backup. Bloody hell. Things are about to get ugly.

Heart pounding, I throw my dagger straight up in the air, and while it is tumbling, with my now-free hand, I grab a temporary ward. I chuck the spell at my feet—but it activates seconds too late, trapping me with the trolls. Not great. I catch my dagger and swing my sword, beheading the first raging troll in a single smooth stroke. Blood splashes.

I slice off a hand of the next unfortunate troll, and the blade in his grip follows, clanging to the concrete floor. The owner of the hand collapses with a wail. I kick the weapon out of the way and draw my dagger across his throat.

A darker green troll, number three on my right, swings his massive, two-handed blade. It slices through the air in a dangerous arc. I dance out of the way and spin from an outstretched hand as troll number four on my left tries to grab me. I kick her in the chest, and she meets the pointy end of the other troll's sword. As they collide, both of them go flying. The dark green troll falls under her. She screams and, with a meaty-sounding squelch, rolls off the blade. He attempts to rise and gets my dagger through his ear.

This is why I don't do hand-to-hand combat outside training. I wrinkle my nose. *It is messy.*

Breathing heavily, I finish the last troll off quickly and cleanly. The temporary ward gives me time to look around.

Relatively safe above me, Forrest whoops as she hangs off the girder with what looks like an orange-and-blue Nerf gun. The plastic gun clicks, and a foam bullet flies past the ward. I turn to see it doink into the forehead of a vampire who was attempting to sneak up behind me.

"Timber!" Forrest yells with obvious delight. The vampire groans, wobbles, and then falls face-first. I can't help but stare.

What the fuckity-fuck sorcery is that? A toy gun, really?

A potion strong enough to take down my ward rolls out of the vampire's hand and clatters harmlessly onto the floor.

Oh.

"Oh, Forrest, well done. That was a great shot!" I yell.

Around me, more sneaking, not-so-carefully hidden creatures fall. Knocked out by Forrest's toy. "The blue bullets make them sleep, red set them on fire, and the yellow ones make their heads explode!" Forrest yells back at me.

"What?" I say with an incredulous splutter.

"Nah, kidding." She drops her voice and puts her index

finger to her lips. "I think yellow makes them pee." She scratches the side of her head with the plastic gun. "To be honest, after the first ten minutes of the weapon debrief, I wasn't really listening." She throws me a bright smile and then clambers higher up. "Wee, this is so much fun."

"Yeah, fun." I scoff. I then watch wide-eyed as Forrest continues to snipe the vampires. After a while, the temporary ward flickers, and the spell fades, but I can't help but grin. The wolf shifter has the vampires on the run, and the fae have backed away to a safe distance from her firing range. They have no idea how to deal with the spell-dipped foam bullets.

Creatures, we don't use guns. Guns are super rare and heavily regulated. There is also this strange thing of honour between creatures where it's all blood and blades. Oh, and not to mention the many spells and nasty potions that will melt your face clean off and turn you inside out. If you have scales or tough gargoyle skin, tiny little bullets are a joke.

Obviously, like me, Forrest doesn't give a crap. I specialise in long-range weapons. I'm trained to find the sweet spot. Not that I have anything with me today, more's the pity.

I throw another temporary ward just as the last one dissipates—it's like I'm skipping a stone across a gross shallow lake. The floor, with the puddles of congealed blood I carefully avoided before, is now our battleground.

The ward snaps into place, the timing perfect. Only Forrest's unconscious vampires are inside with me, so I take the opportunity with adrenaline-fuelled slashes to methodically remove their heads.

If it wasn't for the fact these fuckers would have given anything to kill me, and they kill kids, I might have felt bad.

Once I've finished my grisly task, I clean my sword and blade as I wait for either this last ward to fail or for the creatures to be brave enough to venture out with a spell good enough to destroy it. The sleep grenade burns in my pocket. We are way too close to the action, and I can't bloody use it.

"When did you first turn into your animal? I was nine." Huh? Forrest fidgets with a single long pink strand of hair, wrapping it around and around the end of her finger until it turns white. She has run out of foam bullets and has come down from her perch.

I wince. "Six." I flatten my back against the metal girder and peer around the other side. Shifters don't really shift until the early twenties, maybe even older. Half-shifters—normally half-human—don't shift at all. It's only the pure-bred that gets the privilege of the magic.

Oh, and me. Of course I had to be different.

"Six, whoa, must have been a trauma response. Trauma shifting, bah, it sucks to be us." She grins, flashes nonhuman teeth at me, and flexes her claw-topped fingers. The hair imprisoning her digit snaps, the strand unwinds and floats to the floor, and her freed finger changes colour as the blood rushes back in.

"Yeah. It sucks." I like this Forrest; the dead-eyed, scary Forrest not so much. But this side of her... I think I might have made a new friend.

Something pings above my head, and quick as a whip, Forrest jumps. She catches the marble-sized spell before it shatters. Head tilted, she rolls it between her fingers. "Ooh, that would have been nasty," she mumbles. "The ward is failing." With a flick of her wrist, she pitches it back in the direction it came from. Seconds later, there are a few blood-curdling screams.

She grins, but it fades when she looks back at me. "Why don't you...?" She flaps her hands and lifts her chin towards the ceiling. "Go up to the roof. Get yourself off home. I can handle all this."

All this. She means the dozens of creatures that are creeping closer.

"It's what I do," she says with a shrug.

"No. No way, I'm not leaving you."

Her voice drops, and seemly vulnerable, she wiggles from side to side, and her hands twist together. "I like you, Tru. If we don't die in the next ten minutes, let's be friends." I nod, and we grin at each other and do an impromptu fist bump.

Then... with a last flicker, the ward drops.

CHAPTER
EIGHT

FOCUSED, I sink into the moment, and like a whirlwind, I slice at limbs. Graceful and lethal as I can be, I dance across the festering blood-soaked floor. The vile liquid splashes up my legs.

Forrest fights alongside me, opting for her wolf form. She is all teeth and claws, which is way more effective, I must admit, than any blade. She moves like a wolf possessed, ducking and moving so fast no one can get hold of her, and if they dare to get near, they are severely punished. Underneath all the blood and gore, her beautiful cream-and-red fur gleams in the morning light that is streaming down from the transparent roof sheets.

It is a whirlwind of growls, metal, and claws.

I lose sight of Forrest as a big vampire rushes me. The other creatures dive out of the vampire's way as the twin blades in her grip make the hot air sing. She moves like a warrior. *Whoa, she's fast and controlled.* I block, letting the first blow glance off my sword. Testing her. I stab at her with the dagger in my left hand. Her other blade neatly evades my sword and scrapes a burning cut against my side. I wince. I aim my next strike at her face, but I end up burying the blade in her upper arm. She screams. The pitch goes higher as I yank the sword from where it embeds in her humerus.

I hate this.

I reverse my grip on the sword and hit her on the side of the head as hard as I can with the pommel. She goes down like a sack of spuds, collapsing on her knees and then face-down onto the concrete. I take her head.

I really hate this.

For several seconds, all I can do is pant for air. The creatures around me stare and creep ever closer. I ignore their mutters of disgust, a mix of "rebel leader" and "abomination." I don't care what they think about me. But in the back of my head, I'm worried. I do not know where all this energy has come from. I should be exhausted, but instead, I feel like I've barely warmed up.

An orc swings at me with a wooden mace. Yeah, after the demon kissed my hand, I'm suddenly full of beans. Even after drinking blood from my angel, I didn't get this kind of energy. I'm strong and fast, but I'm not this strong or fast, and my sluggish vampire side is roaring to the forefront as if I have recently fed. Believe it or not, the unicorn part of me is usually my badass side.

It couldn't be the drop of the demon's blood, could it? Nah, it only touched my lips.

I catch the glow of fire out the corner of my eye. Wolf

Forrest is doing some serious magic, but I can't get a good look. I duck underneath the orc's mace as it almost slams into my head. Uh-huh, my nosiness will only end up getting me killed. My full attention must be on staying alive. I jump and spin. Blood sprays over my face, and the mace-welding orc drops to the ground. The thud created by his heavy body vibrates through my feet.

With lashes dripping with blood and narrowed eyes, I peer at the creatures surrounding me. Something snaps in the minions. It's as if they seem to make a silent collective decision, and all at once, the creatures swarm.

Too many. Way too many.

Surrounded as I am, there is no longer any room to swing my bloody sword. The useless blade clatters to my feet as I grab another iron knife. With both shorter blades slashing, I desperately try to gain back the space I need to keep up my fight. But I'm losing hope. I glance at the gold bracelet on my wrist. I have magic I can use. But it's a nuclear option.

I don't want to die.

I'm about to say my goodbyes to Story when the ground rocks and shakes so much that I stumble. It's as if Northwest England has suddenly developed earthquakes, and then there is an almighty angry *roar*.

I drop to my knees and cover my ears. Oh my gosh, and I thought the trolls were bad. Even with my hands covering them, my head screams in pain, and my poor eardrums feel like they could almost explode with the awful sound. Before the roar has had a chance to fade, I watch in horror—like a real-life monster movie, there is a grinding, ripping, and crunching sound, and the entire right corner of the warehouse is just... gone.

I see a flash of massive teeth.

An unfortunate orc finds himself in the way of the vast mouth. The teeth grind, chew, and then the pulpy orc is spat aside.

Ew.

Forrest, still in wolf form, slumps, panting against my leg. The panicked minions pour around us like rats running from a flood. One of them screams the biggest girly scream I have ever heard as he runs past, and I don't blame him. They all scamper away from the teeth, running for their lives to the exit.

Debris rain down from the damaged roof. The morning sun cheerily shines through the now-gigantic hole, and the entire warehouse creaks ominously with distress. A giant nostril, a nostril framed with silver scales, blocks the sunlight. Little pieces of my hair, not restrained by my hat, flutter in the artificial wind, wind created when the surrounding air is forcibly drawn into the cavernous snout as the beast inhales.

The dragon chuffs what I can only describe as a contented sound as his nose confirms we are, in fact, here. A silver eye with a vertical pupil replaces the nostril, and the third eyelid tracks across the eye from side to side and blinks at us.

Oh goody, our backup has arrived.

I shake my head at the mess he has made, but I'm so grateful for his well-timed rescue. Forrest yips and, tail wagging, trots towards the humongous silver *dragon*. A massive scaly, clawed front foot—hand, whatever—sweeps into the warehouse. The building crumbles a little bit more around the silver limb as the dragon, to my amusement, casually flicks a few unfortunate creatures out of his way as he scoops Forrest up gently.

I meet her eyes through his dragony digits and give her a thumbs-up and a nod. "Thank you!" I yell. I wave her away. "I got this."

Wow, that was a close call, Story says softly.

Too close, I grumble. *I thought for a minute I was a goner.*

I dunno. I've never seen you fight like that before. Did you know that female vampire had over a thousand confirmed kills, said to be unbeatable? You had her head off in under two minutes.

I grunt and scramble to my feet. I stroll towards the dragon-made hole. Putting my knives away, I grab my sword off the bloodstained floor as I go. I get there in time to watch the silver dragon—he's shiny like a seventies disco ball—elegantly leap into the air, followed by the powerful beat of his wings. The downdraft causes a cloud of dust and debris to roll towards me. I raise my arm to cover my eyes and hold my breath. When the dust settles, I lift my head. They are now just a pinprick in the sky. I watch until they disappear.

Now that was a hell of an exit.

The *clunking* sound of several car doors opening and closing gains my attention. *Huh, it looks like the dragon brought ground backup.* Men dressed in black combat-style clothing, not dissimilar to my own, approach me in a fan formation. Their cautious armed demeanour is kind of strange for a rescue.

The Grand Creature Council employs some of them, and according to facial recognition, a few work for the Hunters Guild.

Ah. Okay. I keep my hands and weapon where they can see them, and my posture I keep relaxed, even if I feel anything but.

"Tru," says a familiar voice from behind the menacing group. Butterflies explode in my stomach with delight, and I sigh with relief.

Oh, wouldn't you know, it's the missing blood donor himself, Story says.

Story. I growl a warning, and in response, she *humphs* in my head.

Nobody is perfect. I know I only have myself to blame. She called him the *blood donor* a few years ago, and I didn't correct her, so of course it stuck. It's not a derogatory term, but he deserves better than that, even *from me.*

His movement is graceful and liquid. He doesn't walk. He glides across the car park towards me, dressed in combat trousers and a long-sleeved thermal shirt. The top clings to his body, showing off just how toned he is. I greedily catalogue all his features. Seven foot two. Short dark hair, warm skin tone, beautiful golden-honey eyes, wide forehead, high cheekbones, elegant nose, and a firm chin. All those features make up perfection. The most beautiful face.

My angel. "Xander," I whisper.

Without even looking, I slide my unneeded sword away. I know now, seeing him here, everything is going to be okay. Safe. I take a deep breath in as he stands before me. The scent of him, an intense burst of metal mingled with sunlight, hits my senses, and his angel magic dances pleasantly along my skin.

I feel like I have come *home*.

Gosh, how I have missed him.

"Hi," I say as I goofily grin at him. I smile so big my cheeks hurt. Crap, I can feel myself blushing. My fingers wiggle at my sides with the most overwhelming urge to reach out and touch him. I haven't seen him for months, and my soul aches. I wish I could just throw my arms around him like a normal person and hug him.

I guess if I did, it would mortify the stoic angel.

"What did you do?" he growls.

My smile fades, and I frown, not understanding his question. He is looking at me as if I'm a stranger. "What?" I ask, confused.

His eyes take on a hard, stern gleam, and with an elegant hand, he points behind me. I turn my head and follow his finger.

Oh yeah, shit. I want to slap my forehead. Of course I see now what he means. The warehouse looks like I have bombed it.

Dust rents the air, and strewn bodies lie where they have fallen, limbs chopped and torn. The chewed and spat-out orc also makes a grisly sight right in front of the gnawed hole in the building's side.

Then there is me, completely unharmed and covered in dust and other creatures' blood. A shiver runs down my spine in a warning.

I gulp. "Oh yeah. About that."

CHAPTER NINE

A DOZEN or so men file past us and through the dragon-made hole into the warehouse. Blimey, rather them than me, what with the creaking state of the place. If I can help it, I really don't want to venture back inside.

Beside me, my angel is spitting mad. Contempt oozes out of him, and his magic crashes around us like a storm. I can feel the anger radiate from his very pores. I open my mouth to explain, and he glares at me.

Oops. Properly cowed, I snap my mouth closed.

Awkwardly, I rub my gritty face and stand there silently, looking at the floor as he follows his men inside.

The sometimes cold but oh so morally strong angel confuses me. I understand why he is so cross, but you'd think a small, tiny part of him would be relieved that I'm okay. What with all the dead bodies and a chewed-up orc lying about.

I'm alive! Yay? Does he think I fought with the creatures inside for shits and giggles?

I've seen him frustrated and exasperated, but I have never seen him this angry before. It's not like I'm a constant pain in the arse. He hasn't cleaned up a mess of mine since I was a teenager. Yet his very presence and raging anger make me feel guilty.

The warehouse creaks, and I gaze up at the roof. *Gah, I wish he'd just come out of there.* Maybe I could tell him what happened informally over breakfast. A cup of tea would be great. I twist my hands.

Uh-oh. I'm so not looking forward to telling him about my role in this mess. Not that I've done anything wrong. Well, apart from perhaps releasing a demon and destroying the evidence of the demon trap without higher-up permission. I've done everything else by the book.

I hate that he is mad. What can I say? We have a tempestuous relationship.

A good thing is that one of my angel's powers enables him to tell a truth from a lie, so all this nonsense should be quick to clear up.

When I was a teenager, they appointed him as my guardian—I tuck in my chin and keep my head down so either Xander or anyone else can't see me smile. I don't need to stir up any more vitriol, and that's what will happen if I'm caught smiling in this situation. During his guardianship, he gave me his superstrong angel blood and saved my life.

So of course, *bam*, seventeen-year-old me fell head over heels in love with him. I lift my eyes and surreptitiously peek at him as he's checking the bodies that are scattered about. I mean, he's an ancient *superhot* angel. What's not to love?

Then there was this spell, and I had powerful visions of our future together. Those future flashes. Wow! They were incredible. If I hadn't already been in love with him, the visions would have thrown me over the edge. Gosh, I love him with my entire heart. Xander is my everything.

Now nine years have passed, and I can't make my mind up if it was all wishful thinking. The visions. I shake my head. Now I don't know if, over the years, I have just embellished the heck out of them.

As time ticks away and I wait for our epic life together to start, the days, months, and *years* tick by and... and I am still waiting.

I feel like a total idiot. But I can't give up on what I saw. I can't give up on him. Us.

Not for the first time, I contemplate: is knowing about the future more likely to encourage events, or does knowing about the future change things irreparably? What if how I've reacted to things has messed everything up? What if my knowledge has made it so I ruin everything?

Yeah, it's a real head fuck.

Underneath my lashes, I peek at him again, and the ever-present loved-up butterflies in my stomach rage. I've never played games, never been coy, not with him. I've always been open and honest about my feelings. Well, I've not told him I love him, as that would be... well, a bloody nightmare. But he knows I like him. He knows I like him a lot.

Honest about feelings but *not about your role as an assassin*. Oh. *Apart from work*, I correct myself as I push the shitty thoughts to the back of my mind. I've always been honest, even when it's been detrimental to my mental health.

Even when he has repeatedly rejected me. It hurt, but I understood.

A shifter prowls across the warehouse to my angel. He whispers in his ear and then draws Xander away. They move further into the building. *Oh, please be okay.* I gnaw on my lip as my eyes flick back to the unstable roof.

It's not his fault that we have never been on the same page. Heck, we aren't even in the same book. At first, at seventeen, I was waaay too young. Now at twenty-six... I puff air through my nose and pluck at the gold bracelet on my wrist. I'm still too young when compared to a creature who has lived thousands upon thousands of years. Twenty-six years is a blink of an eye. *I've cans older than you*, Xander once said. I'm fighting against the tide of that experience. Of millennia.

Yeah, I fell in love with a gorgeous man who avoids me like I'm a disease. I guess you can love someone with all that you are, but there are no rules set in stone that they have to feel the same way. No rules to say that they must love you back.

And unrequited love?

I huff out a pain-filled laugh. Yep, it's a real bitch.

It hurts. Gosh, how it hurts. Especially when I have to go cap in hand and beg for his blood. Oh, he is lovely about it. Very understanding. His golden eyes look at me with pity, as if I'm a needy addict looking for my next hit.

It's one messed-up roller-coaster ride I can't, won't, get off.

I love him, and... and it is soul destroying.

That's why Story hates him. She sees everything, how we met, the aftermath, and the way he makes me feel. I scuff my boot against the paving stone. It isn't his fault that he doesn't love me back.

Yet.

He doesn't love me *yet*.

After fifteen minutes of uncomfortable silence and me trying to go over in my head what I'm going to say, my angel reappears. My heart misses a beat, and I straighten my spine. His golden eyes are on me as he liquid prowls across the warehouse.

Okey-dokey, now comes the hairy bit.

I'm going to have to tell him what happened and why I am here. I'm going to have to come clean about my seven-year stint as a black ops assassin. Ah, no. He thinks I work at a café, which I do. I work about eight hours a week as a cover. My angel doesn't know that I've been working as an assassin, and I couldn't tell him either. But now that I'm caught red-handed, I must explain. I hope he isn't mad.

As he closes the gap between us, I ready myself to relay a full situation report. I decide to start from the very beginning, but before I can utter a single word, Xander loses his ever-loving mind!

My angel's smoky white magic with little gold flakes whips up and wraps around the tops of my arms. Grabbing me like invisible hands, the magic's grip is harsh, pinching the soft skin on the underside as it violently shoves me against the side of the building. My back hits the metal siding with a bang, and a serrated piece of dragon-chewed metal digs uncomfortably into my spine.

"Ouch," I squeak.

Whoa. I know the whole dismembered-creatures-in-a-warehouse-and-me-covered-in-blood looks bad. But what the heck is this? My angel is more than mad—he is livid. So livid, he has lost control of his magic. I almost look to the sky for a stray lightning bolt as he prepares to smite me down.

If he will just give me a chance to explain... *He's not a bad person*, I remind myself. He just doesn't understand.

While his magic continues to squeeze, he moves closer, his big body boxing me against the warehouse. I'm having serious trouble with this situation, and I've never seen him act like this before, not to me. He's never been a threat to me.

He is my angel.

Shocked, I stare into his beautiful honey eyes. My lips tremble, and I press them together as I forbid myself to not allow so much as a single tear to spill.

"Xander, please stop it. You are hurting me."

"Tell me about the angel."

"Angel?" I croak. My throat is supertight, and my chest hurts. "What angel?" As soon as the words leave my mouth, I know immediately it is the wrong thing to say, as his magic shakes me. My teeth rattle, and my head raps against the building with an ear-ringing thud.

Talk about knocking some sense into me.

The reality of the situation really hammers home. He can be mad all he wants, but that doesn't give him the right to manhandle me. It's like I flip a switch inside me. "Get your bloody magic off me," I snarl.

He narrows his eyes, and I glare at him right back.

"You are hurting me," I say again, this time with a painful groan. Slowly, he peels his magic away. It releases its death grip on my arms, but my angel doesn't move. "What the hell is wrong with you? Get yourself under control." His cold eyes watch me as I rub my sore arms, and I shuffle sideways away from the stabby, damaged part of the building. "Nobhead," I mumble under my breath.

Two men—shifters—to the right of us close in, blocking any escape. I tense, and my back aches. It feels as if I have some metal lodged back there.

Great.

Who the hell is this person who stands before me? Certainly not the man I have loved for nine years. Feeling hurt, confused, and suddenly so exhausted. It has been such a long night. I slump back against the building. As I lean again on the ridged metal, I ignore the cut on my back as it stings. I rub my forehead and dig my thumb into the throbbing groove between my eyes.

I can't speak. If I open my mouth right now, I might cry.

My tongue flicks against the back of my teeth, and my fingers drop from my face. There's also not much air in my lungs as I'm struggling to breathe. If I get a snotty nose, there's a real chance I might suffocate and die. I can't believe he did that to me.

Think.

Is this about me or his missing angel? That is the problem, isn't it? He asked me about an angel. More importantly, who? Who the hell has been spinning lies? Pointing fingers in my direction? My stoic angel wouldn't be losing his mind if he didn't have concrete evidence of my guilt.

Which must have been in writing, as I'm sure there are only a handful of people powerful enough to lie to his face.

The rotten worm wiggling in his ear has scrambled his brain. He has lost all common sense. Then again, maybe it's me? Did my brain scramble at some point last night, and I missed an entire conversation?

You are seeing what I'm seeing? Right? I ask Story.

Yes. Did he... I'll kill him, Story sputters out with indignation. I don't have to see her to know her face is all red and she's standing in front of the observation screen with her hands planted on her hips in her dramatic Peter Pan pose. *He. Hurt. You.* She spits each word out with barely refrained anger. *Mother Nature, I hate him. I hate him so damn much.*

So this is real, and I'm not going mad. This is really happening...

Angel. There wasn't an angel with the kidnapped kids or the vaporised, was there?

No, and Ava's checking for any online chatter. You need to come home now.

With a swallow, I brace myself for another violent reaction as I ask him again, "What angel? Who are you talking about?" Luckily for him, he doesn't try anything again. I'm not willing to stand here like a divvy and take it while he smacks me about. "Xander, are you okay?" I whisper. I eye him with concern.

"What are you doing here?" he asks, ignoring my question and seemly changing tack. I can't get anything from his expression. He's so cold. It's like he is a stranger.

"I'm an assassin," I tell him.

"Don't lie to me, Tru. You are not an assassin." My angel scoffs.

"You know I'm not lying. I've been an assassin for seven years."

"You are not a kid anymore." With a disappointed twist of his lips, he shakes his head. "What happened to that sweet girl?" Then Xander drops his voice and speaks slowly, each word drawn out as if to hammer them into my head. "You work at a café. You are delusional and unstable, and you've gone too far this time. I can't protect you anymore."

"You can't protect me from what?" It's my turn to scoff. Does he hear himself? I can protect myself. Thank you very much, both physically and professionally. I don't need or want his help. Especially when he's like this.

Granted, I didn't tell him about being an assassin, my bad, but secrecy is part of the job. Working black ops is a big thing.

Xander watches the delicate bracelet on my wrist spin as I fiddle with it, the bracelet he gave me. His mouth puckers with disgust as if looking at it, at me, revolts him.

The beautiful lines on his face are hard, sharper than a blade, and his lips curl over his teeth with every venomous word he says. "You are a serial killer. A psychopath," he spits out.

My head jolts back as if I've been slapped, and I stumble back a step. What the hell is he talking about?

"What?" I say in a horrified whisper.

CHAPTER
TEN

A SERIAL KILLER AND A PSYCHOPATH, nice one. I laugh under my breath and rub my arms. Even standing in the bright morning sunshine, I feel frozen and a bit sick. Yeah, he'd better stop with the name-calling, as it's getting harder and harder for me to ignore this shit. The entire unfairness of this situation would drive a lesser person nuts.

No, come on, Tru. He doesn't know what he's talking about. All this is just some terrible misunderstanding, something that we will laugh about in a few years.

Right?

Xander is prone to being a little hot-headed, and he obviously has a lot of stuff on his plate. I open my mouth to beg him to listen... then my pride sweeps in, and I snap the stupid thing closed.

Beg. Him.

Tru, really? Beg?

I tilt my head to the side as I watch him with his chest puffed out like a proud cockerel. I narrow my eyes. Where was he when Forrest and I were storming into a building to rescue kids? Tucked up in bed? Yet he comes here with his merry men and misinformation, throwing his weight around without giving me any courtesy, giving me zero chance to explain. And when I try to, he calls me a liar and a bunch of names.

And I was going to beg.

Eff that.

What the heck is wrong with me? There's a fine line between giving a person chance after chance and being a doormat. My chest burns, and my bottom lip wobbles. The last time I begged someone, I was a kid and got chucked out of my home. My non-uncle made me homeless.

"Tell me about the people you exsanguinated," he asks, breaking the long stretch of silence.

"Are you on drugs?" I croak through my tight throat. I cough to clear the worst of it, but a stubborn lump of emotion doesn't want to disappear. "The people I exsanguinated. Me?" I point to my chest. Is he kidding right now? If the entire situation wasn't so messed up, I'd be laughing my arse off. Apart from his, I hate drinking blood. Why on earth would I drain anyone dry? "And you say I'm unhinged."

It's his turn to rub his face as if he's also had a long night. Boohoo. "Don't play games, Tru." He drops his hand, shakes his head, and again speaks in that same slow tone he used before as if my brain isn't up to understanding the importance of his words without him oh so helpfully dumbing it down. "The people behind the ward. Why did you kill them?"

What? I narrow my eyes as my mind flicks back inside the warehouse. The temporary wards I used while I was fighting crumbled. What ward... Oh, unless he means the one in the nightmare room, the pile of bodies and the woman with the red shoe?

Well crap. If I wasn't already leaning against the warehouse, I would have stumbled.

"Me? I didn't—" My voice jolts to a stop with shock. I don't know how to respond. "You think I did that?" Disgust almost overwhelms me. "Really, Xander? You really think I'm capable of that? I told you I'm an assass—"

"Why are you lying to me?" he interrupts, and I groan at the venom in his voice.

"I'm not lying!" I yell, and we gain the attention of a few of his men who are still digging through the warehouse.

Immediately he calms. His tone switches to cajoling. "Okay, an easier question. Why did you murder your accomplices?"

Oh, here we go.

I scoff, and I can't help the accompanying eye roll. "My accomplices? You think I was in league with those guys?" I nod back at the pulpy orc. "Yeah, 'cause I killed that guy as I didn't want to pay him. You know, the chewed-up one right there." I sarcastically hold out my wrists and tap them together, and in a dodgy London accent, I declare, "You got me. It's a fair cop guv." I drop my hands. "I'm gobby, but my mouth isn't that bloody big. Xander, come on. Even from here, my nose can smell the dragon spit. You are not making any sense." I tap my temple in case the people around us do not know of his gift. "You *know*. You know I'm not lying to you. Okay, okay. Look, if your brain is a little wonky concerning me, fair enough, but you must know without a doubt the dragon does nothing shady. He's the dragon. I was here on a job to save some missing kids. Those dead creatures who you are implying are my accomplices have kill order warrants out against th—"

"Liar!" he screams. Spittle from the word rains against my cheek as Xander flings himself toward me like a madman and slams his hands above my head. I flinch. The echo of his hands on the metal vibrates against my back and rings in my ears.

Seconds tick as we stare at each other.

His livid golden eyes glow.

I'm very much a one-strike-and-you-are-out kind of girl, and he's teetering on the edge of strike number three. My entire body feels warm—and not in the sweaty way, thanks to the demon's spell. I don't think I've ever felt so frustrated in my entire life. I do not enjoy being called a liar, especially when I have done nothing wrong.

"I understand I'm in a compromised position because you don't know and haven't been arsed to ask me for all the facts. But to accuse me of such a heinous crime and call me names..." I grind my teeth. "Next, you'll be saying I'm an unstable hybrid and I need to be put down. You have been my number one advocate for years, Xander. Please tell me what the hell is going on. Who have you been talking to? Who has been telling you these lies?" I blink up at him earnestly. "I want to understand."

And perhaps I stupidly want to fight for us.

His eyes widen, and for a microsecond, I see his doubt,

but with a flicker of his eyelid, it's brushed away. There's no getting through to him. He has made up his mind.

"Where is she!" he screams in my face. "You shouldn't have taken her." I flinch as just above my head, the metal beneath his hands distorts, crunches, and rains little spiky shards onto my head. She? The missing angel is female, and he thinks I've taken her. Why the heck would I do that?

"I didn't think you would be capable of such cruelty as this," he says. The scent of his blood fills the air, the cuts to his palms already healing as droplets of gold blood weep onto the torn metal millimetres from my face.

Huh, how strange. It's right there, but I don't crave it.

I take in the wild look in his eyes. Oh, and there we have it. *Bing,* the light goes on in my head. The world stands still, and I feel like I'm holding on to my love for him by the tiniest thread, the tips of my fingers digging into the slippery emotion as it tries to disappear like smoke from my grasp. If I take a breath, will it dissipate? Fall apart as soon as I dare to exhale?

This has nothing to do with the bodies inside. This is about *her*. His missing angel. Whoever she is, she's obviously way more important than me.

My lungs burn.

Another thing hits me. *Oh no. No.*

I gasp.

Another puzzle piece slides into place, him calling me unhinged and delusional. *That's why he doesn't believe me.* Wow, oh wow. Now that makes a sick kind of sense. If someone is unwell and they believe their own lies, then they're not technically lying, are they? A truth-teller kryptonite.

Uh-oh.

Someone has really set me up, using my angel to do it and... and he believes them. Just like that, my heart cracks.

Boom. Strike three, and you are out.

My mind flits over *our* moments. The sweet memories of me growing to love this man. The times he came to my rescue over and over again and that beautiful glimpse of our future... *Come on, Tru, you aren't a psychic! Who sees the future?* I huff out a muffled, bitter laugh. The burst of power was a delusion. It wasn't the future I was seeing, but what I wanted to see.

A stupid girl's dreams.

Nine years wasted. I will not do this to myself anymore.

Yeah, fuck the visions, fuck our future together as there isn't one. I'm so fucking done.

I feel something inside me break. *Oof*, is it possible to feel your own heart shatter? There will be no sticking back the tattered parts of me with tape. My soul feels like it's dying.

The angel hovers over me, blood all over his hands. My continued silence makes a little vein in his jaw tic. I swallow down my hurt the best I can and instead embrace the anger. It's all I've got left. To start with, he needs to get the hell out of my face. My chest heaves against his. We are so close that our angry breaths mingle. Being near him—I feel like I'm being torn apart.

"'Cause of our shared history, and I know you aren't thinking clearly," I rasp. "I will again ask you one last time, *politely,* to back the fuck off!"

When he still doesn't move, I flash my fangs and *hiss* at him.

With another crush and bang of the metal, the angel pushes off the wall and casually waves away his boys in black when it looks as if they are going to intervene and jump to his aid. Poor baby needs backup.

I turn my head and make eye contact with the pair of them. I deliberately lick a fang. "Don't mess with me. I'm unhinged, remember?" When one of them goes for a weapon, I snort and shake my head. "Piss off, wolf."

He drops his hand, thinking better of it. They both back off.

I nod. "What were you going to do anyway? You ain't gonna do shit." If I were so inclined, it would take a matter of seconds to pluck out their eyeballs. Might make me feel better, somewhere to put the rage. With a dismissive snarl, I keep my hands to myself. "I've just spent the morning, sword in hand, hacking at orcs, trolls, and vampires." I nod at the warehouse. And for what? No good deed goes unpunished, right? To lose the love of my life when he believes anyone but me... I close my eyes to the pain.

There is something to be thankful for, I guess. *At least, at least I'm not crying.* With that thought, my bloody eyes sting. I rapidly blink. *Oh no. No you don't, none of that.* If I start, I don't think I will stop. I grind my back teeth; I can control myself, and years from now, when I'm looking back, this will just be a painful memory. I hope I will muster a single iota, a tiny little bit, of pride in the way I handled myself when my very soul shrivelled up and died.

I huff and nod. He's the one who's going to be sorry. He's the one who is going to feel ashamed when he finds out someone has played him.

Xander is an angel puppet with a hand up his arse.

The problem with me, my biggest fault, is I'm very black-and-white. When someone crosses the line into enemy territory, there is no coming back.

Even if I hurt myself.

I hunch. Story is right. She has always been bloody right. Love is about equality, and we have never, ever been equal. Love is about give and take, friendship, and understanding. He has never even trusted me enough to be my friend.

We never had a chance.

His scent wraps around me, seeping a chill through my bones. The metal mingled with sunlight smell of him, combined with the tinge of blood, makes my stomach drop and roll.

Butterflies.

Piss off, you little shits. I don't welcome their flutter. I used to think butterflies in my tummy were a good thing. A sign of attraction, nature's way of highlighting someone fated to me. The angel has always given me a dancing, bubbly feeling inside, butterflies drunk on fairy wine. Now I see the reality. I see what they are now. They are not a sign of attraction but of warning. Do not engage. Avoid like the plague.

"Take her for interrogation," Xander instructs his men.

Yes, the very worst of monsters are the ones that give you butterflies.

CHAPTER
ELEVEN

GRIEF HITS me like a gargoyle's punch, a solid smack-bang to the chest. A punch so hard it stops my breath, and my entire chest aches. That's what the pain, the emptiness, and the anger feel like. Grief. It's like he has died and come back as a ghost to haunt me.

Am I evil to think his death couldn't have rocked me as hard as his betrayal? It's going to be incredibly hard to grieve for the angel when he is still alive. Worse, grieving for a non-relationship I saw in a *vision* nine years ago.

Uh-huh, what was I thinking?

I hate him. But I hate myself more.

The squishy side of me, the weak part I have kept protected and intact all these years, even through the horrors of my past, is now broken. I can feel it. Feel the broken pieces grinding together, rough edges scraping like the Earth's tectonic plates, causing mini earthquakes inside my chest.

Oof.

How has this all gone so wrong? It happened so quickly, and it doesn't feel real. I guess I am in shock. I know the angel can be a dickhead, but this is on another level of wrong.

The angel signals for his men to surround me. Great. If I'm not careful, this could get ugly real fast. Giving him my back, I turn away from his liquid-honey gaze. I don't want to analyse these feelings anymore, don't want to acknowledge the grinding, and nor do I want to face what's happened. Not here and certainly not now. I mentally take out a dustpan and brush and sweep away the wounded, broken parts of me. Then drop that shit so deep inside my subconscious that it might be lost forever.

Good. I bloody hope so.

I straighten, leaving behind the whimpering, hurt creature I was but seconds ago. The angel is now just a stranger, a man I used to know. I take a deep breath, square my shoulders, and lift my chin. "Let's get this sorted, shall we? Like the good old times. Whoopee-doo, I haven't had a good old interrogation for years." I rub my hands together and spin on my toes, and I'm off.

He follows me. Right on the back of my heels. What the hell? Why won't he just sod off? He tries to grab hold of my arm, but I slip to the side, neatly avoiding him. I stroll towards the cars they arrived in and use the bonnet of the closest one as a shelf. I begin to take off all my weapons and equipment. I'd rather do this myself than have these strangers strip me.

With each piece of kit I remove, I shout out a description.

"What are you doing?" asks a blond-haired shifter as he creeps towards me. The others aren't so bold, but they watch as I carefully place another blade down.

"I'm making sure none of you get sticky fingers. I want everything back." The collection on the bonnet has me scowling. My weapons are disgusting. They all need a deep clean. I hate leaving them like this. "I want everything back *clean,* seeing as I can't do it myself."

"You are mad." A few of the others murmur their agreement.

"Yeah, she's fucking tapped in the head."

"Mental."

Unperturbed, I dramatically sigh and, for good measure, roll my eyes. "And you are all stupid. There are cameras, you bunch of dicks. Micro-cameras are zipping about everywhere." I point and circle a finger. "Everything is being recorded."

The surrounding men frantically search the air for the cameras. The angel narrows his eyes and squints. "I want that footage, now," he demands from no one in particular.

I roll my eyes again. Good luck with that. Ava's camera system isn't for easy hacking. "I'm sure my team will give you access to the footage if you officially request it." He dares to move, to stand by my side. "Here, before I forget." They all tense as I lift my arm, pull up my sleeve and tug the delicate gold bracelet so hard that the magical clasp breaks. It tumbles from my wrist and pools warmly into my palm, glinting in the morning sun. "This is yours."

The spelled bracelet helped me to control a challenging

power. I haven't needed it for a very long time, but as he gave it to me, I loved it and continued to wear it for sentimental reasons. It was treasured. Now it makes me feel sick.

Xander doesn't even attempt to take it. His big muscly arms move to settle across his broad chest. He drops his chin and taps his still-bloody fingers rhythmically against his forearm. Mr Impatient.

I tip my hand, and the bracelet slides from my palm with a flash of glinting gold as the jewellery drops onto the tarmac. Dramatic of me, I know, but after the morning I have had, I think I'm entitled to being a bit of a drama llama.

"What was that?"

"Was that...?"

"She dropped a spell!"

I snort and watch on with amusement as the mighty fine warriors scatter. Some of them dive for cover behind the cars. I raise a single eyebrow at the angel as if to say "Can you believe this shit?"

"My shadow," the angel warns.

My insides jolt when he uses that name. An *effing pet name. Is he for real?* "Don't call me that." I snap. "We aren't friends. I'm an unhinged psychopath, remember," rasps out of my burning throat.

I hate him, and for a moment, I almost contemplate grabbing my sword and giving him a little poke. I look at the dirty blade longingly, and my hands twitch at my sides. I shake my head. "Sorry, did I make your henchman look bad? Did you see the bitten vampire with short brown hair, the guy over there?" I point in the vampire's direction. "He dived like a pro. Very impressive."

If I'm honest, my voice sounds a little strained, but I wouldn't be me without a bit of snark. You know, a sense of humour to hide the pain.

"Must embarrass you to use lesser beings for this mission. What with you being the angel's top representative on Earth? What, were the hellhounds busy?" Hellhounds are old, powerful shifters with fire magic. Trained up to be an elite fighting force. You don't mess with a hellhound.

Xander grunts. From one of his many pockets, the angel pulls out an anti-magic band.

"Oh goody, a present. It's like we are exchanging gifts." It's a nullifying band made to remove every spell and shut down every trace of magic. It works on every creature but is mainly used on criminals.

"Stop looking at me like that," Xander grumbles.

"Like what?" I look him up and down as my feet move into a fighting stance. "What are you, Xander, stupid or a monster?"

His face is blank as he taps the plastic-looking black band against his hand.

Don't fight. Please don't fight them, Story whispers. *You will have to go with him. There is no other way. Ava has a contact, a talented barrister called Mr Brown. We will find you and get you out of this. Just please, for the love of Mother Nature, please keep calm.*

I will, I promise. Like the good friend she is, she says nothing about Xander and what he has said. I can hear the pain in her voice. There will be no "I told you so" from her. *I love you, Story.*

I love you too.

Will you tell D-Dexter... tell him I will be home soon.

That stupid cat. Yes, I will tell the ginger fur ball, and I will feed him until you come home, she says playfully. Overly playful, but that's okay. Story also knows that once the band goes on, our communication magic will be gone and we won't be able to talk again till I sort this mess out.

Lucky for me, I've played with the bands before. Of course I have. If there is something so readily available that can stop magic in its tracks, damn straight, I got hold of one and slapped that puppy on my wrist.

Yep, the magic renders you less than human. Weakness is something I'm familiar with, especially when I was younger. The best way to describe the band's magic is instant human flu. The type of flu where it is impossible to drag yourself out of bed and you struggle to lift your head from the pillow.

Oh, and the more power you have, the more debilitating the effects are. Yay. Not to be big-headed, but I'm pumped to the brim with power. For instance, just on my shifter side, I have the magic of four unicorns. Then sprinkle in the power of my born vampire lineage, and I'm a melting pot of magic.

No way would I allow an anti-magic band to disable me without trying to mitigate its effects. So I trained. It took me weeks and months of repeatedly trying and building a resistance just so I could stay awake with the cursed thing. I've even slapped one on my wrist for fun and then gone to spar with the gargoyles.

That's the only reason I'm confident enough to hold my arm out to Xander.

CHAPTER
TWELVE

KEEP CALM. We love you, and we will sort this out, and you'll be home before you know it. Pinching against my skin, the anti-magic band snaps and wraps around my wrist. *Leave it with me*—Story's words are cut off as the anti-magic activates.

I lock my knees against my body's sudden weakness and continue to glare at Xander. I got this. With my natural vampire healing and its pain management now unavailable, every injury barrels to the forefront of my mind, and with no way to shift so I can instantly heal, my body screams its discomfort. *I've still got this.*

Grumbles and mumbles bubble up from the peanut gallery surrounding us.

"She's not that powerful."

"Are you kidding? She's fucking insane. That's why the

anti-magic does nothing to her. Like a pixie on fairy wine, they gain crazy-ass strength."

"Never seen anything like that. I put one on a human as a joke once, and it knocked the guy sick."

"The hellhounds can cope with them."

"Yeah, didn't I hear that John guy had two stuck on him when the rogue vampire lord captured him, what... six, seven years ago—"

"Nah, eight."

"It was six years ago, you morons."

Throughout their meaningless chatter, wide-eyed, I stare at Xander. The wanker. I give him the big sweet innocent look I've perfected over the years. A look that matches my rainbow hair that screams I wouldn't hurt a fly.

He looks away. "Mike," he calls out, his voice gruff. A smug shifter, the aforementioned Mike comes to call. Wearing heavy gloves, he presents a case so fancy you'd be forgiven to mistake it for a briefcase that holds nuclear codes.

With flair, pizzazz almost to the point of jazz hands, he opens the case. All the other shifters step back, and the vampires shuffle forwards. His smug smile only gets wider as he pulls out solid silver restraints.

Ooh, handcuffs—how antiquated.

So many ways to secure a person, and the idiots chose this method. You'd think locking my magic inside would be enough, but no, they have to put silver on me. Nice.

While Magic Mike and his snazzy silver jewellery have my full attention, another brave soul slams me against the car. I grunt and groan as my hip hits the doorframe. *Shit, that hurt.* Without missing a beat, he grapples my arms behind my back and tweaks my right elbow. His hands are bruising—even though I'm offering zero resistance.

Magic Mike approaches, and the solid silver handcuffs click into place. It's almost like, collectively, everyone holds their breath. Waiting.

Fun fact: I'm not allergic to silver. Being a hybrid does, in fact, have some perks. I do my best to hide my smirk and oblige with the obligatory hissing and pain-filled noises. Not that I have to act much. My body is hurting. I can feel every bruise, every scrape. If I hadn't practised extensively with the anti-magic, I've no doubt I'd be out cold on the tarmac, flat-out unconscious, probably elegantly landing on my face.

The idiot behind me slams against me again, grinding me against the car. The angel does nothing. I laugh under my breath, snort, and then laugh some more. Yep, I'm perfectly mentally fit.

"Oi, perv," I say at the end of my chuckle. "If you rub your pelvis against me one more time, I will rip your dick clean off and make you eat it."

"Yeah?" he whispers in my ear like a proper sleaze.

I turn my head to get Xander's attention, but conveniently, he's looking away. "Angel, do all your prisoners get this treatment? Sexually assaulted? Or am I just the lucky one?" I feel the sudden tension more than I see it. An uneasy hush falls over the car park as everyone cranes their necks to watch. A few of the men shuffle with discomfort. "Yes? No?"

Looks like I'm going to have to deal with this myself. I

throw my head back and get a satisfying hit to Mr Pelvis's nose. He screams. I hum. Simple but effective.

At least the move got him away from my bum, and... as I turn, he punches me in the face. Nice. That's unfortunate. Even I can't block a hit with my hands handcuffed behind my back. I duck another punch, and the vampire's fist smashes right through the car's side window. Glass shards rain around my feet.

"Cameras," I singsong as I lick the blood from my now-split lip.

With that single word, the angel grabs hold of Mr Pelvis by the scruff of his neck and drags him away from me.

Oh look. It's the brown-haired champion car-diving vampire. I must have hurt his feelings before. The horror of a fragile ego. The hired idiots step up to help to restrain him, and he's tossed behind a wall of muscle. Shame really, as now I can't kick him in the face.

You promised Story to behave.

"An anti-magic band and silvered and I can still beat the ever-loving shit out of you. Don't worry, perv. I will find you when this is all over." He bobs up and down, side to side, trying to get to me. Honestly, he's ridiculous. I laugh at his antics, roll my shoulders, and then rotate each wrist as far as my new silver jewellery will allow. My poor elbow is killing me.

The angel runs his hand through his short, dark hair. Frustration and hate bleed out of him. It nips and bites at my skin.

"Thanks for looking after me," I say to him. His eye twitches. "Remember, I'm still a female shifter, super-duper special and oh so rare." I'm not kidding either. Female shifters are rare, and I think there are only ten purebred females in the country. I move, and one shifter, a tiger, stumbles backwards, refusing to let the space between us shrink.

"Half. You are half shifter," a wolf grumbles to himself at the back while toeing at a piece of warehouse rubble.

"Yes, but I can shift." My new handcuffs jingle as I nonchalantly flick a piece of gunk from my leg. Eww, rubbery, is that brain matter? Gross, it is. It takes everything I have not to hop around and squeal. I'm okay with the chopping, but I don't want the aftermath stuck to my leg.

Focus, Tru. What was I saying... Oh yeah. "According to public test results, if I breed with a shifter, there is a high probability I'll have a girl." His brown eyes almost pop out of his head with that little revelation. "That's why my life has been incredibly public. I want people to notice if I disappear." I smirk at the angel and then at his motley crew. "So I could, if I was so inclined, chop you all up into teeny-tiny pieces and get nothing more than a slap on the wrist."

Oh no. Did I hit a nerve? Oops. Bam. Angry angel. His magic whips out and slams into my face. It throws me back a few steps. I hold my ground. Without my magic, that is some feat. At least I'm not bouncing my aching hip off the car again.

Huh, my face feels kind of funny and the skin itches. I rub the side of my cheek against my shoulder and open my mouth to retort, but... Xander's magic has sealed my mouth right up. More than that, as my tongue batters against what should be my mouth, I find only skin. Friggity-frig-frig, what *Matrix* shit is this?

Horrified, I stare at him, my eyes saying what I can't.

It was your fault, you knew you were being a dick. I know. I know. I was almost annoying myself with my stupid quips. I should have just kept my mouth shut.

Now I don't have a choice. I have all this pain and anger. It is overwhelming, and it's all I can feel. His face blurs. Ah, now I'm crying! *Only a little, but what the hell, Tru? Why is he doing this?* I rapidly blink back the stupid tears.

"It's not permanent. The spell will wear off."

Oh, that's okay then. Silly me for freaking out. No bother at all that you've magicked away my effing mouth!

Xander then pulls open the rear passenger door of the car and unceremoniously shoves me inside.

CHAPTER
THIRTEEN

THE ANGEL and two of his more professional men drive us to the nearest portal. I feel vulnerable. I am on my own. The cameras can't follow me through the gateway as the line magic will fry them.

When we step through the magical ley line gateway, to say I'm surprised at what is on the other side is an understatement.

Is this... is this some kind of joke?

Instead of going somewhere familiar, I expected to arrive at the Hunters Guild offices, or I even had a horrid inkling Xander was going to try for a mental institution. What with the unhinged narrative he has about me going on in his head.

But no, it's worse.

Eff my life.

Okay, I admit it; I'm a magnet for trouble. From the

moment I took the assassination contract, things have been spiralling out of my control. Even before I went inside the bloody warehouse for those kids, I had a feeling deep down in my stomach that told me something was about to go horribly wrong. I felt it all night. I know to trust my instincts, damn it, and they were screaming at me. But did I do anything to help myself? No.

As I take my first full breath in, it registers that the air is artificially clean. It is missing the smells of everyday life that I take for granted. As I move, gravity is heavy. I must work harder for each step, a sensation I can only equate to walking through water. *Toto, I've a feeling we're not in Kansas anymore.* The famous line from *The Wizard of Oz* rattles around in my head as I take everything in with wide eyes. I know instinctively we are off-world.

Oh, and the big-ass sign right there is another, bigger hint things have stepped up to echelon levels of effed up.

Welcome to prison intake

Yep, we are on a prison world. Yay. As I shuffle along, my mind is going a hundred miles an hour, and I've concluded that this isn't just some random lousy luck situation of me being caught with my pants down. Xander didn't make any calls after he found me at the warehouse.

No, he planned all this in advance.

The double doors ahead of us whoosh open. Everything inside this first area is super clean and bright, with chrome and metal finishes, a more fancy modern hotel aesthetic than prison.

The angel liquid prowls alongside me, matching my shuffling steps. With only being able to breathe through my nose, the gravity, the anti-magic band, and my hands handcuffed behind my back, just walking is a struggle. My boots annoyingly squeak on the marble floor. I avoid looking at him.

My eyes drift back over my shoulder longingly to the portal, and I notice with little chagrin I've left a visible trail of gross crap on the floor. It has been shedding from my clothes. Amused, I stumble. Xander tries to steady me, and I almost fall flat on my face, avoiding his hand.

"This facility is the best, and they have a stellar reputation. They are also independent of any alliances, so you can rest assured you will be perfectly safe." He clears his throat and rubs his chest. "I know you do your best to make trouble wherever you go, but you won't be able to do that here. Plus you will also get all the help that you need."

The only help I need is to get away from you. Xander clears his throat again. I shoot him a dirty look. *Feeling a little guilty there, bud? Your conscience stuck in your throat?*

Behind a counter that takes up the entire back wall, underneath another cheerful welcome sign, an old lady greets us with a fake smile. Her enormous dark brown eyes and pointed ears show her to be an elf, but her visible ageing shows a human heritage.

My adoptive grandad was half-elf, although he didn't age like this lady. Her fixed smile fades as she looks me up and down, and she tuts at Xander and the shifters behind us.

Huffing a sigh under her breath, she mumbles, "Poor girl." With a scowl and a flick of her wrist and the jangle of a white bracelet, her magic creeps towards my face and removes the angel's horrible spell.

I gasp with relief and rub my lips together. I have a mouth, thank goodness.

"Thank you," I whisper.

I swallow, the sound audible, transmitting my fear through the room for everyone to hear. I'm not stupid. I recognise the danger I find myself in. I'm bricking it. Frightened beyond belief. But over and above the fear and hurt is still the raging anger. I frown and rub my lips together again. I will take anger over those feelings any day.

"Tru Dennison?" she asks, her tone pleasant and no-nonsense as she slaps a datapad down on the desk and, with a crooked finger, points at a highlighted section. "I need a signature." Xander nods and bends over to sign.

As he moves, I catch my reflection on the shiny surface of the processing desk. I look a bloody mess. The phrase *dragged through a hedge backwards* comes to mind. Well, if that hedge was covered in gore. I suddenly feel itchy, as if my skin wants to crawl away from my clothes.

"Excuse me. Is there somewhere I can get cleaned up?" I ask with a wince as my tongue makes a click as it sticks to the roof of my mouth. "And could I trouble you for a drink of water?"

"That won't be necessary, dear," the old lady says as she shuffles towards some shelves. Over her shoulder, she says, "You can remove her restraints. She can't go anywhere. You aren't going to do anything stupid now, are you, dearie?"

I shake my head. "No," I croak. Even if I could ninja up and take the angel and the two shifters, where would I go? The portal we came through is locked down tight.

Is Xander really going to leave me here, lock me up? Or is this a horrid way of getting me to confess? What does he want, a big reveal, a villain speech? Funny enough, I won't confess to something I haven't done.

One shifter catches my eye and gives me a chin lift. I take that as his willingness to remove the cuffs. I spin and give—ah, I remember his name—Magic Mike, the silver keeper, my back. With still-gloved fingers, he carefully removes the heavy silver handcuffs. He then opens the fancy case they came in and returns them to the safety within. *Bloody shifters.* It's all so dramatic. I have my own restraints in silver, steel, and iron. I dump them in a drawer for when I need them. The ceremony of the case is mystifying.

Xander's fingertips brush against the skin of my wrist as he removes the anti-magic band. I can't help my shudder of disgust from his touch, and when the band is finally off, I skitter away from him.

Pins and needles zip up and down my arms when I move them. I feel utter relief to have my magic back as I rotate my shoulders, happy that my natural healing will kick in soon to sort out my various aches and pains. I rub my wrists, trying to get the blood to flow back into them. I have bands of redness and spots of blood where the skin has been rubbed away. The fault of the stupid, perverted vampire. Fighting with him made me strain. I'm lucky. If I was a regular shifter, my wrists would be black with necrosis.

Silver is no joke. It also scars horribly.

Xander doesn't know of my immunity to its effects, and as I stare at my bruised and bleeding wrists, the threads of rage inside me build.

My relief is short-lived as the prison lady returns from her hunt with a white metal collar. It looks very similar to the bracelet on her wrist. She places it down with a clack on the shiny metal counter. Ominous dark magic comes off the thing in waves.

"This collar uses your own magic against you," she says, eyeing me with way too much glee for the situation. Whoa, she enjoys her job a little bit too much, I see. "It has incredible inbuilt power. They made it to keep prisoners under total control. The magic within the collar will keep a prisoner clean, maintain physical health, and keep the prisoner nourished and hydrated. Our prisoners do not need to consume anything to stay alive. They also don't need to use the toilet, have a shower, or change clothes. The artefact meets every bodily function."

Her mean gaze focuses back on me. "If you misbehave, it will also give you a little shock. A short, sharp correction so you will know immediately to change your behaviour. So handy."

I wrinkle my nose as she lovingly caresses the collar. *Yeah, soooo handy.* I have to clamp my lips closed so I don't snarl at her.

She smiles at Xander. "Prisoners can't protest. They cannot use food or the lack of food to hurt themselves." Her eyes sparkle as her wrinkly hand continues to stroke the collar. "We don't want a bunch of skeletons going to court. That wouldn't look good." She titters. "What with over a year of waiting time for cases to be heard."

My brain skips, and my thoughts screech to a halt. What? Wait... a year? What? My heart jumps in my chest. No, no, no, that can't be right. Can it?

Tru, don't you dare freak out. Story said she had a fancy barrister, and she said she will sort everything out. I will be out of here in a few days. No way can anyone find me guilty of anything. I have done nothing wrong.

"The suicide rate is zero, and we haven't had a report of violence towards our staff for over a century. Using a collar system also means we don't have to move prisoners around unnecessarily." She looks back at me with a rictus grin. "You can all just stay in your cells. It cuts down on guard work-load and costs immensely."

Unnecessary movement? Erm, what about creature rights and mental health? The collar is an excellent idea in a hospital setting, when a patient can't fend for themselves. But in a prison, really? Taking away a person's basic needs is needlessly cruel. But what do I know? Any bad people I encounter, I'm usually there to kill them, not lock them up. I shrug. I shouldn't be here too long. Story wouldn't leave me here to rot, and Xander is just trying to frighten me.

I hope.

I rock back away from her hands as she reaches towards me with the collar. Xander oh so helpfully steps up and holds my head steady. My hands ball up into fists at my sides. The old lady, as she moves closer to me, smells like rotten wet leaves. Metal, sunlight, and rotting leaves. The combined scent of the pair of them makes me want to heave. It takes everything in me to keep still and not rip away from their hands.

The old lady hums as she reaches around my neck, and with a *snap*, the collar clicks into place.

I wobble away from them, heart pounding. I hold my breath as I wait for something to happen… it takes another few seconds for the dark, rank magic to bury itself underneath my skin. In a flash, my dirty black combat clothing is gone, replaced by a white long-sleeved top and trousers. Cautiously I lift my hands to my face. My skin is squeaky clean. My unrestrained hair hangs loose, its heavy weight down my back. A strand sticks to my cheek, and when I brush it away, I notice that my multicoloured tresses are gone, replaced with white, colourless strands.

Whoa. They like the colour white, don't they? Crikey.

For the time being, I can cope with white hair. It's preferable to having no mouth. At least they didn't shave my head.

I feel odd, not weak like the anti-magic band, but not full of life either. It is like all my vitality is being sucked into the collar. I no longer hurt, nor am I thirsty. The sensation is strange. Numbing. The old lady unconsciously strokes the bracelet on her wrist. That's why she was strong enough to remove the angel's mouth spell. The creepy collar-and-bracelet combo must allow her to use the magic of the prisoners.

"You cannot use any magic or shift into your animal form. So please do not try as you will dislike the punishment. Now..." She flips a few pages on the datapad and then squints up at me. "You're a hybrid? We don't have a hybrid procedure, so you will have to pick a creature. Do you want to be treated as a..." She glares down at the document. "Unicorn or pureblood vampire?" She stares back at me and taps at the side of the datapad.

Neither. I'd rather be home in bed. I lick my lips—glad I still have them—and puff out a small breath. Choices, choices.

"What would be the difference?"

She rolls her eyes and folds her arms underneath her

breasts. "Well, as a shifter, I would appoint the unicorn leader as the guardian for your care." That would be my father's mother, my birth grandmother, Ann. She would love this scenario. Ann would use my predicament as leverage and have me married off before I could blink. "Same with the vampires. The vampire leader would be appointed." Atticus, the vampire leader, isn't so bad, I guess. Better than Granny Ann any day. "Oh, and as a shifter prisoner, I would give you time to shift, which is currently half an hour per week. You, of course, wouldn't get that as a vampire prisoner, but I would add blood to your collar's magic ration."

"It is dangerous not to shift," the angel pipes up. *Why does he care?* "I'll be her guardian. I've done it before, and I can then give her my blood."

He can sod right off. "Yeah, and that got me into this mess. No, thank you." I give him a fake-ass smile that screams "nobhead."

He stares back at me with a look that screams "you will do as you are told."

"No, I can't do that," she says with a smirk. "You cannot be her guardian as you have signed all her intake forms. That would be an obvious conflict of interest, unethical, and a breach of our rules. It is clearly written in the contract you signed. Please see section 4.8634."

"Vampire please."

"Tru," he growls my name with a reprimand.

"Ignore him. He's been a prick all morning," I say to the old lady.

"Righty-o, vampire it is." Her thumbs go like the clappers, and with a final satisfied nod, she pops the device back on the desk.

"You are making a mistake," Xander murmurs next to my ear.

"Not your pig, not your farm," I snarl back at him—it was one of my grandad's favourite sayings—and lean away. No idea why he wants to cosy up to me now. He needs to learn the meaning of personal space.

The datapad on the desk pings. The prison lady's head tilts oddly as she looks at it with a scowl. She scoops it back up and reads the message with a *humph* sound. "The vampire leader has replied, and he's already on his way." She lowers the datapad and peeks at me through her eyelashes. "That's very unusual. Aren't you a special little princess?"

I shrug. What can I say to that?

The kiss mark on my hand, which nobody has said anything about, throbs. I surreptitiously brush the tip of my finger over it. Static builds underneath my skin.

Magic, when magic shouldn't exist. Now that's interesting... powerful stuff. A shiver runs down my spine as my mind wanders to the demon. I wonder what he's doing now. The kiss pulses as if it understands I'm thinking of him—freaky.

Somehow with it on me, I don't feel so alone, which is even freakier. Perhaps I should kiss the scar? That's what he said, wasn't it? Kiss it, and he'd come? I snort. I wonder if he meant an otherworld prison break. Doubt it. I push the thought of the demon away. No way do I want to add a pissed-off demon to my issues. I can rescue my damn self— well, with a bit of help from my friends.

"Will it be possible to speak to my family and barrister please?"

"Only your guardian, and he will have all the details you will need." She claps her hands. "Okay, that's it. Thank you, gentlemen. You can all go. Shoo. Shoo. I'll take things from here."

Xander shakes his head and uses his extra bossy tone. "No, I need an interrogation room. I must talk to the prisoner—"

"Not today, you don't," she says. "You should have done all your chatting before you arrived. Intake and administration come first. Look, pretty boy. If you haven't heard this about us, take it from someone who knows. Princess here will be more inclined to speak to you after she has spent a few days in our care. You will be happy to know they always break." Her rictus grin is back. "We will knock that fighting spirit right out of her."

Ah, right. Bloody great.

CHAPTER
FOURTEEN

THEY STASH me in an interview room to wait for the vampire leader. As I'm waiting, I check out my snazzy white clothing. It's so odd. I can see the white cotton fabric and touch it, but I might as well be naked as it doesn't feel like I've got anything against my skin. I attempt to lift the bottom edge of the shirt just to get a closer look at the material and get a love zap from the collar for my trouble.

And by love zap, I mean I find myself on my back, wedged halfway underneath the table and chair with no rhyme or reason how I got there. *Ow!* My mouth tastes like ozone, my lips are buzzing, and my teeth ache. I also bet if I peeked in a mirror right now, my hair would be standing on end and I'd see the residual static crackling within the strands.

Bloody hell, for a second there, I think the collar stopped my heart. Ah, I won't be doing that again. The bloody thing packs a punch. No wonder the old lady had a sick sparkle in her eyes as she explained the collar's punishment setting.

"Okay, I get it. No touching the clothes," I grumble.

Moaning, groaning, and using the table leg as a guide, I drag myself off the floor and onto wobbly feet. I slump back into the chair just before my knees buckle. I feel like crap. It doesn't help that my body has gone into shutdown mode. I was wrong about the collar's effects. The longer it is on, the more drugged I feel. The damn thing is horrible.

The door to the interview room whooshes open. I keep my head down, and I don't even bother to raise my eyes. Fingers crossed, it's another visual check, and I'm not about to get a reprimand. The prison guards have been popping in and out all aflutter. They are making me feel like I'm a museum exhibit or, worse, an animal in the zoo. It's the same old come look-at-the-hybrid bullshit.

The chair across the table moves. Oh, and there it is, the pitter-patter of my heart as it picks up its rhythm. The creature in the room is powerful. Nice to know adrenaline mitigates some of the collar's effects as the fight-or-flight hormone floods my system.

"Apologies for keeping you waiting," says a deep cultured voice.

Intrigued, I lift my chin from my chest, and my alien long white hair flows around me, settling annoyingly against my neck and covering half my face.

We take each other's measure.

Atticus.

The pureblood—born, not bitten—vampire leader is here. Head of the Vampire Guild and the Vampire Council.

I have met Atticus before. He is forever eternal and never changing, and he looks exactly the same.

Dressed in an immaculate navy suit with a short, clipped-to-the-scalp, no-nonsense haircut, his eyes are a dark brown. I had once upon a time thought that they were black, but after seeing the demon's bottomless eyes, I now realise they are brown. Handsome, if somewhat plastic-looking.

Purebloods have this airbrushed quality, so perfect that they don't seem real. They give me the heebie-jeebies. I'm glad I don't look like that. For all my hybrid weirdness, I still look kind of human.

Apart from some basic information on what his job is, he's an unknown... a mystery to everyone. Atticus is a recluse. He rarely goes out in public, and nobody knows where he lives. He certainly isn't a TV vampire. Purebloods tend to be famous.

He scares the bejesus out of me.

It is then I realise I'm slouching, and I didn't reply to his greeting. I sit bolt upright. "No problem, sir." Last time I'd met him, he'd been straight talking and non-game-playing. I hope he is the same now. I know he's not about to put his neck on the line to get me out of this predicament, but I appreciate his time nonetheless.

The thing I don't get is why did he come so fast? I know I'm impressed with my self-importance, but I'm not this important. So what is going on?

Still watching me, he's sort of frozen to the floor. With his hand resting on the chair, he breathes in a sharp, angry breath, and his nostrils pinch together. My entire face scrunches up with a frown. *Did he get me confused with somebody else?* Well, that's not entirely unexpected, and it must piss him right off that someone has made a mistake. To have to drop everything and come here for a half-pure-blood and a waste of his valuable time.

Instead of sitting, Atticus bends down to my level and asks, "May I?" His eyes are fixed on the collar. Ah, I see. That's why he is so mad. I nod. With a cool hand, he gently cups my chin and tilts my head to the side. With his other hand, he moves my hair so he can get a better look. "Barbaric," he snarls. He drops my chin and makes a *humph* sound at the back of his throat.

Elegantly he adjusts his suit and sits down. "I would have answered the summons to this horrendous world at some point this year, but I'm here now because of a favour." He digs into the inside of his navy jacket and pulls out a Don't Hear Me Now ball. He drops the expensive potion to the floor. The buzz in the air that follows the impact tells us the privacy spell has been activated.

Atticus rests his arms on top of the metal table between us, sits forward in his seat, and stares at me intently. "How do you know Kleric, the demon prince?"

"A prince," I squeak. Bloody hell. I had no idea he was a prince! "Imethimlastnight," I blurt.

Atticus leans away from me with confusion, his eyes flicking to the collar with concern.

Uh-oh. He thinks it's scrambling my brain. *No wonder. What the eff was that, Tru?* Blood rushes to my cheeks as I take a deep breath and try again. I repeat myself. This time I speak slower. "I met him last night. They trapped him in a demon circle, a killing circle, and I... erm... I released him." I duck my head and wince. "Was that bad?"

"For you, no."

"Oh." What can I say to that? That's good, right? What the eff is going on today? The big-ass blue demon is a prince! Bloody hell. It's not every day you find a naked prince in a warehouse.

"He told me to tell you you've got yourself into a bit of a pickle. Does that mean anything to you?"

I clear my throat. "Yes, it does." Gah, bloody cheeky demon. When he was in the circle, I said that very thing. I rub my face and sink back into the chair. I drop my hands on my knees underneath the table and give the still-red scar a prod. The demon's kiss. Not just a demon, a prince. *Kleric, you are hilarious.* The scar throbs, and a wave of magic skitters under my skin. Again, it is like he is listening. Wow, that is still freaky. "The message does make sense. It's a private joke."

"Good. I have also had your friend Story blowing up my phone, demanding answers, and your barrister is causing many legal issues for the Vampire Council and Shifter Assembly. Rest assured, Miss Dennison, your chosen family knows where you are, and I will inform them that, for the time being, you are safe."

For the time being, uh-huh, that sounds great.

"Will you be able to get me out of here?"

"No."

"Oh okay." I tuck my hair behind my ear. "So, erm, what do I do?"

"You wait. There have been some serious allegations against you, Miss Dennison, and you have upset some pretty important people over the years. Creatures who are more than happy to take this as an opportunity for petty revenge. The angel…"

I see a flash of his right fang, his only sign outward of anger.

"…Xander believes he has irrefutable evidence against you. The unicorns are happy to let you rot here unless you decide to take a unicorn mate." He holds his hand up when I splutter. "I know, I know. You do you, Miss Dennison, I don't care. I'm informing you so that you don't expect them to ride to your rescue. For now, the demon's favour will keep them at bay, and I'll tie Xander up in legal knots for free." He smiles briefly. "But for now, you are going to have to sit tight until we get all this sorted out, and unfortunately, it's going to take a while."

"How long?" My stomach rolls and flutters, and I sit forward and stare him down. How long will I be a prisoner with this horrid black magic collar around my neck?

Atticus rubs his face. "I don't know. It takes an average case two, maybe three years to be heard…"

Everything stops.

I can't hear anything over and above the rush of panic that is taking over my brain. Is he serious? Two, maybe three years? Yeah, this is one big joke. My legs tremble underneath the table in preparation for me to jump up and run.

Perhaps this is just some interrogation technique? Atticus is throwing out these ridiculous numbers to freak me the fuck out, and any second now, Xander is going to pop out and yell surprise and throw a party popper spell.

This can't be real, can it? This is a nightmare.

"I didn't do anything," I mumble.

"Hey, Tru." Atticus snaps his fingers in front of my face, and I blink at him. "Miss Dennison, I said on average. I did not say you. Normal people don't have a demon prince going to bat for them, pulling in favours." One of his black eyebrows rises. "You have made a good impression. Kleric has more political influence than Xander, but like everything in this blasted world, it takes time."

"Okay, thank you," I rasp as I flop back in the chair. I hunch and bury my head in my hands. I'm not going home today, that's for sure. As soon as I get that in my head and deal with it, the better the time will be while I wait. *I'm innocent.* How could the angel do this to me? Why? I could be stuck here for months or years.

"Your mother was an incredible woman." His quiet words snake through my panicked thoughts, and I drop my hands from my face. It's rare for anybody to speak of my mum. I didn't realise he knew her, which thinking about it is silly. Atticus has been head of the vampires for centuries and has undoubtedly met every pureblood. "When she fell in love with a unicorn, I told her nothing good would come of it. Your father was incredibly charming, and it was only a matter of time before she lost herself."

He's not telling me anything that I don't know. Charming, yeah, just enough to get into my mum's pants. I bet. Otherwise, my dad was a horrible person. The evil bastard killed her.

"Vampires, as you know, love with our entire hearts. We fall in love, and unless something horrific happens, we love that person for eternity, never able to love another. The soul bonding. It is a vampire's greatest treasure and a vampire's greatest curse."

I blink at him. *What the hell is soul bonding?* He must see the confusion written all over my face.

"What? How could that be? You didn't know?" Horror shines in his eyes, and he rubs his face. "I forgot your mother passed when you were a little girl. You were six, were you not? No one taught you our ways." Looking thoroughly uncomfortable, Atticus tugs at his navy jacket sleeve and adjusts his tie. "What a pity. It sure explains a few things. It also means that you are unaware of your soul bond with Xander?"

I can't breathe.

More effing magical bullshit, and things suddenly make sense.

Atticus nods sadly. "I am so very sorry, Miss Dennison. I'm sorry that the vampire community let you down. You didn't have the necessary information, and I presumed wrongly that you bonded to Xander on purpose. It makes so much more sense that you didn't know. I lost my mate a long time ago. Even death doesn't remove the bond. I feel for you. I'm sorry to tell you now you have bonded with him. You can never let him go." He sighs and rubs his chest. "There is nothing worse for a pureblood vampire than unrequited love."

"Half," I whisper.

"Pardon?"

"I'm half-pureblood vampire, and as you said, I'm also half unicorn."

His eyes watch me with intelligent consideration, and after a moment, he nods.

"As you said, unless something horrific happens, this soul-bonding, soul-binding malarkey is forever. What happened today ticks that box, don't you think? *Horrific.* Xander put me in here." I wave to indicate not only the room but the prison.

How can I go from loving someone with my entire soul one moment to hating them the next? I don't know. It's like a switch has been flipped, and I can see beyond my hopes and dreams. The reality is a slap to the face. I twist my hands in my lap. "Earlier this morning... I felt something inside me break. My soul shattered." I meet the vampire's eyes and say with pure conviction. "I'm done with the angel. What was holding me to him has been irreparably damaged, and I could kill him with my bare hands. All I feel for him now is hate."

CHAPTER FIFTEEN

AFTER THE MEETING with Atticus concludes, and the vampire reiterates again the need for me to be patient, a polite but weirdly silent guard escorts me to my accommodations. The guard is dressed in a pristine white uniform with white boots. The odd boots, with thick, padded soles, I notice, don't make a sound as we walk down what feels like an endless corridor.

When I'm shown into my cell, the door closes with a firm finality that creeps me out, and utter silence greets me.

When I imagined the cells in an off-world prison, I thought they would be cold and slimy. Mediaeval. Water drip, drip, dripping down the walls, so much so that the walls would glisten with dampness and green mould and rats. Rats would run around trying to take a bite out of you. But no, here it is all white, bright, oh so clean and modern.

I spin, taking in the small space and all the white. Four sides of white, six if you count the floor and ceiling.

It's disorientating.

The bed along the back wall is white. I step forward and give it a poke. It's a rubber mattress with no covers for comfort and nothing to block out—my eyes drift to the ceiling—what will probably be a constant, *white* light.

White—something about the colour pisses me off and stirs an old memory in the back of my mind. I huff out a frustrated breath and dismiss the annoying thought for now. It'll come to me. The superfiltered air is entirely still, and the muffled silence makes my ears ring. No doubt this room is soundproofed.

I'm left alone with only my thoughts to entertain me.

What the old lady said at intake now makes complete sense about the prison breaking me, and that's when it clicks and the memory slams into the forefront of my mind.

I remember.

They are using the white torture method.

Huh, that's why the colour was so familiar and it resonated in my head. When I was younger and my grandad was still alive, I read about the torture technique extensively. I found it fascinating—what can I say? I was a weird and morbid kid. White torture, oh, and it's a doozy. A torture method that breaks the mind. It is a form of sensory deprivation with a focus on learned helplessness.

No matter how strong you think you are, this right here is unbeatable, and I won't be the exception. My fingertips brush against the wall. Being the creature that I am with my heightened senses, I'm probably more at risk of this method than a human.

I stand there, contemplating the meaning of life and the mistakes that led me to this messed-up situation I find myself in. Hidden speakers in the ceiling click, and white noise plays. Of course it does.

Eff my life.

Slowly, turning in a circle, I clap my hands. The clapping sound is so odd within the heavy, muffled silence of the cell. *Clap-clap-clap.* "Bravo," I say to the white walls and to the guards behind the hidden cameras. "This is some messed-up psychological shit. Very impressive." Whoever has set me up has done a wonderful job. The entire unhinged narrative, on record, then sending me here. I shake my head and laugh. The bastard who set this all up is trying to make it a reality.

Madness.

Uh-oh, if I don't have a psychotic break from this room, it will be a miracle.

No, I wasn't unhinged when I walked into this cell, but sadly, I will be when I leave. All creatures have evolved to react to stimuli, and when nothing exists, our brains will desperately try to find something, anything to react to. Heck, it'll only be a matter of days, perhaps a week, before I begin to hallucinate.

I flop down on the bed, and I pull up my memories. They fed the prisoners I read about white rice on white plates. They also made mealtimes sporadic, so the person did not know if it was night or day. I lift my eyes back to the ceiling, especially with the constant light. It messes with the circadian rhythm.

But this prison has also stepped up a gear. I chuckle and shake my head again. My fingers airbrush the collar—unless

I want to swallow my tongue with another friendly correction, I don't dare touch it. *The bloody collar.* I don't get food or water. I don't get the sensation of running water to wash my hands. I'd have rather sat and festered in my filth than be subjected to nothing. No sensation.

The collar takes care of everything, so I can't break up my time. Soon my brain won't even know if I exist, as all there will be in my world is white.

It's villainous. It's genius.

Destroying me from the inside out and not having to lift a finger. They don't need to break my body, it's too valuable, but they are happy to break my mind. I groan and close my eyes. Now, I don't know whether my knowing what's going to happen to me will make things better or worse. I'm not sure.

On my back, I squint as I lift my arm in the air. With barely a brush of a fingertip, I trace the kiss on my hand. *You better hurry getting me out of here, demon prince. If you don't... there will be nothing left of me to save.*

The kiss pulses. The wall to my left flickers. It blackens. What the fu— That's not right. A portal? No. I scramble up. If I listen hard enough, I can hear the moans and screams of... animals? It's enough to send my entire body into a tizzy, and my back hits the wall. I hug my knees to my chest. I don't understand. I stare at the flickering wall.

The demon's magic rhythmically pulses up my arm.

Are you doing this? Maybe *what* is he doing might be the better question. I wiggle to the edge of the bed, the white rubber concaves underneath my weight. I don't move. My back is so poker straight that the muscles throb as

I stare with disbelief at the wall. It flickers again. Blackness. Movement. This is his magic.

Surreptitiously my eyes flick about, and I wait for the collar to zap or the guards to come into the room with bats. When no one runs into the room, I relax. My best guess is, like the demon kiss on my hand, only I can see the wall.

Is that a... is that a hell beast? I tilt my head. The wall is like a window or a television screen into another world as there are animals and creatures within the blackness. Huh, look at that. Kleric has given me something to watch.

I huff. Wow. A man, a demon I met a few short hours ago, is offering me kindness. No, more than simple kindness. He is saving my mind. My heart twangs.

What the heck does he want?

CHAPTER
SIXTEEN

A GROWL COMES, and five seconds later, there is a barking gurgle. I count to twenty in my head, and a roar echoes around my cell. On cue, five seconds later, the tail of a massive animal comes into view.

"Hi, Spot. How are you doing today?" I mumble as the black tail flips towards me and then disappears back into the abyss.

It didn't take me long to work out that the magic-made view—dubbed the sanity wall, as I would climb the walls without it—is on a constant replay of an eight-hour loop as the sequence plays out three times within a twenty-four-hour period with the third loop helpfully running darker to simulate night. I take that loop as an encouragement to sleep. The magic helps immensely as I can work out roughly how much time is passing and the time I'm spending sleeping and exercising.

It gives me a much-needed routine, and it's just enough to keep my brain active.

I don't know for sure how long I've been here, but I think I'm on day eight. Eight periods of sleep anyway.

In this cell, a day feels like a week and a week feels like a year. Time is not my friend, and the insurmountable amount of it ahead of me gives me too much damn time to think. To think about him. I pick apart everything, every word, every emotion, looking for evidence of the soul-bonding magic bullshit that ruined my life. My feelings are all over the place. I go from hurt to grief to anger and back again.

As I wait for Spot to chase Fred—a birdlike animal—I smoothly hold the plank position. I've always been very into exercise. Keeping my body strong in my book equals staying alive. It's always been a priority, and I have never just relied on my natural gifts as there is always somebody out there who is bigger, stronger, and better trained.

Working out in this cell is tricky. The room is seven by seven feet with a narrow bed that reduces the floor space to a rough seven-by-four rectangle. Pilates, yoga, and my various and extensive martial arts training are keeping me busy. I can mix it all up to fit within the space. Close-quarter fighting techniques, perfecting my fighting forms, and creating new fighting styles are all things I have been meaning to work on. Building that muscle memory and, importantly, keeping my brain healthy.

Even with the sanity wall and the exercise, I'm not doing great.

I've concluded, I guess part of overthinking, it's not a lack of conversation that is making my mind slip into madness. I never did like people. It's the lack of touch. Not skin-on-skin, but stuff.

I have no blankets to snuggle with.

It wasn't until I came here that I realised what a tactile person I am. A snuggler. I like nothing more than to bury myself in a soft oversized hoodie and blankets. I didn't even realise the importance of the sensation of things against my skin until it was taken away. Also taste, the lack of food in my mouth, water on my tongue, and the simple sensation of liquid going down my throat. It's all so hard.

The bloody collar ensures my body has nutrients and is healthy enough. Enough to be kept alive, at any rate, and despite all the exercise I'm doing, I'm maintaining weight.

Sure, it might be my fear, but the thought makes a sick kind of sense that they intend the collar to be a permanent body addition and for their prisoners to never go back to everyday life. And really, in this scary reality, who can feed themselves when their mind is messed up? Now I worry that when I go back home, which I will, I won't be able to chew or swallow. When does it get to the point where my body and mind forget what to do? Will I even remember to wash? Will burying myself under a mountain of covers be alien? Will silk feel like glass on my oversensitive skin?

My eyes follow Spot as he flashes across the wall, missing Fred by a scant inch. With a small moan, I move into the splits.

I've always seen myself as superstrong, the first to jump into a fight even against insurmountable odds. Cocky. There have been times I've wanted to give up, but somehow I've always found a way of pushing through, even if I had to do it on my hands and knees and crawl.

But this, this is the hardest thing I have had to face. He —Xander did this to me, sent me to this cell to rot, and he broke something fundamental inside me just before he did it. Yeah, I don't know what or who I'm going to be when I finally get out. Even with the demon's help, I can feel myself slipping away, and I only have hope to cling to. The unending belief Story will get me out. With Ava's help, she is unstoppable. Add Kleric, the prince, and Atticus into the mix, and it shouldn't be long till I'm home.

Hope will no doubt bring me to my knees. Hope, the bitch, is so bloody fickle.

I lift myself from the splits into a perfect handstand. Crap, my body itches; my unicorn wants out. I point my toes, put my right hand behind my back, and keep my balance perfectly on just my left hand.

When I was a kid, I thought I could change the world. Save people and shit. For a time, I did. I made a tiny difference. But you know what? Looking back...

I peaked too early.

When I get home, I'm going to shift and not turn back. Live outside with the wind in my fur and rain on my back. The world can burn as far as I'm concerned. I don't care anymore. I will keep my chosen family safe, and that's it. Fuck everyone else.

Please. I don't want to go mad.

CHAPTER
SEVENTEEN

I think it's day fifteen when the door opens for the first time. I blink up from my wickedly wonderful, twisted yoga position on the floor. A guard in white, a different one from before, waves me up with two fingers. He doesn't even glance at the sanity wall, so the theory that no one else can see it is at least confirmed. No one can see it but me.

Cautiously, I follow him out of the room. Bloody hell, I feel like an epic adventurer stepping into the great unknown. In my head, I understand it's just a prison corridor, but for me, being stuck in a tiny white box for so long and leaving, if only for a moment, the feeling is indescribable.

Scary.

As we walk down the corridor, moving and actually going somewhere feels really weird. The opposite of jumping off a treadmill, when your body feels like it's still moving fast, I feel like I'm moving too slow. I plod slightly behind the guard. It doesn't bother him in the slightest that he has me at his back.

We arrive at the same interview room I had used before when I met with Atticus. The guard opens the door, steps aside, and waves me in. Somehow, as I move through the door, I expect the vampire to be there. The riot of butterflies in my stomach should have been the first warning. Instead of Atticus, it's him.

Xander.

My top lip twitches with a barely repressed snarl. I almost step back into the corridor and run away. But as luck will have it, instead, I freeze in place.

Phew. I don't want the collar to zap me.

Flopping like a fish on the floor with the angel standing over me, yeah, eff that. That's nightmare fuel. For that reason alone, I'll be a good little prisoner and get that five-star review. Prisoner of the year. What can I say? I'm an overachiever. Unlike Atticus, his red tape to keep the angel at bay didn't last very long.

Xander isn't sitting. The twat is not even looking my way. Dressed all in black, he is standing with his back to the door, looking at his phone, his big fingers jabbing frantically at the tiny keyboard.

The guard pulls out my chair, and I politely nod a thank you as I sit. His brown eyes widen. Look at that. My politeness has surprised him. *Not what you were expecting?* Awareness of surroundings is probably unusual at this stage of incarceration. My mind should be a puddle of goo. Sorry, I'm not on schedule.

Xander puts his phone away and turns.

A breath gets stuck in my chest, and it burns. His honey eyes are the first bit of proper colour I have seen, and the memory of them does not do them justice. They are so bright. Blinding. So much so that I struggle to focus on his face.

"You look so strange with the white hair," he says.

Without permission, my body jolts and my shoulders creep towards my ears. His voice is so loud. Roughly fifteen days, a lifetime alone in the white room, and the first words I hear another person say, I can't make sense of them. My nose wrinkles. It is like the language centre in my brain glitches, and I take a while to translate them. He could be speaking another language. *Come on, brain.* What did he... ah, yes, my hair and the lack of colour must be jarring to him. Though he has seen it before, I bet I still look freaky. The white tresses, as well as the white clothes, must wash my skin right out. Almost unconsciously, I flick a wayward strand from my neck.

After I escape this shithole, I'm going to destroy any white in my wardrobe—not that I have anything white, really. As well as a magnet for trouble, I'm also a magnet for dirt. But anyway, I'm going to wear nothing but bright, colourful clothes. White is going to be banned from my house, and I'll paint the walls pink.

Nah, not just pink, but all the colours of a rainbow.

He stares, waiting for me to speak. I scratch the back of my head and yawn. "Th-they can't have rainbow hair ruining the wh-white aesthetic," I croak out. My tongue feels weird. I flick it about in my mouth a bit. Perhaps it's the numbing effect of the collar or, more than likely, my melted white-tortured brain. Each word I speak becomes easier though. Huh, I'm glad I have been talking to Spot and the animal gang within the sanity wall. I need to keep doing that and practice a little more. "Rainbow hair wouldn't fit with their white torture method."

"White torture?" The shock on his face is genuine.

Is he for real?

I kick the chair away from the table and hold my hands out wide so he can see me and my cute white outfit. "This isn't a fashion statement. Did you not notice the guard's white uniform and his padded boots? Was it not in the brochure or mentioned in the forms that you signed? The fine print? No. I guess not if it isn't ringing any bells." I shake my head and explain. "It is a sensory deprivation technique—"

"I know what white torture is," he interrupts hotly.

I shrug. "Okay then, whatever." I tried to explain. He thinks he knows so much more than me, he can crack on. *Ooh shiny*. My finger traces the edge of the desk. I don't want to look at him anymore, don't want to look into his liquid gold eyes as he talks oh so casually about the lack of pigment in my hair, as if it's my choice. I snort. The hate I feel is shocking and overwhelming. He's such a dick.

Yeah, if I keep looking at his shitty, horrid, handsome face, I think... I think I'm going to dive over the desk and start smacking him.

Punching him.

Eventually, my hands will find his neck, and I won't be able to stop squeezing. No matter what he does. I will squeeze and squeeze and squeeze his neck till his last breath. The air in my throat shudders, and I close my eyes. If I do that, I'll be here forever. They will never let me go.

And I so desperately want to go home.

Xander looms over me. "Tru?"

I ignore him.

"Tru, will you stop rocking and look at me?"

Am I rocking? Oh, look at that. I guess I am. Rocking is a self-soothing movement. I didn't even know I was doing it. I frown. How strange. It must have become a habit without me noticing.

"Tell me about the angel." He pulls the chair back, scraping it across the floor, which sets my back teeth on edge.

He sits.

I groan.

Not this angel shit again. He's like a broken record. Tell me about the angel. Where is she? Blah, blah, blah. I'm positive he expects me to break and throw myself into his arms, crying as I confess my sins. He said I'm unhinged, but if I am, I'm not the only one.

"Tru, look at me. Listen to my words. Tell me about the angel."

I lick my lips. *This is my chance.* I couldn't for the life of me be able to add up the countless hours I have spent in my head planning what I want to say to this man. I've practised for days.

Xander slams his hand down on the table. I jump, and I bang my knees on the edge. *That wasn't very nice.* Do you know what else isn't nice? A fist to the face. With the urge to do violence beating like a heartbeat in the back of my head, I plant my bottom firmly in the seat and hook my left leg around the chair leg for good measure so I can't quickly launch myself at him. When satisfied with my silly and useless precautions, I force my eyes up to meet his.

My anger leaks out in my words. "Apart from you, I have never met another angel. Tell me I'm lying." I wait. His face is carefully blank. "It has been what? Fifteen days?" I raise an inquiring eyebrow. Useless. He gives nothing away, so I do not know if I am right about the days. I fold my arms underneath my chest—so I don't grab him—and slump back in the seat. "Did you not get access to the official paperwork from Atticus about my job with the Assassins Guild? Did I lie about that too?" I hiss the last few words, too angry to yell.

"I received credible information from a trusted source," he says.

"Uh-huh, did you now? I've got to commend your commitment to believing a *trusted source*"—I do little bunny ears to highlight the words—"over nine years of friendship."

"Come on, Tru." The angel tuts, a condescending smile on his face as he shifts ever so slightly in his seat. "I wasn't your friend. I was your little crush and unfortunate blood donor."

The bastard leans across the table and pats my hand.

My vision blacks out. I see red. I squeeze the chair with my calf to make sure it's still wrapped around. *An effing crush.* Is. He. Serious.

"I couldn't in good conscience allow you to be out on the street. You are a psychopath, Tru."

I blink a few times to wash away my anger. "I am?" I beam a smile at him. Perhaps, going off his wince. It's a little too manic, a little too wide. What can I say? My social filters have slipped, and I can't be arsed with adjusting my mask. "Wow, and who told you that?"

The angel rubs his mouth and flexes the fingers of his other hand. His arm muscles strain and bulge underneath his shirt. "I have seen it with my own eyes."

"You have, have you? Huh." I nod and let out a bitter laugh as I flap my hands up in the air and gesture for him to get on with it. "Okay, armchair psychologist, please, please tell me what psychopathic traits I have." I lean back in the chair and wait. Silence greets me. "Go on, don't leave me in suspense. I'm listening... please tell me." I cup my ear.

"You kill people."

I snort and smile as I shake my head. "Really? So. Do. You. Are you a psychopath too?" I clap my hands with fake glee. The sharp sound and movement make his eye twitch. "We could start a club. We could invite the hellhounds." I chuckle.

With a deep sigh and a snappy movement, Xander ignores me. He undoes his cuff and rolls his sleeve up to his elbow. Showcasing golden skin, prominent veins, and bulging muscles.

"They have permitted me to give you some of my blood *if* you answer my questions." With his index finger, he slowly, sensually strokes his arm.

Is he effing serious?

"Yeah, like that is ever going to happen. Given a choice between drinking your blood and toilet water, I'd rather lick the toilet."

"Why is a demon prince helping you? How do you know Kleric?" He utters the demon's name with such revulsion, and something wild flashes within his eyes.

Kleric causing you a bit of trouble, eh? What a shame.

I roll my eyes and puff out my cheeks. "I don't know him." I don't. Not really, so I'm not being untruthful. I don't know the demon and have no idea why he's helping me.

"Lie," Xander growls. His chair creaks with his weight as he leans across the table, taking over the space.

I shrug and point to my temple. "The angel lie detector thing, it's no longer on the blink? Or do you just pick and choose what fits your narrative? Why don't *you* ask Kleric?"

"I could use a truth potion."

"Ooooh." I dramatically shiver. "And... Fine, go right ahead. It's not like I can do anything. I'm, after all, here against my will. What's stopping you? Don't let a little thing like the law and creature rights stand in your way."

We glare at each other, and he looks away first.

"I loved you." There I said it. Past tense. Loved. I nod when his head snaps back, and he cannot hide his shock. "It wasn't a crush."

Heavy, he sits back in the chair.

"Pureblood vampires have this... thing." I wince, embarrassed, but I must get this out. He needs to know, and I can't hold on to it anymore. I need to give it to him, like a full dog-poo bag, he can carry the shitty burden instead of me.

"I didn't even know it existed. It's all hush-hush. I'm sure you know all about it." *Bloody Mr Know-It-All.* "No one had bothered to tell me. What with all the hybrid stuff? No one gave a crap. When you dumped me here to rot that day, I had a meeting with Atticus, and he had to explain it. I soul bonded with you." I smile at him softly. "Soul-deep love. I wouldn't have been able to hurt you or lie to you even if I had wanted to."

I let my words sit between us for a few minutes. Xander's face is carefully blank.

"It's the reason my father could kill my mum. She wouldn't protect herself. She couldn't hurt him back." *Mother like daughter.* My fingers twitch, and I look at his neck. Or maybe not. "I would have burned the world to keep you safe. To make you happy, there would have been nothing, nothing, that I wouldn't have done for you."

I drop the anger, drop the sarcasm, and with a lump in my throat, do my best to explain. "I had visions of our future together. Xander, they were so vivid. Gosh, our future together was glorious. I will always grieve for future us." A single shitty tear rolls down the side of my nose. He tracks its path before I hastily wipe it away.

"For over nine years, I did my best to stay away 'cause it was best for you, and I guess I also had a lot of growing up to do. Nine years. I assumed we were at least friends. But you..." I laugh at myself. "While I would have burned the world for you, you would burn *me* for the world. An angel's life is worth more than mine. Nah, that's being generous. It's worse than that. Anyone's life is better than mine. You will sacrifice me to save anyone you think is more worthy.

"I'm just a parasite, right? The hybrid. With my little crush and my disgusting need for your blood. When some manipulative bastard fed you a load of lies, you jumped on the chance to be rid of me, so much so you couldn't even be arsed to ask for my side of the story. Xander, you are an idiot. Your so-called source played you. And you? You lapped that shit up."

I continue to stare into those cruel eyes of his that are now so sad. He can sod off. He doesn't get to feel sad. He doesn't get to be the white knight anymore. Give me a villain anytime over this dickhead who will still do his best to convince himself that he was in the right.

I hold my hand up when his lips part. "Don't worry. It's gone. What you did, throwing me around that effing car park like a rag doll, calling me a liar, handcuffing me with silver, letting that vampire assault me while you watched..." My voice breaks, and I shake my head when he tries to speak. "Sealing my mouth shut with magic and then sending me here to this hell. You fractured my soul.

"I'm not telling you to gain anything from you, and I sure as hell don't want your sympathy. I want nothing from you except the respect to leave me alone. I just wanted you to know." My voice drops to a whisper. "It wasn't just an effing crush, you arsehole, but I'll tell you what. I thank fate every single day that you never reciprocated. Worse than being broken would have been stuck with you as my mate. Did I lie about that too?" I shift in the chair and unhook my leg. I'm not going to even attempt to rearrange his face.

He isn't worth it.

He never was.

"Those who can make you believe absurdities can make you commit atrocities," I say, quoting Voltaire. "Look, I don't want to talk to you anymore, and to be frank, your time would be better spent looking for the real culprit of your missing angel. So unless you are willing to bring out the thumbscrews, I'd like to go back to my cell please."

"Tru, I am sorry. I didn't—"

"Just fuck off. Oh, and Xander, are you listening closely? Please don't come back."

"Guard!" the angel yells. The door whooshes open. "Take her back to her cell."

I stand and leave him with his head in his hands. Maybe the final stage of getting over someone is to tell them to fuck off.

CHAPTER
EIGHTEEN

DAY THIRTY-EIGHT, I think. *No one is coming. I'm never going home.* My shifter magic itches all the time. For the first few weeks, the unicorn felt as if it was biting through my skin, liquefying my bones. I relished the pain as it was something to feel, and it made me feel alive. It gave me a sick kind of hope that my body still belonged to me and not the black magic collar wrapped around my neck. But then... the itching. I got used to it. It's still there, but it blends like background noise into the back of my mind.

The mattress lets out the tiniest squeak of protest. What? Oh, I'm rocking. Rocking so fast that even the hard, unyielding rubber is struggling with the movement. *None of that*, I hiss as I lock my back muscles tight midmotion. I can't keep doing that rocking shit. I look down at my twisting hands, and I pick at a nail. The ragged, swollen cuticle bleeds.

I need to talk and do my daily practice, even if it's only for my ears. If I don't practice, I'm frightened I will forget how to speak. So the following words I say are out loud. "I know it's wrong." My voice drops to a shame-filled whisper. "But I keep wanting to aggravate the collar, like attempt to strip, just so it will electrocute me. So I will feel something." I laugh with an edge of hysteria. It fills the tiny white room. I sound manic. I brush my index finger over the already-healed cuticle, the collar at work, healing the minor injury like it never happened. It's aggravating. I pick at it again.

"Feeling anything is better than nothing. Even if it is pain." *How messed up is that?* At least I haven't done it yet. Electrocuted myself. It's just as messed up as hope. Believing Story and my friends would get me out of here. You hear of people disappearing all the time, and their families never get answers. I'm a statistic. One of many. Atticus hasn't come back, nor has the angel. I lock that thought down, as thinking of him will only send me into a rage.

My thigh bounces. Back in the car park, I regret I didn't fight. I should have. If I had fought, I would not be here now. Yeah, I should have killed them all.

No one is coming. I'm never going home.

I stare at the rapidly healing nail bed, and my eyes catch the outline of the demon's kiss. I flip my hand over to see it better. It trembles as I bring it closer to my face. My mouth hovers, and my breath tickles warm against the sensitive skin. If I just... I close my eyes with disgust, and my hand slaps down on my still-bouncing thigh. I can't. It would be the equivalent of selling my soul.

The demon's voice echoes in my memory. *A gift. A*

promise. I will aid you in a time of need. All you do is kiss the same spot, and I will find you wherever you are.

The cuticle bleeds. It heals and then bleeds again. *No one is coming. I'm never going home.*

My lips meet the raised skin.

CHAPTER
NINETEEN

My lips heat, my hand throbs, and my heart hammers like crazy. Fear? Excitement? I have no bloody idea. I scurry to the far end of the bed, knees to my chest, and I press the nodules of my spine and shoulder blades into the wall. As if I can just disappear from what's coming.

Must be fear.

What the hell did I do? What was I thinking? I should have kept my damn lips to myself. Uh-oh, I've done it now.

Loneliness and my need to go home has killed me. *It's better than bleeding out one nail at a time. It's better than going mad.*

The sanity wall ominously *creaks*. Oh crap. Black smoke trickles around the edges, building consistency till it pours inside the cell, bringing with it the choking stench of sulphur and ash. It tickles the back of my throat. I cough, and my eyes burn. Rapidly I blink and watch in disbelief as the smoke whips around in a frenzy, and right before my eyes, finally, it accumulates together and solidifies, forming the shape of a man.

A demon now takes up all the available floor space.

The back of my head scrapes against the wall as I tilt my head to take all of him in. Wow, I forgot how massive he is. He drops his chin to look down at me. His gaze is filled with a storm of emotion.

He's pissed. Royally pissed.

"Your lips finally touched my kiss," he says, breaking the silence of our stare-off. His refined, deep voice makes a shiver rack through me. His endless black eyes leave mine to drop meaningfully to my still throbbing hand.

I tuck it between my thighs.

"I never thought you would."

Neither did I.

Whoa, was he always so beautiful? Beautiful and intimidating. His skin is the colour of the sky. I dig my nails into the rubber mattress in a desperate attempt to retain what little grasp I have on reality. Am I dreaming? Is he here with me in this cell?

With a curl of his lip and a flash of serrated teeth, he takes in my cell. Stretching out his arms, he touches each side of the room with ease. He grunts. "This cell is worse than I thought. You weren't kidding about all the white. I hoped you were being dramatic."

"Are you here? Or have I lost my mind?" I finally rasp some words out of my gaping mouth.

"I'm here."

I move before I can think about it, push from the wall and launch off the bed.

Kleric lets out an *oof* as we collide. I clumsily tackle hug him. My arms find the narrow part of his waist. They still don't go all around, and I cling to him like a monkey.

"Your self-control is impressive." He finishes with the tiniest of chuckles.

"I don't feel very impressive," I mumble into his rock-hard chest. I press the full length of my body against him. He's so warm.

Bloody hell, Tru, I can't believe you are hugging a stranger. A demon. But I guess it is better than hugging the next guard you see. Yeah. Uh-huh, what the heck am I doing? I can't... I can't seem to let go. It should mortify me. I would have been mortified if I was still the girl I was when I stepped through the prison portal. That Tru would have smacked me around for being so bloody naïve, so damn stupid.

He feels so amazing. He smells so good. See, even my nasty inner voice is on board with the hugfest. I wince. I really need to let go.

I know nothing I say now could explain to him why, as a complete stranger, I am hugging him so tight. There's no excuse. Nevertheless, I've got to try. "I'm sorry. I'm so sorry. My control is a mess," I blurt out. My lips brush against the cotton of his T-shirt. The fabric is so soft.

I've been alone for so long.

I flinch when his tail flicks behind him, and the strange appendage pats me awkwardly on the head. The bloody thing is solid. His hands, I then notice, are well away from my body and are still widely outstretched. My breath catches in my throat, and I slam my eyes closed. I can feel the blood rush to my cheeks, and my entire face radiates heat. *I'm assaulting him, assaulting a demon prince, and he's being polite enough not to touch me back.* That's the thought that makes me let go. Starting with my death-grip arms around his waist, I prise away from him.

I move, pinning my fluttering hands to my sides as they make grabby motions at him. Backing away. "I'm so sorry."

His pretty black eyes shine, crinkling at the corners with a genuine smile. Kindness. "I don't mind. We are friends, are we not? You have been in my head for over a month now. I might still be a stranger to you, but I know your voice better than my own."

I don't understand... I roll his words around my cotton candy head and then add in what he had said before when he first arrived. *You weren't kidding about all the white.* That combined... I groan. No. That can't be true, can it? Can this get any worse?

Doh. Of course he could hear you. It's how he knew to make the sanity wall. I suspected it, but it is so much easier to lie than to be honest with myself. I've been chatting to the demon this entire time.

He hums under his breath. "I have wanted to tell you for weeks the way you dealt with the angel?" He kisses the tips of his claws. "Bravo. What you said to him was way better than what you had practised."

I groan again. Yep, he heard it all.

"You dealt with the angel beautifully. He scurried away with his wings tucked in, never to return."

"You heard all that?" I rasp.

He lifts a thick eyebrow. Yeah, it was a somewhat rhetorical question. "You broadcasted the entire conversation to me."

I spin—as best I can within the small space—giving him my back. I can't. I can't look at him. Gosh, I feel dizzy and hot. "I'm sorry. I am so sorry I've been rambling at you." Slumping in defeat, I press my forehead against the wall. "Oh no. All this time, I haven't shut up. How the hell have you got anything done?" I throw my hands in the air, push away from the wall, and slump onto the bed.

I slap my head into my palms and dig my fingers into my eyes, another bad habit I've cultivated. I press my eyes so hard that when I stop, I see colour. The flashes of light are what I like to see.

Crap. I'm so effed up.

The mattress dips as he sits beside me. "I've enjoyed your voice inside my head," he mumbles. He gently tugs at my wrist, pulling my palm away from my face. He's extra careful not to touch my oversensitive skin. It's been one of my big mental-moaning complaints.

He heard me, and more than that, he listened.

Okay, wow.

It's then I have to mentally grapple with my brain to stop myself from picking through all the endless days, the hundreds of moments I spoke to him directly. I'd drive myself crazy if I did that. I need to let it go. This demon, this stranger, knows me better than anyone. The inter-working of my mind, as I've had no filter for weeks. I've shared so much of myself with him. Unknowingly perhaps, but it's done. I should, I guess, try to say something, anything to scrape back some of my dignity. But my dignity has gone. I am a shell. Broken. No, I'm not bloody broken. I'm just dented a bit, that's all.

Instead of freaking out, I need to acknowledge I was

never ever alone. He was with me, and he came when I called. A stranger. I can do this. I swallow, take a breath, lift my head, and turn to face him.

The blueness of his skin against all the white is a welcome sight. The colour is so beautiful. "I—" I almost say sorry again, but I snap my mouth closed, refusing to let myself apologise one more time. I mean the words, but endlessly repeating them will only diminish their strength.

He waits patiently for me to continue. The airflow in the room has changed. Who notices shit like that? Airflow? But my senses are heightened by being stuck in this room. Kleric makes the cell bearable, dare I say, cosy. Ha, cosy. The demon is so bloody big; he takes up the entire bed. To give him more room, I wiggle away and perch on the edge. Precariously, I balance on half a bum cheek. I don't want to risk any more hugging incidents.

"This is so weird."

"No weirder than me transporting myself across ley lines to another world, a fortified one at that, because of a promise and a kiss." He gives me a self-deprecating smirk.

"Will you get in trouble? Being here?"

"No. The guards can't see me or sense my magic."

"Good. That's good." I nod. Leaning forward, I plant my hands on the mattress and stare at him intently. No longer able to ignore the biggest, most important question, the elephant in the room. My heart begins to pound, and my stomach flips. I blow out an audible breath to steady myself as I ask, "Can you... will you take me home?"

CHAPTER
TWENTY

"No." A firm no with zero explanation. My bottom lip wobbles, and I hunch into myself. I can't... I can't hold all this emotion inside me anymore. It's too big. I was so elated to see him, and now all the pain and misery I've been hiding inside erupts with a burning, heart-wrenching sob. I can't keep it inside, and it hurts as it spills from my lips, filling the room with my agony.

"I wanna go home," comes out of my mouth with a wail.

I break. I cry.

I haven't cried since this all started, not once. Not even for him, the nobhead angel. All this time, I've been so bloody brave. But I'm done. I am so effing done with this shit. I break down in front of the demon.

"I—" Sob. "Wish—" Sob. "I—" Sob. "Was dead," stutters out of my mouth.

Mortified at my words but unable to take them back, I take a shuddering breath and do my best to control myself just so I can get my next words out. I must say them, as what is left of my tattered pride demands me to.

"Please, Kleric," I beg. My eyes burn and sting as I look at him through the blinding haze of tears.

He frowns.

"Please don't let them see. Don't let them see me like this." I still have a trace of that pride. I am not letting it go. "I don't want the watching guards, this evil prison, to see me break. That's all they have wanted from me all this time, for me to be broken. Please don't let them see." I hiccup and swipe my arm across my face.

"I'm blocking as much of the collar's magic as I can, and my magic is obscuring us from the guards. They can't see shit. They think you're working out," he growls. "I'm sorry, but I can't just sit here and watch you cry. Forgive me for this." He moves. His massive hands converge on my waist, they wrap around me, and he scoops me up—as if my athletic, six-foot form is dainty and light as a feather. He spins me around until I'm sitting sideways across his lap and his massive arms wrap around me. Kleric hugs me against his chest. "Tru, brave chimera, you are breaking my heart."

He rocks me.

He strokes my hair.

"Hush, it's okay. You are okay."

I bury my face in his muscled chest and cry my heart out. He continues his murmuring, reassuring sounds, and his enormous hands alternatively stroke my hair and rub between my shoulder blades.

When my epic crying jag slows to sniffles, Kleric whispers in my ear. "Are you listening?"

I nod.

"I'm not being a selfish prick. If it was in your best interest for me to take you home right now, I would. I would have already done it. If you leave now, you will be hunted, your life will not be your own, and they'd hurt your friends and your family. Story."

I hold my breath.

"Yes, your bossy best friend has practically stationed herself at the Demon Embassy. They will hurt her. Please, just for a few more days. Give me a few more days to sort this mess out, and I'll get you out of here. I promise."

He waits. Time is nothing between us as his words soak in.

I look up at him. My lashes are damp, and the sticky mess of tears on my cheeks makes my skin feel dry.

Big blue thumbs swipe away the dampness.

"Okay," I mumble. "Thank you."

I can do a few more days. I curl back in his arms. The welcome heat radiating from Kleric seeps into me, and one by one, each of my tight muscles relaxes. As the demon breathes, I breathe with him. Each shaky breath gets easier as my lungs open back up. If I listen hard enough, if I strain my collar-muffled ears, I can hear his heart beating. Moving my head, I press my ear to his chest. I smile. Yes, I can hear it, feel it, and my heart echoes each thud. The sound is comforting.

I close my eyes and then start the arduous task of gathering the tattered, frightened parts of me back together, hiding the fear and panic under that bloody dreaded feeling of hope *again*.

Nah, less hope, more trust. I can trust him.

"You feel so warm, nice." The smell of him, sulphur and ash, tickles my nose. "You smell of sulphur."

"I'm sorry." He tries to pull away, but I cling to him like a child would with her favourite giant teddy bear.

"No please. I like it." I shouldn't like the scent. Most creatures find it abhorrent. The rotten egg smell causes worry, anxiety, and resentment.

Kleric grunts. With the tip of a clawed finger, he lifts my chin. His black eyes flick across my face. "Beautiful chimera. No one likes the smell of sulphur. I normally mask it better."

Chimera, that's nice. He called me that before, and he also called me beautiful. After all the crying, I must look like a blotchy mess. I smile shyly at him. "I do. I like it."

"Liar, your nose is full of snot. You can't smell a thing. Here…" One-handed, he lifts me. My eyes widen as he grabs something from his trouser pocket. He plops me back down and passes me a clean cotton *monogrammed* handkerchief. "Don't look at me like that. I'm a prince," he grumbles.

I grin and laugh. It is husky sounding, thanks to my tears. "Yeah, a stinky prince. Thank you." We grin at each other.

One thing, one thing I wouldn't mind the evil collar dealing with, and that's my snot. It should have at least got rid of it. I bet it would have if the demon wasn't here doing his magic mojo. I fiddle with the handkerchief.

Oh-uh. I've never had to blow my nose while lying across somebody's lap, a hot somebody. There is no way of doing it in a ladylike way. Turning so he can't see anything, I cringe as I blow. Shyly, once I've finished, I hide the handkerchief in my palm as if I'm about to perform a magic trick.

Kleric smirks at my antics, and his black eyes sparkle. He cups the back of my head with his big palm to hold it steady as the other works into my hair. Deftly, the demon undoes the plait. I hum with pleasure at the rhythmical swipe of his claws as they comb through the strands. Some newly finger-combed hair brushes against my cheek. I scowl at the horrid white hair. I hate it.

My bright multicoloured hair used to drive me crazy. Rainbow hair causes a lot of assumptions. I had to work hard to get taken seriously. Handy if a creature is at the pointy end of my sword, but it was frustrating. Until it was gone, I did not realise it was such a massive part of my identity. It made me, me. I know it's ridiculous. It's just hair. I cannot explain it even to myself.

Kleric reaches forward and wraps the strands around his index finger and pulls them away from my face. The white hair changes... the colour slowly shifts. Gone is the horrid white, and in its place are vibrant strands of pink and blue. My hair. I let out a small, surprised squeak.

"There you are. That's better," he grumbles. "For our eyes only, till you get that collar off. It is the least I can do. I know it's only a small thing, but I hope it goes towards making you feel more like you."

"Thank you," I say around an enormous lump in my throat. He is kind. I catch movement. Spot's tail flicks.

"Where did the inspiration come from for the sanity wall?" I husk.

Kleric dips his chin. "The spell had to be a memory," he replies. His voice is equally gruff. "When I was ten, I broke my back doing something stupid." His lips twitch ruefully as I tilt my head back. "I fell from a cliff. I was hunting for wyvern eggs. Okay, no lies between us. I wanted to take a peek at the babies. They were so cute. I didn't want to hurt them. I fell. My dad was so mad he dumped me in my room and let me heal naturally. It took eight hours."

"It was your view," I whisper, immediately understanding what he's alluding to and the significance.

"It was the view outside my childhood bedroom window. While I healed, I was in so much pain I remember every second. The only way to stop me from screaming the place down was to concentrate on what was going on outside. I'm sorry. It was the best I could do."

"I'm sorry that you got hurt. It helped me more than you could know. Your kindness kept me sane."

He squeezes me against his chest. I want to talk about Story and find out what Atticus has been up to, but before I can, the demon talks. "The collar." His voice turns serious, and I tense up. "It feeds you, but no one here has considered the magical blood you usually consume. Whatever that thing generates as nutrition isn't good enough, and as a consequence, the vampire side of you is starving. If you remember, when we first met, I mentioned the angel was neglecting his duty as a donor. You were already on the edge. Being locked up here has exasperated the problem. It's something that you need to fix now while I'm here. Otherwise, when the collar comes off, not only will you have to deal with raging, angry unicorn magic, but you will also be starving."

I understand what he's saying, and it's something I've already thought about. It's the "something that you need to fix now while I am here" part of his speech that my mind is stuck on.

"The collar only masks the issue, as it was never meant to come off." Kleric pulls on the neck of his cotton T-shirt, and the fabric rips. He nudges me towards his throat. "Drink," he grinds out.

I freeze.

I can't. I can't do that.

"I've never... I don't... I've only ever taken blood from the elbow or synthesised bottle blood," I rush to explain.

Crap, I can feel my face glowing red with embarrassed heat. I can't drink from his neck. That's way too intimate.

"From *him*, you take from the arm, the elbow, like an old-fashioned human doctor drawing blood. How clinical. From me, you drink from the throat. Now drink." The claw on his thumb pierces his throat, and a single bead of dark green blood drips down his neck.

"Drink."

My greedy eyes fixate on the line of blood as it steadily rolls down his throat. "Why? Why are you doing this, helping me?" I rasp around my fangs.

"You saved my life."

I scoff and roll my eyes. "Yeah, sure." Huh. Talking to him, I feel like me again, even if it's only for the moment. It's nice. Well, if I ignore the blood dripping down his throat. "I scuffed some chalk on the floor. That's hardly saving your life," I lisp.

Kleric watches me with an odd look in his eyes that I don't even try to interpret. It is probably the fact I'm wasting his blood—it is now soaking into his T-shirt—and he expects me to jump on his neck like a starving animal. I would never... Gah. I can't think. The scent of him, his blood, is scrambling my brain.

His arms tip me closer to him, and he cradles the curve of my skull. Kleric leans his head down, his mouth barely an inch from mine. His body entirely encompasses me. "Use me. Let my blood heal you, beautiful chimera. Use me all you want. I'll be your monster." The heat of his hot breath fans across my lips. The scent of him fills the cell. It's all I can smell. I can't help the small moan that spills out of my mouth. I can almost taste him on the tip of my tongue. His blood is full of such power. The demon prince packs a punch. The need for his blood roars inside me until it's strangled by the collar's dark magic.

At this point, I don't care if he's trying to manipulate me. He's here now, wanting to help. I couldn't give a shit about his agenda.

I know one thing: I don't want to go feral. A vampire in a feeding frenzy isn't a pleasant sight. Most are put down instantly. Bitten vampires are worse. The virus in their system attacks their control. At least purebloods, the born vampires of the species, have a little bit of extra control. But even the best of us can go nuts from starvation and become killing machines, too sick to function. I've seen it with my own eyes.

"You are always trying to give me your blood," I grumble as my lips inch closer to his throat.

"For a reason. It will help your body, repair your mind,

and give you the strength to deal with this shithole for the next few days until they hear your case. Please trust me. My blood will help."

"Do you know what you're signing up for? I will understand if it's just this once. It doesn't have to be a permanent thing."

"I know what I'm doing, and you will never need to take blood from anyone else," he growls.

Okay then. If he's sure, I guess one little nibble won't hurt...

Trust. I need to trust him. I do trust him. Swinging around, I straddle his lap. He is so wide my knees don't touch down on the mattress. I hold on to his shoulders for balance, and my soft breasts graze against him as I lean forward till my nose brushes against his neck. He tenses, and I reassuringly pat his chest.

Uh-oh. This is awkward and strange. I'm not used to touching people in this way.

My lips ghost against his throat, and my tongue darts out. His skin is smooth underneath my tongue, salty. The trace amount of his blood hits my taste buds, and it is familiar to me. Strangely so. Similar to chocolate. The pulse in his neck throbs, and the muscles in his throat tighten. It's as if he's biting down on his back teeth. I lick up his neck, following the trail of blood like a proper weirdo. I can't help it.

"Tru, I am not a damn ice cream. Stop stalling," he says with an uncomfortable groan as his pelvis twitches beneath me. "You're making being a gentleman incredibly *hard*."

Oh? Oh! My eyes widen. Embarrassed, I bite down.

The taste of him explodes in my mouth.

CHAPTER
TWENTY ONE

MY BODY IS BUZZING. Heck, at least I know where the power boost came from when I was fighting in the warehouse. It wasn't the demon's kiss or his magic forehead tap. It was his blood.

The sneaky prince.

Somehow the single drop of blood he dribbled on my lips must have got into my system. Without realising it, I must have licked my lips.

I hum and roll onto my back. I turned into a fighting machine from *a drop* of his blood. After a few mouthfuls of Kleric's blood yesterday—even with the collar on—I can feel my entire body glow with health, and in my head, I feel incredibly content.

Yeah, I'm content in this shitty white cell. What's up with that? It's like Kleric has wiped my mental struggles away with demon snuggles and a gulp or two of his blood. I've even stopped rocking.

Xander's blood is incredible, but Kleric's blood… it's like he made it for me, and I've never heard of anything like that, perfect plasma. This isn't saying much because I obviously know nothing about vampires. The soul-bonding, binding bollocks prove that. I rub the back of my hand. I also thought the demon kiss would be gone, like a marker. Now that I've used the favour, I thought the magic would disappear. But it's still there, bringing me comfort. Comfort?

Blimey, I'm not right in the head. I groan and throw my arm across my face and rest the crook of my elbow over my eyes to block out the ever-present light. For what is the millionth time, I force thoughts of the handsome prince out of my head and instead contemplate all the different foods I'm going to scoff when I get home.

In my sleep, I keep seeing fields of ryegrass and clover. Unicorn me wants to gorge. I'm also craving chocolate, as that's what his blood tastes like.

I don't hear it, but I feel the change in the air as the cell door opens. My heart jumps, and I drop my arm.

"Come on," grumbles a guard. "Time to go."

I almost fall off the bed when it registers he spoke to me. Is he new? "What?" I croak as I turn my head and squint at him.

He huffs and rolls his eyes as he mumbles something nasty about prisoners and mangled brains under his breath. Slowly, as if he's talking to someone from another realm who doesn't speak the language, he repeats himself. "Time… to… go."

It's time to go? *Kleric, I am going somewhere*! I yell in my head as I scramble to my feet.

Three strides and as I step past the doorframe, I pause. My trembling hand rests on the wall inside the cell. I take a deep breath. My entire body is shaking, and I feel a bit sick. I peer over my shoulder back into the tiny room.

Will I be back? I bloody hope not.

Yet I still can't help but lock this moment down in my memories. My eyes drift across to the now plain white wall. The sanity wall is gone, it is no longer needed and has changed back. That alone is practically screaming a message from Kleric that it's okay for me to leave and I can trust what's happening to a certain degree.

The guard coughs, and when I look at him, he scowls. With obvious impatience, he waves me forward, and not waiting any longer, he turns and trudges down the corridor.

With a last look at the cell and a middle-finger salute, I scurry to catch up.

Outside the room, it's even worse than last time. I hate this place. This time we don't stop at the dreaded interview room. Instead, the guard leads me straight to intake.

The portal is just beyond that door, screams inside my head, and my feet squeak against the marble floor as I move to stand in front of the long shiny metal desk. I lock my knees and do my best to keep the panic and fear from my face. Nothing seems real. The walls are moving. Throbbing backwards and forwards. It's like looking at an object in the desert when the heat makes it ripple. The walls are doing that. *Rippling.*

With dread, I contemplate how I will cope with more people. I can only imagine what a circus the court is going to be, and I can only imagine if I had to do this before Kleric gave me his blood.

Whoa. I am so grateful.

I rack my brain for anything I can use to ground myself with. Anxiety techniques or something. I come up blank, so I concentrate on simply breathing. I stare at the counter and breathe. That has to be better than hiding in a corner and screaming. Right?

"Look at you," tuts the same old woman as she shuffles around the corner with a look of disappointment plastered on her face. "It's like we never locked you up." She narrows her eyes as she looks me up and down. "Fresh as a daisy," she spits out. "Thank Mother Nature that you are leaving us. Never in all my days have I had such a difficult prisoner. All those demands," she spitefully grumbles.

Demands? I blink at her. *I haven't spoken to anyone.*

A wrinkly finger snaps out to point at my chest. "Listen here, missy, if I book a prisoner into a white room"—her pointy finger drops and aggressively stabs at the desk— "they stay in a white room. We are a prison, not a hotel."

The guard rubs the back of his head and shuffles as the magic from her bracelet swirls around the room; the dark, angry magic mixes with his fear.

"I'm not a personal assistant." She sniffs. "You have way too many important friends. The contract is the contract. I told them to read section eight, clause ten. I told them to blame the angel." She tuts again and slams a datapad onto the desk in front of me. "I am very disappointed in you. Not one freak-out to make it worth my while in dealing with your crap. You, girl, you are not normal." Her wrinkly hand goes to caress the collar on my neck, and I deftly step back. "I wasted my beautiful collar on you."

She nudges the datapad towards me as I continue to stare at her blankly.

"If they find you guilty, the administration team has told the Grand Creature Council in no uncertain terms that you cannot come back here. You are a public relations nightmare. A magnet for trouble. Because of you, we have had dozens of cancellations."

Oops, and there goes my five-star prisoner review.

I shrug. Shame.

"Will you remove the collar?"

"No," she snarls. "It goes with you. Jackson here will accompany the collar and return it when your verdict has been read. All the rules still stand."

There are rules?

The jabby finger is back. "Sign here and here." I can't believe she expects me to read this when I can't even focus on her face.

"How long have I been here?" I ask as I drag the datapad across the counter towards me.

The old lady scowls and snatches the datapad off me. She flicks a few pages. "Forty-one days and eight minutes."

Forty-one days I will never get back. I swallow.

I need to be grateful. It could have been much longer. The demon kiss heats my hand, and in response, I lift my chin. Huh, my count was out by two days. I roll my wrists. That's not bad. Kleric's sanity wall did its job, and I survived.

I'm not out of the woods yet as there is still the farce of a trial. But experience has taught me I can keep my heart and soul in the past and never move on, do the whole *why me*, and let the bad experiences ruin me. Or I can confine stuff to the past as a terrible memory, a memory that will one day strengthen me, and I can use this shitty experience to help someone else. I can't let this prison ruin me. I won't. If I do, they win.

Revenge is a much better use of my time.

I look down at the datapad, and the lines and words on the screen wiggle together. "What am I signing for? I can't focus."

She tuts again. "That will be the collar. We can do a verbal confirmation." She leans over the counter and presses a few buttons. "Confirmation of prisoner 765375. The prisoner is being released to court with guard Jackson Blanchard. Prisoner, please confirm you have been safe and physically unharmed while in our care and that during your incarceration with us, all your needs have been met."

Unharmed? What the f... I shake my head. What about the mental aspect of their care and the collar of doom?

"You need to confirm out loud please." We scowl at each other. "I need vocal confirmation, and before you say it"—she waves her hands and smirks—"yes, yes, the little white cell blah, blah, blah, answer the question. Did any member of our staff hurt you?"

"No."

"Good." She pokes the screen. "There, the documents are updated." She glares. "Well, what are you waiting for? Off you go. The door is that way. Don't let it hit you on the way out. Jackson, bring back lunch."

WE STEP out of the portal, and the smells of everyday life hit me. I have to lock my knees so I don't crumple to the floor. We are back on Earth. It would have been nice to see the sky, but being somewhere else rather than the prison is welcome. Even if it is just the Grand Creature Council's government building, it is one more step towards freedom.

"This way," Jackson grunts.

The world around me is manic as we weave through the crowd of people. I trail behind him like a good little girl, and I focus on a single spot at the back of his head. It keeps my head up and stops me from panicking. The last thing I want to do in this environment is look like prey. Even if all these people, this building, and the abundance of space is freaking me out. Realistically, I know there isn't a crowd. Ten people milling around in the lobby of a building isn't a crowd. It just feels like it to me and my understimulated brain.

Leaving a white torture cell to come here with no time to adjust is needlessly cruel. I wish they'd given me time. Internal me wants to go all fight-or-flight. But with the collar on, anything I do wrong will get my ass zapped. So doing nothing and focusing on one step at a time will have to do for now.

Thinking about my steps, my lips twitch. I'm bouncing. I didn't think about the impact of training so hard in a realm with heavier gravity. Isn't that how Superman in the comics could fly, 'cause of the difference in gravity? I dunno.

But I feel like I'd be able to leap small buildings in a single bound even if my balance feels off. Of course the collar is still sucking the vitality and magic right out of me. So it's going to be fun when the evil thing comes off. Let's hope my head doesn't pop off along with it.

The guard mumbles something to a woman at a desk, and from the lobby area, we go into a quiet side room to wait. I breathe a silent sigh of relief and...

A sharp blow to the back of my head knocks me off my feet, and everything goes black.

CHAPTER
TWENTY TWO

THE WORLD COMES BACK to me in dribs and drabs, the blackness of my vision swirls, and my eyelashes flutter as I come to with a groan. The egg on the back of my head throbs along with my heartbeat. Immediately I cut off my pain-filled moan and instead use all my senses to catalogue where I am. I'm sitting in the most uncomfortable wooden chair. I blink a few times, then lean to the side to see they have magically secured my hands behind me and have attached them to the back of the chair.

Ooh, they mean business.

I twitch my little finger, and the spell around my wrists responds by getting tighter and tighter till my bones painfully ache. Ah, I better not do that again as now I can't feel my fingers.

I turn my throbbing, itchy head slowly—itchy as it's rapidly healing, thanks to the collar. Where the hell did they bring me? For the moment, I ignore the three stooges huddled by the door and instead take in the room. The distinctive sandstone walls tell me we haven't gone far. I'm sure we are in the same building. If not the same room.

I blink a few more times. I'm supposed to be safe in court, talking to my legal counsel, and not getting my head caved in. I can't believe the buggers knocked me out.

How embarrassing.

This kind of stuff always happens to me, and it's always when I think things are getting better or when I say something stupid like "Oh, things can't possibly get any worse," and then *bam,* fate hits me in the back of the head.

As my eyes continue to scan, they land on the prison guard, Jackson. Bored with my assault and battery, he leans casually against the wall. He shrugs when he sees me watching him.

I glare, and as the seconds pass, I can see the racking tension in his neck and shoulders as I remain motionless, expressionless, as I imagine peeling the skin from his bones. Ha, not really, but I'd happily give him a slap.

"You are not my problem. We already signed you out of the prison. I am just here to guard the collar, not the neck underneath it," he sniffs.

Dick.

For a twitchy guy, he isn't very bright. If the old lady at the prison scared him shitless, he has no idea what he has got himself into with me. "I can make it look like an accident," I whisper ominously.

"Hades is here," mumbles a guy with a heavy London accent.

Oh goodie. Hades is coming, whoever the eff Hades is.

A sharp rap on the door follows his warning. The three bad guys all stand a little straighter as the door to the room opens. I grind my teeth as I wonder which one of those arseholes knocked me out. A new guy strolls into the room.

He stops, and his pupils expand, drinking me in. I can imagine the state of me, sticky blood dripping down and pooling on the white collar that is tight around my neck while seeping into the white prison top, turning it pink before it fades as the magic collar cleans everything up.

Like it never happened.

"They smacked me on the head caveman-style," I say as I turn my glare to the three guys behind him. "Thanks for that." I narrow my eyes and make sure to remember their faces. One day soon we will have a little chat.

I'm sick of men hurting me.

I've got a list going to make sure I hurt them right back.

The new guy's rainbow eyes narrow. A unicorn shifter, one that I've never met. For years, my grandmother has been throwing eligible shifters at me. Poor guys. I can be a bit of a blow to the male ego. It wasn't the fact that they weren't handsome, intelligent, and oh so impressive. It was the fact that they weren't my angel. Now with a clear head and the lack of angel fever buzzing through my system, I'm still not very impressed. I would rather be alone than mate with a unicorn.

"Out," he says. The three stooges move as if their arses are on fire. The prison guard remains in place. "You too."

"I have to—"

A trickle of power. "Get out." Only a trickle. Either that's all he's got, or he doesn't want to throw his weight around. It's enough to motivate Jackson. He scurries out the door.

"If I remove the restraints, will you behave?"

"I have no choice. The collar hurts me if I don't," slips out of my mouth. I barely refrain from rolling my eyes. *Nice one, Tru. Tell him all about the fun zapping collar while you are magically tied to a chair and vulnerable.* I blame my sore head and the fact I've been in a torture cell for six weeks. It's going to take me a few days to build my filter back up.

Trial by fire is an entertaining way of rapidly getting my head back in the game, though I'm still not overly concerned... Inside, I smile smugly.

Kleric knows where I am.

Stepping around the chair, I feel his breath on the back of my neck as he leans towards me and releases the spell on my hands.

"Thanks." I rock back, and the chair creaks as I roll my shoulders. My neck clicks in my ears as I rotate my head from side to side.

"You don't look like a unicorn shifter," he says.

I rub my sore wrists and shrug. "What can I say? The prison washes the colour right out."

"Your blood is green."

My blood was red with slight golden flakes from the angel. I swipe my fingertips across my neck and rub the blood between my finger and thumb. Ah, I do see he's right. It's still red, but it leaves a greenish tint on my washed-out pale skin. I hold my hand up towards the artificial light, and the greenish blood sparkles. Green flakes dot the red blood like sparkling glitter.

Huh, interesting. *I guess I am what I eat.*

"Demon," he snarls with realisation. "You have demon blood." Fists clenched, he moves towards me as if he's going to strike.

I hold up a bloody finger, and the digit makes him pause. "Hybrid. So, *Hades,* now you've got my attention. What do you want?" I tuck my arms underneath my boobs, and my jaw clicks as I yawn. I flash my fangs for good measure. Even with the collar on, I'm still a predator.

He takes a step back.

Ah, now he gets it. "Tick-tock, Hades, time is ticking. You'd better speak fast, as my cavalry is almost here."

"Your grandmother says hello, and she is expecting you on Sunday for dinner," he blurts out.

Ah, so that's what this is all about. Granny Ann is pissed she couldn't access me while I was in prison, so she wants to flex her muscles here instead. I nod at said muscle. It's her way of saying "I can play nice or I can hurt you. What I do is up to you."

Bored with this power-playing bullshit, I probe the bump on the back of my head. The stickiness on my neck has already disappeared, and the egg I felt on the back of my head is gone.

Hades scowls at my dismissal. I think he's expecting a little bit more from me, some tears perhaps. *Tears,* I mentally scoff. I can handle shit like this, and to be honest, I'd rather be knocked about than go another second in that bloody prison cell. That was the lowest I'm ever going to get. This, this is child's play, and I can deal with it just fine. I raise an eyebrow. "That's it? No further messages?"

He shakes his head; he still looks utterly baffled, and he still doesn't get why I'm not scared.

"Okay, what day are we on?" I pick at my nail, and when the niggly pain registers, I close my eyes for a second and drop my hand on my lap. *It will just take time.*

"Monday."

"Ah, right. Tell my grandmother that I received her message loud and clear, and I will see her on Sunday. Time?"

"One o'clock."

"Perfect." I smile. "One o'clock Sunday."

I have no intention of going to Sunday dinner. Eff that.

There's a commotion outside the room, and I can't help grinning when the colour drains from his face and he goes ashen. I did warn him. A few more thuds and what sounds like minion bodies hitting the walls followed by a couple of screams.

Silence.

"Yippee-ki-yay, motherfucker!" The door flies off its hinges, and with a mass of pink hair streaming behind her, Forrest crashes into the room. She stands on the door, riding it down like a surfboard as it slams to the floor.

Hades lets out a squeak, and his arms come up to cover his face.

As the downed door creaks in distress underneath her feet, Forrest looks around with a disappointed frown. "Huh. That's it? Kleric promised me a challenge." She dusts her hands off on her pretty dress and pouts for a second until her odd eyes focus on me, and her nostrils flare as she takes in the room's scent. "You are bleeding," she says with a growl.

"I'm okay. Hades here wanted to give me a message, and now that he has, he's leaving. Aren't you Hades?"

Hades scrapes himself against the wall—as far away as he can get from the tiny shifter—and creeps towards the door.

Forrest moves to block him.

"It's okay. He can go." I'm not one to kill the messenger.

Forrest steps to the side and mutters in her rough, gravelly voice, "Bad unicorn. You should know better."

Hades runs out the door.

"Kleric rang me. He's stuck in an important meeting. It's about your case, so he couldn't come himself."

Thank you for sending Forrest. I'm safe, I mentally tell the demon. "Thank you so much for riding to my rescue."

"Meh, looks like you had everything in hand. Oh, just a second... Does this belong to you?" Her purple trainers clunk against the wood. My lips twitch, and I can't help a small chuckle as I see the bottoms flash with rainbow light. She pops her head out and drags the shaking prison guard back into the room.

"I guess. For now, he's my prison guard."

The feisty wolf shifter snarls at him and pushes him against the wall, and if it's not clear enough, she growls at him to *stay*. Then she prowls towards me.

Awkwardly, I stand. The fiery shifter looks so mad.

Making a hum in her throat, she steps closer, and then Forrest shocks the shit out of me as she—ever so gently—gives me a hug. Eyes wide, I pat her back. "I'm sorry about how things went down. I'm so sorry I left you," she rasps.

"Not your fault. You left believing I was safe. I believed I was safe. Unless you are a psychic, no one could predict what was going to happen. I'm fine."

"Fine." She scoffs. "Really?" She moves, keeping hold of my arms, and her strange eyes flick to mine. She looks at me with a haunted gaze. A gaze that likely mirrors mine. The wolf shifter has been through some shit. "Well, anytime you need a friend, you've only got to ask. Oh, talking about friends, I need to introduce you to your barrister, Emm—" Her eyes widen, and she coughs to clear her throat. "Mr Brown!"

On hearing his name, a man shuffles into the room. Carefully he steps to the left, away from the fallen door and to avoid the shaking prison guard who has tucked himself in the corner.

"We need to get someone to fix that door," Mr Brown says. He's thin, with wispy blond hair and pale, watery blue eyes behind thick-rimmed glasses, and he is wearing an ugly brown suit. He lifts his head and smiles at me. Then straightaway, his eyes home in on my hand, on the demon kiss. "Oh," he gasps.

"What?" Forrest asks as she narrows her eyes at Mr Brown and then at me.

Mr Brown shrugs and gives me a small, secretive smile as he pulls up a chair and sits. "Oh nothing. No bother, Miss Hesketh. Now, Miss Dennison, if you are ready, let's begin."

Whoa, Mr Brown is a demon, and he can see Kleric's demon kiss.

CHAPTER
TWENTY THREE

STANDING IN THE CORRIDOR, I feel shaky and sick as we wait to be called. The door leading to the courtroom is ajar, and I can't help peering inside. It's a proper English courtroom that you see on television, all wood panelling. On the left is a bank of massive stained-glass windows that make beautiful colourful patterns on the floor. My trial is thankfully closed to the public, so the seating gallery at the rear is empty. I don't think I'd cope very well with more people. Whatever Kleric's blood did, it helped immensely, but only time will heal my oversensitive mind.

Inhaling deep, heart pumping wildly, I push my fingers into my eyes, *shite*. The most influential members of society are on the Grand Creature Council, and they aren't known for their mercy. I'm about to plead my case, and I'm so bloody frightened.

I'd rather die than go back to that cell.

Forrest is on my left, and Mr Brown is on my right. I welcome being wedged between them. About twelve feet away from us stands a wolf shifter. He must be a bodyguard as he has been following us around. Short hair, and a foot taller than me, he has a cruel look in his green eyes.

With his mean energy, the shifter blocks the corridor, and his very presence keeps Jackson away from us without even trying.

The prison guard awkwardly cowers in the corner. The guard is having a terrible day. They should have sent somebody else. He's so used to his prisoners locked in the cells and in their collar-drugged state that he can't handle this.

Well, the shifter bodyguard is mean unless he's looking at Mr Brown. He watches the demon barrister intently; whenever the demon moves or speaks, his green eyes soften.

Forrest squeezes my hand.

I turn and give her a wobbly smile. Oh. "You have a little something..." I point to a spot of blood on her dress.

Forrest drops her chin and scowls. She gathers the material and flicks the dried blood with a fingernail, and then she looks left to right to check the coast is clear. Once satisfied, she shifts. It's a blink and you miss it transformation. Instead of turning into her wolf, Forrest shifts back into herself. Her dress is now immaculate.

The bodyguard scowls, and Forrest scratches the side of her face with her middle finger.

I huff. I have never considered doing *that* before, and I did not know that you could shift and snap back to a human like that. So incredibly handy in a fight! I need to practise shifting without turning into my cumbersome animal form. If I can snap back to human, I'll be able to heal during a fight.

As we shift, the magic vibrates and scrambles all our molecules. In the process of shifting, any naff or damaged cells get instantly replaced. So we don't age. A shifter shifts, and we are as good as new in seconds.

Or, in Forrest's case, I frown. *Dirt removal*. I grin. I didn't consider it an option or an alternative to a shower.

Forrest is either lazy, a dirt magnet like me, or an evil genius.

A fly buzzes. It keeps annoyingly buzzing, and I peer around for it. I find the poor insect near a ceiling light, frantically struggling in a spider's web. I can see the black spider busily wrapping the fly up. It makes me anxious. He is trying so hard to get away. My hands clench. He's so wrapped up that even if I wanted to, I can't help him, and I also can't deny the spider a meal. But I feel so guilty as he fights for his life. I have to look away.

It's then that a harried-looking human waves us inside. I can still hear the frantic buzzing as I follow. I try not to think of it as an omen and that, in this situation, I'm the fly.

Mr Brown points to the raised lectern where he wants me to stand. On my own, with my knees knocking together, I shuffle towards the right side of the courtroom and the dreaded oak lectern. I feel like I'm going to the gallows. I pause. All my fear I lock down tight in the back of my mind, and I tell myself I am not the damn fly.

I lift my chin and float across the remaining distance as if I'm wearing a crown and a beautiful dress, not the shapeless white prison outfit.

People only hurt you if you let them, and I have nothing to be ashamed of. I have done nothing wrong.

I take the two small steps up, and the wooden platform creaks underneath my weight as I turn to face the front of the room. I tuck my hands behind my back. It would ruin everything if my fingers held on to the dark wooden edge of the lectern for grim death.

I wish Story was here. I know she would be if she could, but it isn't safe, and she also isn't allowed. I scan the room and meet Forrest's eyes. She beams at me with approval. After a slight nod to my friend, I focus ahead and do my best to keep my face blank.

Eight council members representing their people slowly trickle out from their chambers and settle into their seats, shuffling notes and talking quietly between themselves and their aids. I don't dare look at them, and even if I wanted to, I can't focus anyway. Panic is making my vision fuzzy.

I concentrate on one person, the blonde witch in the centre. She smiles at me, but it doesn't reach her violet eyes. She clears her throat, and the entire courtroom becomes silent.

"On our docket today is Miss Tru Dennison," the woman says in a monotone voice.

I bow my head respectively when everyone's attention turns sharply to me. *Thud-thud.* My heart picks up its pace.

"Charges of kidnapping, assault, and murder."

I keep my face blank, my body stiff.

"Let our records state, after careful deliberation, the Grand Creature Council unanimously finds the defendant *not guilty* of all charges and will compensate for the time

165

served. Thank you, Miss Dennison. You are free to go." She slams down a gavel. "Next case..."

What? That was it? That was my trial?

I'm flabbergasted. As if I'm no longer in the room or in my body, I meekly allow Mr Brown to take hold of my hand and carefully guide me back down the steps and out of the courtroom. "Let's get that collar off you and sign your release paperwork," he mumbles.

"That was it?" I whisper.

Mr Brown nods. "Your demon and the head of the Vampire Council have been working diligently behind the scenes. My firm is also the best for these types of cases. Now everything is official; you can relax." He pats my hand. "You are free to go home, Tru. We just need to deal with the collar and see what compensation the council is offering and if you want to accept it. This entire saga has been a massive public embarrassment, and my professional advice is you need to take full advantage."

I can go home. Is this real?

Dimly, as if I'm in a fog, I watch as Forrest bounces behind us, her trainers flashing. Followed closely by the green-eyed bodyguard and Jackson. My eyes drift to the ceiling; the fly is silent.

"My shadow, we need to talk." His voice makes my limbs lock up, and I stumble. In the darker corridor, a tired-looking Xander, dressed immaculately in a suit, liquid prowls towards us. He nods at the bodyguard as if they have known each other for years, and an entire conversation passes silently between them.

The bodyguard returns the angel's nod and herds a

snarling Forrest, a frightened Jackson, and a protesting barrister away.

"What the heck, John—" Forrest's protests are cut off as the door slams shut.

Leaving us alone.

Oh, here we go.

I puff out my cheeks and wash my palm down my face. I'm bloody free. All I want to do is get this bloody collar off, shift into my unicorn form, and go home to my family. Have some ryegrass. I don't want to deal with this. Whatever this is. There is no need for another confrontation with the ex that was not an ex. Hell, I will be content if I never see him again. He is lucky he's approaching me now while I still have this evil collar on. At least it will stop me from killing him.

I can feel his volatile magic battering away at me. His boots tap mine, and he looms, hemming me in. He glares down with fire and fury. I pull my mask on tight, and I keep breathing. That's my job, to just keep breathing and to keep calm.

Then I feel him. I feel Kleric coming as much as I hear the thud of his boots on the tiles. I'm hit with a wave of his sulphur scent as he stomps around the corner and into view. I close my eyes in relief, just as a punch of white-hot need slams into me. It is unexpected. I shove it back down. I'm sure my face is blooming a bright red—there is something about Kleric that makes me crazy.

"Xander, I've been meaning to ask you, what the fuck kind of nickname is that? My shadow? Really? Couldn't you think of something better?" Kleric's voice is heavy with sarcasm as he reaches down and takes my hand, giving it a reassuring squeeze. I squeeze back, and he pulls me, twisting so I'm against his chest. Warm magic slips through him and into me. It calms my heart and clears my head.

Xander narrows his eyes, and his lip lifts with a snarl as a massive blue arm wraps around my waist.

"That's the problem with you," Kleric continues. "When you envision Tru, you see her creeping behind you in the dark, highlighted only by the light coming out of your arse."

Every muscle in Xander's face hardens. His eyes hold mine for a heartbeat as the muscle in the back of his jaw ticks.

I don't know why he is so mad. Is it because Kleric is sticking up for me? Or more likely he doesn't like to be interrupted.

Kleric though is on a roll. "My shadow. Give me a break. Tru is more than that. Hell, she's full of light. Any idiot can see it. Fate gave her the rainbow hair of her unicorn heritage for a reason, just so she can stand out. She wasn't meant to be in the dark. Your shadow." He tuts, shakes his head, and his tail flicks behind him, agitated.

"I'd rather not have a nickname, thanks," I grumble under my breath.

Kleric's lips twitch, and Xander grunts.

"Well, I wouldn't." I stare down at the horrid white prison plimsolls and shuffle.

"It blows my mind that you couldn't see what was right in front of your face." Kleric's claw tips my chin, and his eyes soften as he looks down at me. "I can. From the moment we first met, I couldn't take my eyes off you. A beautiful chimera."

I appreciate the rescue, but this public display of affection is a little too much. His beautiful words have left me dazed, but they don't make this conversation any less awkward. Kleric's thumb brushes my glowing cheek.

Okay, so I will admit a childish part of me wants to shout at the angel, "Look at this. Someone—a hot-male someone—sees me." But I don't. Instead, I clear my throat and ask the question that has been bugging me. "Do you... erm... call me chimera 'cause I'm a hybrid?" I've decided I'm just going to pretend Xander isn't even here. He doesn't exist.

"No," Kleric says, brushing a kiss so fast to my forehead that if I'd blinked, I'd have missed it. Only the memory of it exists on my skin. "I call you chimera as you are a beautiful dream."

"Uh," I reply eloquently.

What the f... *I'm a beautiful dream.* I swear my heart misses a beat and my stomach flips, and a feminine part of me does a happy dance. I rub my forehead with shaky fingers, and his black eyes trace the movement.

Our moment is broken by the livid angel. "What do you know? You are still a kid," he snarls.

I blink up at Kleric. A kid? What?

"Now get lost. I need to speak to Tru *alone*."

I shake my head. I'd rather not.

"Kid? Yeah, we are all children compared to you. You'd think after countless millennia you would have got smarter, kinder, and have learned a little patience. No, not you. Instead, you get worse with every year that passes."

"How old are you?" I mumble out of the side of my mouth.

Once again, he looks down at me with those endless black eyes. "I'm four years older than you; I am thirty."

"Oh." Wow. So young!

"I will not ask you again. Step aside, demon."

"I can't. Unlike you, I want to protect her. Come on, Xander. Can't this wait until after she gets the life-sucking prison collar off from around her neck?"

The angel looks at the collar with a frown.

"Don't you think you've done enough to her? You sent her to an off-world prison, for fuck's sake. You know the justice system on Earth is rotten. She could have been there for *years*."

"I might have overreacted."

Ha, ya think?

"Damn right you overreacted. It's all about you and what you want, isn't it? Let her go man, or at least let her go home and have a shower and something to eat before you start your bull-shit. Her grandmother's men have already attacked her today."

Xander drops his focus back onto me. "Ann hurt you? Are you okay?"

"Am I okay?" I mumble. A maniacal giggle rips from my mouth as I thumb the courtroom behind me, and with a grimace, I tell him, "No, I'm not okay. I am far from *okay*. But getting bludgeoned is nothing compared to..." I rub the back of my neck, sigh, and drop my head in defeat. What the hell is the point of all this? The white prison shoe scuffs the floor. "It is what it is," I mumble. "Talk. I'm listening. What do you want, Xander?"

His golden eyes look up at the ceiling as if he's thinking, and the hair on his chin crackles annoyingly beneath his nails. "The angel." He grunts out the two words with an exasperated sound.

Arrah! Not this again. Rage and annoyance slam through me, and I move on instinct without thinking. My hands shove him hard in his chest. The collar reacts not a second later, and I feel like my insides are burning. A whimper slips out, and blood fills my mouth as I bite my tongue.

Kleric catches me before I hit the ground. He holds me in his arms as we sink to the floor and grunts as the collar's magic electrocutes him too. Sitting on the tiles, he cradles me in his arms.

"I'm sorry," I whisper. A lone tear rolls down the side of my nose. I feel like a stupid fool.

"Your heart stopped," he says as he brushes my hair away from my face.

"Yeah, the collar, it does that." My voice is rough; I must have been screaming. "I'm fine."

Kleric closes his eyes and rests his forehead against mine. The hurt, fear, and violence thrumming off him are off the charts. It's almost ready to ignite with a single spark like a gnash from his razer teeth.

"Tru, I'm sorry. I didn't know. I didn't mean for that to happen," Xander says as he leans towards me. My body stiffens, and I lift my eyes from Kleric to *him*. "I can heal you." Golden magic zips around the angel's fingers.

I lick my lips and, with the demon's help, scramble unsteadily to my feet. I avoid his glowing hand. "Please don't touch me. I know what you want, Xander. You want me to find your missing angel."

He averts my gaze and stares at the floor. "I have been told you're the best, and I will pay you—"

I hold a shaky hand up to stop him. "You don't need to pay me." *Pay me. Has he always been this bloody dense?* I grind my teeth, and my nostrils flare with indignation that I can feel down to my very bones. The angel doesn't know me at all. "This shit with your angel. Did you think I would just sit around and wait for their next move? The person who did this to me isn't getting away with it. It is all connected, and it is now very personal."

Kleric shoulder barges the angel out of my way as I limp past. I head towards the door where good old Jackson, the collar-releasing prison guard, has fled.

"Xander, I'll be in touch. I've got a plan. I'm going *hunting*. I will not stop until every single creature involved with this debacle is dead."

Dead, or at least punished. After all, I have the perfect prison in mind. A manic grin tugs at my lips. Oh, and his missing angel. I'm going to rescue her or find what rock she is hiding under, drag her out by the hair, and throw her at Xander's feet.

For her sake, she had better hope it is a rescue.

CHAPTER
TWENTY FOUR

FORREST WATCHES me with concerned eyes. She looks fine, not a hair out of place, but the silent bodyguard has a bruise on his cheek. Mr Brown looks mad. Kleric slips inside the room behind me and closes the door with a firm click. My eyes close for a second with relief when Xander doesn't follow.

I clap my hands and with an overly bright voice say, "Okay, let's get this collar off." All eyes turn from me to the prison guard. Jackson digs into his pocket, frowns, and tries the other side. With noticeable relief, he pulls out a thin potion vial. Everyone continues to stare at him, and his entire body shakes as he shuffles forwards. He thumbs the cork, and with a *pop*, the vial opens.

Hand hovering over my throat, he rolls the glass between his fingers and, with a twist of his wrist, like a sommelier about to pour an expensive bottle of wine, he drips the potion onto the collar.

The collar clicks, swinging free. I catch it before it hits the ground, and holding the horrific thing gingerly by my fingertips, I pass it over to the guard. When he takes it, my hand flutters out at my side. I have an overwhelming urge to wipe the collar's residual grossness off on my leg, but I can't as I don't want to touch the horrible white trousers.

The area around my throat feels cold and weird. Locking my knees, I brace myself as we all wait for something, anything, to happen. Like when the collar was first snapped around my neck, nothing happens. My eyes flick around the room, and when my gaze finally lands on Kleric, his eyes crinkle in the corners as he frowns back. *What now?* I rub my neck. The skin feels thin and shiny. I then tug at my hair.

Job done and the collar secured, the prison guard makes a hasty retreat. He yanks the door open and disappears down the empty hall. The door slams shut, and as the sound fades in my ears, something... happens. There! I tilt my head. The dark magic is growing weaker. I can feel it. It peels away from my skin layer by layer, sloughing off, and with its fading grip, my magic bubbles up inside me. My vampire magic is shockingly intense, full to bursting with health, thanks to the kindness of the demon's blood donation. My shifter magic is a tiny whimpering thing, only a weak brush of fur against my insides.

As the collar's magic breaks down further, the white uniform finally dissipates, and my head rolls back with relief as the black fabric of my combats replaces the dreaded white.

Oh, thank fate I'm not naked.

I huff in a breath and instantly regret it as the smell of me hits my nose and tickles the back of my throat. I gag. I glance down at my clothes. Six-week-old sweat, blood, and brain matter are still plastered to my skin.

Gross.

And the back of my neck and hair are also crusty with blood from earlier; at least the bump on my head remains healed. Yeah, got to look at those positives.

Forrest's cheeks puff out as she holds her breath and wrinkles her nose. Mortified, I dare not look at Kleric. This is so embarrassing. I can't believe we cuddled when underneath the magic I looked and smelled like this.

"Crap, they've made me into a zombie. I sure as shit smell like one."

No wonder the white clothing felt odd. This was the real reason the collar zapped me for attempting to touch the prison clothes. It looks like the prison didn't care at all about the aftermath of their evil spell. Who cares if your prisoners are clean if you don't need to see or smell them? It was all bullshit. Smoke and mirrors. The uniform and the cleanliness were all an illusion, but I guess the accelerated healing wasn't, thanks to the state of my head, and if the collar's magic didn't give some form of nutrients, I'd be dead. So there is that.

The old lady at the prison smelt like rotten leaves. I wonder what she looks like without the bracelet on. Did the magic make her age prematurely? Or was it another illusion?

Mr Brown pulls out a datapad. "I will update your file. The prison's collar gave only the illusion that you were perfectly healthy. Would it be okay to take photos for evidence?" he asks.

I shrug. "Yeah, that's fine." No, it's not bloody fine, as if I want anyone else to see me like this. Kleric rubs the back of his neck, and I hop from foot to foot as I glance around the room. A Forrestesque plan forms in my head. The room is big enough, I guess. "Can I please turn into my unicorn?"

I can't stand the smell of myself. But I need to double-check that my animal form is allowed in this government building before I shift. I've already been zapped once today and don't want to chance another magical punishment. I know Forrest did her sneaky shift before to clean her dress, but I don't think I will have that level of control after six weeks and black magic eating away at me. No way can I snap back to my human self like that without practice.

"There isn't any magic in the building to stop you. It's safe to do so. Just give me a second to take these photos." He opens his hand, and a small camera zooms into the air. After a few moments, which feels like forever, he gives me a nod. "Go ahead."

Kleric shunts a few chairs out of the way without being asked to make more room. "Thank you," I whisper. I still can't look at him.

Forrest claps her hands and mumbles, "Unicorn, unicorn, unicorn," under her breath. She joins her finger-tips together underneath her chin like a James Bond villain, and her eyes shine with manic glee. She watches me in a way that would, under normal circumstances, freak me the eff out.

If my skin wasn't crawling. *Crap, I've got to get rid of this smell.*

The shifter magic comes sluggishly, opening like the petals of a dying flower. Quicker, it blossoms until it's like a burning flame. Shifting is never painful, but this, this isn't a regular shift. My magic fights within me against the hold of the residual magic from the collar. The black magic has dug its way into my cells. I groan in pain and lean forwards to grip my knees. I need to make sure to just bring out my unicorn form and not include the bloody wings. No way those babies would fit in this room, and nobody wants feathers in their face.

The pain fades, and my white furry legs wobble like a newborn foal.

I almost have a Bambi moment when my iridescent hooves slip on the shiny floor tiles. They have zero grip. I scramble for purchase, and when I'm finally steady, I snort, wiggle my ears and swish my rainbow tail. Ooh, that feels good. I eye the floor sadly. *I wish I had room to roll.*

It's then that I hear the commotion.

The bodyguard, John, has his arms wrapped around Forrest's waist. He has her lifted so her feet dangle. He's stopping the excited shifter from coming closer and touching me.

"Come on, John, she doesn't mind," she whines as she twists to the left and kicks his shin. He groans and shares an exasperated look with Mr Brown.

Mr Brown's thin lips twitch, and his blue eyes sparkle.

I clop a few careful steps and nudge John until he drops the wiggly wolf shifter. I blow my unicorn breath into her face. Forrest grins. I nose her hand, and she gently runs her hand up my muzzle. Her fingers tickle my whiskers, and she trails her fingers up my nose, moving my forelock out of the way to rub an itchy spot underneath my horn. "I know it's weird to stroke you, but I can't help it. You're so pretty. Unicorns are so secretive, I've never seen one of you shift before."

"You are beautiful but emaciated," Kleric grumbles. I let Forrest have one more stroke before I back away so I can swing my head. Oh, yeah, he's not wrong. My ribs are showing, and I look like a hat rack in my equine form. Shifting replaces cells; it can't replace fat. Only a few good meals will do that.

"Still okay to take photos?" Mr Brown asks.

That's fine.

Before I can nod, Kleric answers for me. "She said that's fine." I blink at him.

Mr Brown smiles to himself as he taps the information into the datapad.

You can hear me? I ask the demon directly. I didn't think I was still transmitting my thoughts to him.

Yes, and without the collar on, you should be able to hear me back. I snort, and my hooves clatter as the shock of his voice in my head makes me flinch.

What the fuckity-fuck-fuck magic is this?

Don't panic. We can talk about it later.

Okay, later. I give him the stink eye. What the hell is happening with me and the demon? I have never heard of mind-to-mind contact without an active communication spell.

At least you no longer smell rotten. Eau-de-unicorn is so much better than "I had a full-on battle and didn't wash for two months" awful stench. And you had the gall to call me a stinky prince.

I laugh, which sounds like a mix of a high-pitched whinny and choking. Bloody demon.

Forrest's eyes flick between us. She is utterly fascinated.

Mr Brown takes dozens of photos, and once he's happy, I take another few moments to stretch out my limbs. My poor body is dying for a good run. I've dreamed of this moment for weeks.

Well, not this moment, not like this. I wanted my first freedom shift to be in the middle of a field. *Mmmm, ryegrass.* My stomach rumbles. My body is screaming at me for the basics. I'm starving.

Shifting back is something I don't want to do. Life would be so much easier as a unicorn. But if I want to get out of this building through the tiny—to me—creature-sized doors, I need to return to my human form.

One last snort and I pull the magic into me. Turning back, I glance down at my body to check. My once-tight combat clothing hangs off my thin frame, which I didn't notice before with all the grime. At least everyone can breathe normally.

Kleric passes me a glass of water.

"Oh, thank you," I utter.

"Take your time. Take small sips. Can we have a doctor check her out?" His massive hand causes me to shiver when he unintentionally tickles the shell of my ear when he tucks a strand of my hair.

"I don't need a doctor, Kleric. I'm fine. My shifting sorted everything out." My hand shakes as I bring the glass to my lips; in the back of my mind, I'm worried I will choke. Which is daft as I gulped down Kleric's blood and everything was working just fine. As Kleric has already said,

I have to take my time. I take the smallest of sips, and the heavenly water swishes around my mouth.

Kleric's warm voice trickles into my head. *You okay? I've ordered you a salad. It should be here in a few minutes. Do you need blood?*

I'm good, thank you. Still sipping the water, I narrow my eyes. *Is that bodyguard, John, a hellhound?* Now my senses have rebooted, I can feel his wolf and fire magic blasting at me.

Yes.

Ha, and Forrest was kicking him. Though comparing the two of them, I narrow my eyes. I think Forrest has the edge—the tiny shifter is way stronger than the hellhound slash bodyguard on the power scale.

Mr Brown settles himself into a chair. I groan when he nods at me to also take a seat. It looks like he's ready to discuss the council's terms and compensation.

Great.

CHAPTER
TWENTY FIVE

FORREST DROPS me off outside my building. As I get out of the car, I barely have a chance to say thank you, wave goodbye, and get my toes out of the way before her little blue Citroen zooms off down the street. I roll my eyes when I clock the I LOVE UNICORNS sticker in the back window. The wolf is obsessed.

The ward around the building recognises me and lets me in. We have been living here for the past four years. Avoiding the lift—I'm not ready for any small spaces—I trudge up the stairs to our second-floor flat, and with each step, I go over what has happened today.

I agreed to the massive lump sum of compensation from the Grand Creature Council. Even though as a collective they had nothing to do with me being locked up, Xander is a member, and they are all for buying my silence.

Yeah, that had the fingers of the Angels Guild all over it. I had to sign documents that I wouldn't go to the press.

We also talked about a surprise job offer. According to the Grand Creature Council, how I handled myself during my incarceration was exemplary. So I did get that prisoner five-star review after all, whoopee-doo. I guess the job is something I will consider.

Kleric returned to work, and when we parted ways, he gave me a kiss on the cheek—a normal one, not a weird demon kiss. My hand flutters up to my face. I can still feel the memory of his lips. I sigh as I pass the first-floor landing and start on the next set of stairs. There is so much up in the air. He's kind and protective, and when he looks at me... I throw my head back and groan. I am so not going there.

There is no way I can let the big-arsed demon-shaped blue plaster plug up the holes in me. Yeah, and that will not go wrong. Who rebounds from an ex that wasn't an ex with a demon? Me? How stupid. No way.

I chuckle bitterly. My love life is a joke. I am a joke, and magic has been way too involved in my choices. I scowl down at the scar of Kleric's lips on my hand. I no longer know which way is up, and if this is all just some magic-induced psychosis, I've no idea if my feelings are real.

Now, I might trust Kleric to help me out, but I don't trust myself.

Gah. We still need to talk about our mind-to-mind conversations, and I need to learn to block him from my mind. I shake my head. I'm so done with everything today. I need to spend time at home, even if it is just for tonight, eat and have a bath to decompress. Perhaps I will do both together.

I push open the fire door and shuffle past my neighbours. There are three other flats on this floor. At the end of the hall, I quickly undo and toe off my boots, holding them by the laces. I pause with my hand on the handle. *They know I am coming.* My stomach twists with nerves, and with a deep breath, I open the door and step inside.

It smells so familiar of home and family. I have to fight down the massive lump that forms in my throat and blink back tears. "Hello!" I shout, dropping my boots on the mat.

It takes only seconds for Story and the kids to converge, screaming, "Welcome home!" and "We have missed you!"

I freeze at the door as their little bodies hit my legs. *I don't want to hurt them.* Crikey, where did that thought come from? Six weeks ago, we fit. I didn't even have to think about moving around them as we were so in sync, but now, now I'm not in control of my body, and I'm frightened I'm going to mess up.

Hurt them. *Step* on them. My heart misses a beat. *Crap.*

I freeze, and my lips curl into a semblance of a smile. I know it's false and that the smile doesn't meet my eyes, but fake it till you make it, right? Of course Story's family is my family. It will just take time to get back to normal.

Page climbs up my leg using the pockets of my trousers, and Novel swings from my ear. She's always been the fastest, and she sprinted up the side of my body like a speed climber. "Tru, we have missed you so-so-so much," she squeals.

The kids' voices all join in as the best kind of chorus, talking over each other to get my attention. Jeff huffs and puffs. He hates climbing. His pink face is a darker shade.

"I've missed you too, so-so-so much. I can't believe how much you've all grown," I croak.

"Look!" Novel squeaks. With a puff of fairy dust, beautiful orange wings appear. I blink at her in shock. "I'm just like Mum! I'm a pixie with pretty fairy wings! Get in!" She fist pumps the air and spins on her toes.

Jeff scowls.

Story has a mixed heritage that Novel has clearly inherited. A *fixie* is what one of our friends called Story, and the unique word kind of stuck in my head. She's a pixie-fairy mix with a pixie father and a fairy mother. It's a no-no within her community. But Ralph, her mate, sees what I see and absolutely adores her. I love that she's happy.

"Wow. Novel, they are absolutely beautiful! The orange contrasts perfectly with your lemon skin tone. They are gorgeous." Novel beams a smile at me.

Story watches from a few feet away, sniffles, and rubs at her face.

I shake my head and blow her a kiss. *I love you*, I mouth.

I love you too, she mouths back.

A tiny pink hand pokes up my left nostril, almost making me sneeze. Jeff, now that he has got my attention, dances onto my left shoulder, away from my twitching nose. "I've grown an entire millimetre," Jeff says as he stands on his toes—stretching his body adorably—and puffs out his chest.

"Jeff, I can tell. You are *massive*!"

He grins and sticks his tongue out at his sisters.

At the same time Story reprimands him. "Jeff! What have I told you? Do not stick your hand in Tru's nose. And don't be mean to your sisters."

I realise then that my cheeks hurt. I almost want to trace my mouth to feel the alien, genuine smile that is spreading across my face.

"You look like shit," Story says in her singsong tone, ruining my lovefest.

My smile disappears. I understand what she's saying, and if I look in the mirror, I'd no doubt be horrified.

"Mummy said a bad word," five-year-old Page grumbles as she pats my face and kisses my cheek. I gently stroke her back with my index finger.

My potty mouth has had a complete overhaul since Story's kids were born. "I know, naughty Mummy. I missed you, little nugget."

"You look hungry. I'd offer you a sip of me, but that's all I'd be. A sip." She giggles. "I'd be a drop before you drain me dry," Page continues morbidly. She holds her green arms out wide and says, "I'm not even as tall as a pint."

"You're not even as tall as half a subway."

"I'm three six."

I nod sagely. She means three inches, six millimetres. "I know. You are so big." I lift my eyes from Page and smile at my friend. The tiny sapphire-blue pixie with her rose-gold wings grins back at me. Story and her kids have a strange sense of humour that matches mine perfectly.

A tear springs out of nowhere. Like a proper numpty, a single unchecked tear rolls down the side of my nose.

"Hey, hey, stop the blubbering. If you don't, it will be a mass flood, and we'll drown!" Jeff yells as he holds his arms up to cover his face.

A laugh slips out. "I've missed you guys so much."

"Tru is being a silly billy," Page says as she again pats my cheek. Ew, thinking about it, her hand is kind of sticky. I wince.

Story claps her hands. "Right, come on now. Leave Tru alone. I know you have missed her, but you all have things to do before dinner."

The girls scamper down my body. Novel's wings are not strong enough to fly.

Wide-eyed, a still sweaty Jeff groans. He stamps his foot and looks at me with pain-filled eyes. He then morosely looks down at the floor, dropping the biggest hint of his life. "It's miles away," he grumbles, sticking out his lower lip just in case I didn't get it.

I inwardly grin as I solemnly flip over my hand and offer him my palm, and like a lift, I carefully lower the wiggly pixie to the carpet.

"You spoil him."

"I know."

Jeff gives me a cheeky grin, and all the kids scatter.

It's then that I see Justin. He hovers away from me like his feet are stuck to the floor. He holds a bottle in one hand, and with his other, his fingers dig into his auburn hair. His expression flickers from concern to abject horror with a splash of righteous rage thrown in. I can smell the fear and pain he's trying desperately to hide.

"Hey."

"Hi." He rolls the bottle from hand to hand, and I frown. "I got you a magic blood substitute from Tinctures 'n Tonics." He wiggles the bottle and names the expensive magic shop where I buy all my potions. Justin twists the bottle so I can read the label.

"Wow, Justin, that would have cost a mini fortune," I whisper.

The vampire shrugs, gulps, and blinks back tears. "This month's wages... all my wages. I didn't know what to do or what to feel. Whenever I've been frightened, you have brought me blood. You've always been the strong one—" A sob breaks away from his control, and I hold my arms out as he rushes towards me, and the vampire gives me a hug. His familiar scent of rot fills my nose—bitten vampires have a touch of death in their odour. "I was so scared for you."

I gently rub his back. "I'm so sorry I frightened you. I'm okay."

"You're so thin," he wails.

"They didn't hurt me. I promise I'm okay."

He pulls back. "Are you?" His eyes drill into me, into my soul.

I shake my head. "No." I can't lie, not to him. But I give him a small, hopeful smile and brush the tears from his face. "But I will be, especially when you open that bottle." I nudge his hand and wiggle my eyebrows.

He nods and rubs his eyes. "Let me grab the glasses." He rushes away.

"Ralph has just gone to get food with Morris. They are picking up your favourite. Why don't you get changed into something more comfortable? You should have time to have a bath." Story flutters towards me, and landing on my palm, she wraps her arms around my index finger. She hugs me, and I gently wrap my fingers around her and hug her right back. "I missed you so much," she says, her eyelashes wet with tears.

"Oh no. Please don't cry. You'll set me off again. It was only six weeks; I've been away much longer."

"Yeah, I know, but this time it was different."

I sigh. I feel a hundred years older. "Yeah, don't I know it." I look around for Dexter.

"He's in your bedroom," Story mumbles, correctly interpreting whom I'm looking for. "He's sulking. I told him you were coming home today."

She lets go of my finger, runs up my arms, and perches on my shoulder as I head towards my room. It is then that I notice there are boxes everywhere. "We got the house?" I ask, my voice saturated with hope.

Out the corner of my eye, Story grins and holds a strand of my hair as an anchor as she jumps up and down. "We got the house!" she squeals.

"Wow." We got the house. It doesn't seem real. "Wow," I say again. "That is amazing. You are amazing. Thank you so much, Story, for everything."

"Justin and Morris, as you can see, have already started packing. Oh! That reminds me. You will need to sign the paperwork and pick up the keys sometime this week. I have a witch already lined up to install our new wards, and Ralph—" she bites her lip "—has ordered building works for a proper burrow. I hope you don't mind?" She finishes the last part in a rush.

"You don't have to ask. You've worked as hard as I have. We've never had a proper garden or acres to play with like this. Of course I don't mind you building a home for you and the kids." Story nods, and the worried frown in the middle of her forehead disappears.

Story's family at the moment has the smallest of three

bedrooms. Inside their room, they have a setup where everything is reduced to the size they need. Their home is adorable, and I can't wait to see their plans for a proper burrow. It's not natural for pixies to be living in a flat.

"Just make sure you also have the witch put wards in place. I know the kids enjoy fighting spiders, but I want you guys to be safe, and you also don't need to be a hundred per cent traditional in the design, unless you want to, so maybe plan for water and electricity. As it's what you guys are now all used to."

"Yeah, that's a good idea."

"I have some things to do, but after, I will take some time off to renovate the main house, freeing up the budget as there are loads of work I can do myself. Oh, and I just got a shit ton of compensation from the Grand Creature Council. So we are good for the next fifty years."

"Wow, okay. That's good to know." Story grins, and Justin follows us with glasses clinking. We step inside my bedroom, and I firmly close the door so little ears don't hear what we have to say. My room is painted a dark grey, and it looks and smells like Justin has recently cleaned, and if I'm not mistaken, he has kindly replaced the covers on my king-sized bed with a fresh set—my favourite bee bedding and bee cushions in a cheerful yellow. I have a real bee thing going on, and it's even slipped into the kitchen with bee plates and mugs.

"Thanks, Justin," I say, touching the soft cover. He smiles and takes the bottle and the glasses over to my dresser.

The floor-to-ceiling windows look out at the lake and

Stanley Park. The day has turned dull, and it's raining. Dexter is sitting on the chair in front of the window.

"Dexter. Hi, baby boy, I've missed you," I coo. He straight up ignores me. Turning his ginger head away, he lifts his chin and closes his eyes. "Dexter?" *Nothing.* I know better than to go to him. If I do, he will run away. My bottom lip wobbles.

"Your weapons are clean and have been put away," Story quickly says, nodding towards my weapons store and dressing room.

"Thank you." My feet sink into the thick carpet as I shuffle across the room and step into the bathroom to run the bath. My shoulders sag. Crap, my fae monster cat hates me.

"He will forgive you. We have an emergency can of tuna that might speed things up," she whispers.

"I think I'll have to break out the salmon," I whisper back.

"I'll text Ralph to pick some up." She pulls out her phone. "So... you can't put it off any longer. Start from the very beginning when the bloody angel shoved you into that car and tell us what the hell happened, how you ended up in a prison. Also, please for the love of Mother Nature, tell me you haven't forgiven *him.*"

Justin hands me a generously filled glass of synthesized, magic-infused blood. "Thank you." I take a sip, and the magic dances on my tongue. I do my best not to gag. It looks like no matter the brand or bottle, blood and I aren't friends. *Unless it's from a hot demon vein.* My cheeks heat. I take a deep fortifying breath as steam fills the bathroom.

Story zips from my shoulder and sits on the rim of the sink.

"Well, it all started going to shit when a demon kissed my hand..."

Justin chugs his blood with wide eyes.

CHAPTER
TWENTY SIX

I DON'T THINK there's anything better than putting the world to rights with my best friends. I cried again while in the bath after Story and Justin left. Talking about what happened was hard. When I pulled the plug and watched the water swirl down the drain, I let things go. I know healing my heart will take time, and however much I tell myself everything happens for a reason, my poor tattered soul doesn't quite believe me.

After my bath, I change into leggings and an oversized hoodie just in time to hear the front door slam. I slip out of my room and pause, taking the time to store this moment in my brain as the delicious scent of pizza fills my nose. Over and above the murmur of adult voices are the cheers from three hungry pixies.

"Pizza! Pizza! Pizza!" is their collective pixie chant. The kids are on the dining room table, dancing around a massive

Trolls Pizza box—the cardboard box has a winking troll in a chef's hat, holding a loaded slice of pizza.

My mouth waters.

"Stop dancing about and sit down," Ralph tells them as he pulls a chair out for Page.

We have a weird setup with a pixie table in the centre of our dining table. It works. I love that we can eat together. The kids all run to their table and sit.

"Papa, I'm starving," Page whines.

Ralph pushes her chair in and strokes her green hair, and kisses her forehead. "A few more minutes, sweetie. We all need to learn patience."

"I'm going to faint," Jeff grumbles.

Ralph grins at him and ruffles his pink hair on the way past. "You'll be fine."

"Yeah, be patient," Novel says, nodding wisely.

Oh heck, everyone is waiting for me. I hurry across the room. "What else do we need?" I ask with a smile as I look around the tables. My stomach gurgles, and the kids giggle. I pull a funny face.

"Told you she looked hungry," Page whispers. Ralph smiles at me, trying his best to hide his worried frown.

"I'm okay," I mumble.

"We've got everything. Sit down!" Justin yells from the kitchen as Story zips into the room and takes her seat. I slide into my usual chair, and the kids all continue to grin at me. Morris—Justin's human partner—strolls into the room with a smile on his face. When his eyes meet mine, he awkwardly stops, and Justin almost ploughs into the back of him.

"I'm okay," I whisper.

193

He adjusts his glasses, looks at the kids, and visibly grabs hold of himself. He rolls his shoulders, and the smile gets firmly put back in place.

I adjust my plate. Obviously, my zombie look didn't disappear now that I'm clean and in different clothes. I guess I've never looked so gaunt before. At least I don't feel weak.

"Okay, let me do the honours." Justin flips open the pizza box. "Are you guys ready?" he asks as he rubs his hands.

"Ready!" the kids scream as Story and Ralph laugh.

Morris puts the garlic bread on the table and a bee mug of tea in front of me. As he sits down, he pats my hand.

Justin wiggles his fingers and pulls out an enormous slice. It is dripping with cheese, and it takes some careful jiggling to get a particular persistent string of gooey cheese to let go. Balanced in both hands, as the slice is that big, Justin places it on the table-sized plate in front of the pixies. Who all cheer. "It should be cool enough to eat." He grins and sits.

I grab a slice and pop it on my plate.

Morris pours me a glass of water, and Justin fills their plates. Morris peeks over at the kids, who are all busy stuffing their faces. "So are you going to tell me what happened?"

"Xander," Justin and I say in unison. I take a massive bite, and I close my eyes as cheesy goodness hits my taste buds. Cheesy heaven.

"Tell Morris what the dickhead did," Justin growls as his hand tugs at his dark auburn hair. Like Story, Justin lost patience with Xander years ago.

I was just too blind to see it.

Morris leans forward, ignoring the pizza on his plate, which is a sin. I glare at him, and he smirks, rolls up the entire thing and takes a massive bite.

"I was set up—"

"Pert?" An inquiring meow interrupts as a ginger head butts against my calf. With a flick of his tail, Dexter wraps himself around my leg.

It looks like I'm forgiven—he must have smelled the salmon in the kitchen. I lean down and scratch his ears.

"No shit, you were set up. Come on now," Morris begs. "Tell me everything."

IN MY SUPERSOFT BED, everything feels odd. I huff and wiggle, kicking the covers off as they are too heavy and the bed underneath me is too soft. My skin feels itchy, and so does my brain. After an hour of this, lying in bed with my thoughts torturing me as I watch the shadows dance across the ceiling from the headlights of the cars on the road that runs alongside the park, I've had enough. There is no way I can sleep.

I sit up, stuff my cushion behind my back, and grab my phone from the table next to the bed. I message Ava. *Hey Ava, have you got a lead for me?*

Dexter, on the pillow next to me, opens an eye and gives me a dirty look.

"Look, you decided to sleep in here with me, buddy. Deal with it."

He yawns, stretches, and with a flick of his tail, jumps down. From the glow of the screen in front of my face, I can't see where he goes.

I've sent you all the data, is her curt reply.

I thank her and grab the datapad which was left next to my phone. Justin has also charged all my electronics. The vampire is an absolute star.

I pull up the information, and while it loads, I tuck my knees into my chest to balance the datapad. Gosh, my legs are so thin. I studiously ignore my knobbly knees as I read everything.

According to Ava's notes, the missing angel, *Robin*, was last seen seven weeks ago entering an art deco-style building, the old cinema on Dickson Road. It closed down about two years ago. Ava analysed all the footage, electric and water usage, and she's convinced there might be a chance Robin is still inside the building.

If Ava thinks the girl might be still there, then I do too.

The cinema has had trespassing issues in the past, and—again according to Ava—the ward will be a difficult one to get past. I tap my finger against the datapad as I think. She's been there for seven weeks, so she must be getting help and food from somewhere. Unless... the poor girl is dead. I rub my eyes with my palm and groan.

I force myself to flick a few more pages. Details of what Ava could find out about her, which isn't much. Then there is the photo. Robin's beautiful smiling face lights up the screen. With short curly blonde hair and baby-blue eyes, she's adorable.

I know better than most people that looks can be deceiving.

I jump out of bed and change into my black workwear

and load up with potions and weapons. As I click everything into place, my body moves like a predator. I feel like my old self. Add in hunting, and I'm back to being me. This is a much better use of my time than lying in bed.

I slip the phone into my pocket. I have a stack of new phones and sim cards ready to go. It's frustrating as they get so easily damaged. The clothing-retention spell doesn't shift technology and all those moving parts. Clothing is fine, and my swords and all my weapons, with some trial and error. Even the potions will shift, but tech... Nah, the spell I drank to keep my clothing with me will have none of it.

Going old school, I scribble a note for Story. I should be back in time for breakfast, but you never know, and I don't want to wake her with a text. I grab my boots and tiptoe to the front door.

A clunk of glass on wood almost makes me scream. Justin puts the empty bottle of blood substitute on the side. "Tru? Where are you going?"

I rub my chest above my hammering heart. "Justin, what are you doing sitting in the dark? You scared the crap out of me."

He huffs, "Sorry, I nodded off. You can't sleep?"

"No."

"Do you need help?" he asks as he eyes my combat gear. His expression is so earnest. I move to where he's sitting on the sofa and kiss his cheek. It took a long time for him to accept my affection. Like all of us, Justin has a harrowing past.

"How many weeks have you been on guard duty?" I brush his hair back. Justin looks down at his hands. He can't fool me. "Thank you so much for keeping everyone safe. I'm home now, so let me take over the burden. I've got this." I tug his hair and meet his tired eyes.

"But you are so... You've only just got home," he whispers.

"Please, Justin, get to bed. Look..." I pull out a temporary ward and wiggle it at him. Then I chuck it on the floor next to the front door. The ward blooms, adding to the security of the already-secured building. It is a higher-strength spell and will last for a few days. The expense makes me cringe a little inside. But it's worth it to give my friend peace of mind.

Justin pulls a face at the shimmering ward and grumbles, "You didn't have to do that."

"No, I didn't, but it was for me, for my peace of mind. We've had a horrible few months." I don't add, as I'm trying to get him to go to bed, that it will make me feel better while there's some idiot running around trying to ruin my life.

Justin nods and rubs his face.

I squeeze his shoulder. "Helping you guys fixes me. Do you understand?"

He nods.

"Please, will you get some sleep for me? For Morris?"

He nods again.

"Good. I love you." I kiss his forehead. "And I'll see you in the morning."

CHAPTER
TWENTY SEVEN

I PARK my old gunmetal grey Land Rover Defender 90 on a side street near the train station. When I open the door, the wind almost rips it from my grip, and when I'm halfway down the road, the heavens open, and I get pelted with stinging rain.

I hunch. *Gah, why did I come out again?* I could really do without the rain and the wind. I lean forward into the said wind. "Yep, I'm living the dream," I mumble. At least I'm not cold thanks to the weird spell Kleric did on my forehead when I first met him. It is still regulating my body temperature, which is nice. But the rain is soaking me to the bone and dribbling down the back of my neck. I wince. Yeah, it is not so nice.

At least it gives me a valid excuse to hide my face from anyone who drives past. I trot across the road, and with hands in my pockets, I spin, blinking the rain from my eyes as I huddle tightly to the shop's window and take advantage of the awning. Huddled in the dark, I take my time to thoroughly check out the outside of the cinema.

It's a beautiful building with a domineering facade, clad with off-white tiles with a prominent tower on the right. Five narrow windows over a fixed large red CINEMA sign. Underneath is a wide canopy with broken tube lights, one of which rattles as it swings in the wind.

Ava wasn't kidding about the ward. Oh boy, it's a doozy. The hair on the back of my neck rises, and from across the road, the ward feels alive, like it could peel itself from the building and follow me across the street.

It crackles and hums, and when a plastic bag caught by the wind hits it, it goes off like a sparkler, turning the bag into a smoking brown lump on the ground. *Crikey.* Ordinary people don't have the spells to break a ward like that. I'm not an average person, and tonight I'm carrying thousands of pounds' worth of potions, a plethora of witch and fae spells, and even I haven't got the juice to get inside that building. There is no way I'm getting past that spell.

Damn it. What do I do now? Longingly I look back to where I've parked my Defender, shrug, and run back across the road and continue my slow stroll down the side of the building and onto Spring Road. The off-white facade of the cinema turns to red brick, and the power of the ward buzzes against my lips. There is a firmly sealed black fire door, some steps, and another fire door. I keep walking, passing more magically sealed black metal doors. I hit Lord Street and the back of the building. I continue my stroll.

Checking the back of the cinema out, my heart sinks. There is no way inside. I'm about to turn around, and that's when I see it, a black gate. I tilt my head and narrow my eyes.

It's a loading area, and the black entrance gate is attached to the wall of the newish office building next door.

Oh hello.

The gate is a weakness! I can only imagine that they couldn't spell all of it, as it would affect the next door's exterior wall if they did.

Working on the hunch, I pull out a coin and chuck it, aiming for the gap between the gate and the wall. The quid sails straight past. I grin and do a mental fist pump. *Yessss.*

I move closer. The office building just keeps on giving as they have a decorative metal railing with a brick gatepost to separate the narrow strip of the garden from the road. I almost laugh out loud. The gatepost is a stepping stone as it perfectly aligns. *How handy is that? It's as if they're begging me to break in.*

Without preamble, I vault onto the post, my back scraping against the wall of the office building with inches to spare as the ward is sparking against my nose. I leap over the gate. I land lightly in a crouch in the empty loading bay and hold my breath to listen.

In my head, I count to thirty. When nothing happens, no alarm sounds, and no one shouts a warning, I stand.

Even if some creatures are nocturnal, doing this late was definitely the best decision. Plus no one will expect me out tonight, seeing as I've only just got out of a nightmare prison. I allow myself a small smile as I slip my leather gloves on and head to the back loading door, scooping my pound coin up as I go.

This door has only a basic ward. It's long-lasting but

not dissimilar to the one I just used at home. Digging into my pockets, I find the right spells. I throw the first one at the ward, and it dissolves on contact. The second spell unlocks the door with an almost silent click. I grab a handful of micro-cameras and throw them in the air to record what I find, and then I activate the third spell, which will give me cool floating lights.

I pull out a short sword and cautiously stand to the side just in case this door has a nasty surprise waiting for me on the other side. I dim the floating lights to nothing, dig my gloved fingers into the edge, and the door creaks as it swings open. I wait. As the seconds tick, everything remains quiet, so I slip inside.

The place smells of dust and dampness.

This really is a beautiful building. I'm glad to see the art deco theme follows from the outside. I brush my fingers against a decorative panel. The fittings are original. It's such a shame that the cinema had to close. I hope whoever buys it will retain its beauty.

Coat and hat dripping, I take out my phone and send the micro-cameras to check the building. This is a vast space for me to clear on my own, and without them, it will take me the entire night.

Silently I wait in the dark; my eyes are fixed on the screen. Behind me, the wind and rain lash against the loading door. The cameras sweep. Screen one of the cinema is breathtaking, with modern cinema seats, but with the screen inset within an art deco stage, *with curtains*, even the lighting looks original.

My heart rattles against my ribs, and my stomach dips. *There are footprints in the dust.* I think I've pinpointed her location. All I want to do is follow the scuff marks, but I know better than that. I don't want anyone sneaking up behind me. So I take my time to check the entire building with the cameras and leave the heavily foot-stepped area for last. The entire downstairs and upper floors come back free of any creatures, save a couple of mice.

I finally slip off the soaking-wet gear and dump it in a dark corner next to the loading bay. I don't need my wet things to impede my movement.

Phone away and sword in hand, I brighten the globe-floating lights. They bob about behind me as I ward everything, leaving only the front and back exits free. If I wasn't so pissed about my stay in the prison, I'd be sweating buckets with the cost of all this, but I drop the spells as if I've got money to burn.

You can't spend any money if you're dead.

Finally, I can stalk the footprints. They lead to a staff door and a lone set of stairs. I extinguish the bobbing lights that have followed me faithfully around the building and send the cameras ahead again. *Please be there.* I pull out my phone and watch as the cameras reveal a small staff area—an old break room with a kitchen, seating area, and a family-sized bathroom.

There's a pile of covers on the otherwise-empty floor, and without a care in the world, Robin is sitting in the centre of them, watching a film on her phone and merrily having a snack. I watch as she happily chomps on a bag of Walker's salt-and-vinegar crisps.

I sag against the wall and breathe out a silent sigh of relief. *Hell, we found her, and she is alive. We did it.* Ava is a star. I glance back at my phone to double-check the missing angel isn't restrained. No, and she looks a damn sight healthier than me. For seven weeks, she has been holed up in this building. The question is, why? To get one over on me? I don't know her. I've never met her in my life, and I can't wait to ask her why.

I double-check the cameras are recording and flick a button to set the cameras to follow me, then add the time and date. Also, as a precaution, I send the live feed to Ava as, at this point, I can't be too paranoid.

I tuck the phone away, and soundlessly, I keep my weight on the edge of the treads as I move up the stairs towards her.

When I reach the top, I toe the door, step inside, and drop another spell at my feet, blocking the door with a temporary ward so she's locked in with me. For the next few minutes, Robin isn't going anywhere.

"Hi," I say with a pleasantish smile.

Robin gasps, and recognition flashes in her eyes. She drops her phone as she coughs and splutters, choking on a crisp. *Poor girl.* The phone slides down the covers to the floor with a clatter, and the movie on the screen continues to play, giving us an ominous background noise. *How nice.*

"The angels have been worried sick about you. They have been searching for you for weeks." I poke a few boxes of food with my boot. "You seem okay. You're not hurt, are you, Robin?"

"W-w-what?" she stammers. "Who are you?" Her eyes go comically wide, similar to the look Jeff gave me this afternoon.

She's trying to play me.

The wide-eyed butter-wouldn't-melt look was cute on

Jeff. On her... I want to give her a slap. Which isn't very nice, but I'm not a nice person, and my giving two shits about her has fled. My life has been falling apart while she's having a nice old time watching films on her phone. When her dramatics don't get the immediate response from me she expects, Robin shivers in fear. I roll my eyes and point my sword at her.

"Keep your hands where I can see them."

If I was a guy with her innocent, beautiful face—her photo did not do her justice; Robin is exquisite—and cherub-like curls, not to mention the angel's grace power that leaks out from her pores, I would have been fighting with my instincts to give her reassurance, but sucks to be her as I'm not a man.

"Hands," I growl.

Robin brings her hands up. One hand is suspiciously curled, and with a lower-lip pout and tear-filled baby-blue eyes, she... She chucks a potion at my head.

Now that is not very nice.

I use my sword to bat it away. It *tinks* against the blade and flies behind me, hitting the ward.

Ah, my first mistake. The ward drops, and Robin rabbits.

She takes the chance I gave her, and she's off. Racing away. She runs out the door and thunders down the stairs. As she gets to the bottom, she turns and throws a knife at my chest. I wince as it misses me by a hair, and the blade hits the pretty doorframe. She throws a punch, which I easily block. Robin then knees me in the side. I chuckle. I can't help it, sorry, but it was that pathetic. She spins and runs off again.

Oh. I blink. She's superfast. I'll give her that. I slide my sword back into its crossbody scabbard and follow her into the lobby. I smirk when she almost breaks her nose as she slams into a ward that is blocking her way. Instead, she pivots, and before I can stop her, she's out the front door.

The ward lets her pass, so I hold my breath. No idea how helpful holding my breath will be if I get zapped. *Am I going to end up a brown splodge on the pavement?* I cringe, but I still hold my breath as I throw myself through the front door and into the killer ward.

CHAPTER
TWENTY EIGHT

I'm alive! Thank fate for that. The ward didn't react to me. I guess it only kills creatures and plastic bags trying to get in, not out. That's good to know. I chase Robin across the street and hoof it down Springfield Road. My weapons jingle as I run, *my second mistake* of the night. Checking my gear is the number one rule. I'm usually silent. I should have tightened the straps. It's my weight loss's fault.

Gah, I need to get my head on straight.

My boots pound the pavement as I follow Robin onto the promenade and towards the raging sea. Sprinting across the tram tracks, she passes the thousand-year war memorial and the Cenotaph. She volts over the white metal railing and drops onto the lower level.

Where the heck is she going?

The wind whips at my hair, and the sea spray burns my eyes and stings my face. Bloody hell, this isn't the night to be down here. At least it's no longer raining. I need to end this quickly. Gravity is on my side, and it seems I can run faster. As my legs pump, I reach out with my gloved hand to grab her shoulder.

She stops dead in her tracks and uses my velocity against me. As I skid past, she spins on her toes and kicks me. I grunt as her heel hits my sternum, and the impact, along with help from the wind, throws me back into the concrete barrier of the seawall. Unfortunately, it's only waist height, and my momentum keeps on going.

My third mistake, I think as I topple over the seawall. For a few seconds, I'm airborne, and then I'm falling into the thrashing sea below. I hit the water headfirst, and the impact jars my neck. Wow, the water is cold. I somehow manage not to gasp, and as I desperately clamp my mouth closed, I drop like a stone.

My body tumbles and spins. I don't know which way is up or down. Instead of panicking, I observe the water as I let out a controlled scream. The bubbles go up, so I follow them, kicking my legs and clawing at the water, desperate to get some much-needed air.

The closer to the surface I get, the more the waves roll and churn. It's like being in a washing machine. When I reach the surface, I breathe more seawater than air before another dirty brown wave drags me under. It twists my body, and I crash against the seawall. *Oof.* The impact hits directly on my right shoulder. I take another gasp of air, and then I'm under again. The sea is doing its best to make me a statistic and kill me.

No point fighting against the sea. It's a good way to drown.

This time when I pop up, I swim sideways towards North Pier. I know from walking the length of the wall over the years there are some stairs. *Over there.* I think. *I hope.* When the tide is in, they're invisible, but when the tide is out, the stairs and wide ramp are one of many ways to access the beach. I wince as my right shoulder burns.

I'm so thin the meaty part of me, my *bum,* wants nothing more than to flip me over and float me like a buoy. If it wasn't so dangerous, it would be funny. After ten exhausting minutes, my poor shin impacts the concrete steps, and I drag my exhausted carcass out of the water.

Breathless and panting, I roll on the step like a piece of limp seaweed and drag myself further up. My wet top scrunches up, and the concrete steps scrape my back. The waves churn angrily below my feet.

"Crap." I groan. "What a stupid mistake. I'm so off my game."

The story of my life is that I am always hit hardest when I'm not ready for shit, mentally or physically. Yay, this time it is both. I'm a mess and trying to ignore the fact that I'm not right, that the glue I've used to piece myself together still hasn't dried.

I wobble to my feet. "Can't believe the girl tried to kill me, stupid cow." My chest aches, and I scowl as I give it a rub. Robin got me good; that was an impressive kick. Serves me right for laughing at her before. Sometimes it pays to be humble and not be such a cocky arsehole.

Lesson learned. At least I've established the fun fact that she isn't a victim. I scramble up the rest of the stairs, climb over the rusted chain and the swinging DANGER HIGH TIDE KEEP OUT sign.

Hands on my hips, I search the area for a flash of the girl's blonde hair, even though I know she is long gone. Damn it. I was in the water way too long. Ah, my bones ache, and my wet clothing makes everything worse. Frozen and teeth chattering—even Kleric's spell is having trouble fixing my temperature with this wind. Underneath my glove, the kiss on my hand burns. I have a massive urge to ask Kleric for help, but I lock that thought down tight. I don't need his help.

Think of the devil, and there is a gentle tug in the back of my mind, a caress followed by a rough, sleepy voice. *Are you okay? I sensed... Tru, what's going on?* Kleric asks.

Ah, crap.

Where are you? Can I help?

I'm fine. I just went for a little dip in the sea, I tell him.

The sea... what? Tru, it's three in the morning. Shouldn't you be at home in bed? He sighs, and I can almost feel him rubbing the bridge of his nose and shaking his head.

Yeah, I know, big guy. I'm a pain in the arse. I check my weapons. Good to see I haven't lost anything. With everything so loose, I'm lucky.

No. I was hunting. I brush my matted, salty hair away from my face. At least I'm no longer cold; it's like the demon is sending heat through the kiss. Nah, it must be the forehead spell kicking in. *I found Xander's missing angel. Well, Ava found her. I went to pick her up, but I messed up.* I rub my arms and stare out at the crashing sea. *Yep, I royally messed up, and she got away by kicking me into the sea.*

Or maybe I didn't mess up. This might work out for the better. Unless she's an evil mastermind, Robin didn't do all this alone. I've never met her before, and according to the information Ava found, I doubt she had the time to pull this all together.

She's a pawn. A puppet. I need to find out who holds her strings.

If I had caught her, it's not like I could rough her up to get her to talk. No, I'd have to hand her right over to Xander, and she'd disappear along with everyone involved. At least this way, losing her cinema hideout, she will run right back into their arms.

I'm sorry you lost her, but I am glad you are okay. Sweetheart, you could have drowned. What do you need? Do you want me to come and get you?

The soft squidgy part of me perks up. I slam that part of me so damn flat. *Nope, I'm good, thank you. I need to shift and get back to my car. Sorry I woke you.*

Anytime. Can you... can you please let me know when you get home? So I know you are safe?

I cough to clear a weird lump in my throat. Seawater. My soft squidgy side swoons. *Yeah, I can do that. Night.*

Night.

Shaking my head and clearing my throat, I tug at my soaking-wet clothes. I guess there is no better time than the present to learn a new skill. I shift. I do my best to concentrate on directing the magic and stopping myself from turning into my animal form. I think *human*.

All four hooves clatter against the concrete pavement. I roll my eyes and snort. *Nice one, Tru.* I shift back. "Crap, perhaps I haven't got the power to snap back like Forrest," I grumble.

I walk back the way we came, and a glint of a lens catches my eye. The area is full of security cameras, and this one is pointing in my direction. The camera dips. It gives me a friendly nod.

I grin. Ava. She's hacked into the security system. The micro-cameras will be somewhere about, running down their batteries while fighting against the wind. I know they wouldn't have followed Robin as I programmed them to stay with me. When I sent her the live stream, no doubt Ava will have seen that pathetic excuse of a fight, and I would bet a four-leaf clover she is already tracking Robin.

Smiling now, I feel better. I need to get to my spare phone and call her as, without even having to check, my poor mobile is definitely dead. If my dip in the Irish sea didn't break it, my shift has finished the job.

First though, I need to go back to the cinema and pick up the phone Robin dropped and have a poke about to see what evidence she has left lying around.

My phone is like a lump of coal in my hand. Shifting this time has really messed it up, probably because I tried to flip back to human and made the magic spike. I drop it into a bin on the way back to my Land Rover. I've got my coat, hat, and a bag of Robin's stuff, including her mobile, a weird off-world angel brand.

I rifle through the car and find the spare phone. Huh. It rings as soon as I turn it on. "You took your time," Ava grumbles. "Do you know how late it is? Some of us are more human than superhero and need to sleep. Drop the girl's phone off at my lockbox." Ava's lockbox is a small studio flat off Park Road.

"How did you—"

"How did I get your number? I connected the phone while you went for a swim and changed the sim card number with your network, so you have the same number. I even uploaded all your apps so you can put away your micro-cameras."

"Oh, thank you."

"You are welcome. Now drop off the phone. I tracked the girl, and she's at your house."

"What? What the heck!" My heart misses a beat. "My *house,* not the flat, the new farmhouse?" I splutter.

"No, you ninny, the house you've owned for years but never set foot in. The one in the unicorn gated community."

"Oh," I say. "Ava, you scared the crap out of me. She is staying in *that* house." I groan and rub my eyes. I'm so tired they are burning. She's right about me not setting a hoof in that house. I forgot about it. It was part of a big inheritance and a way of manipulating me to be a good little unicorn. A noose. No way was I using that rope to hang myself. I still have the keys and the deeds in a drawer somewhere. Next, Ava will tell me which drawer I stuck them in. I shake my head. I don't know how she even knew about the house, though Ava knows everything.

"So she's at the unicorn house? Cheeky cow, who let her in?" I ask. It didn't necessarily mean that the unicorns were involved.

"Your grandmother."

Well, okay, now that's interesting. Another setup? I bang my head back on the headrest. Bloody great.

"I will forward the proof to your datapad. I have video, audio, and photographs," she says with a yawn.

"Thanks, Ava. Will you keep an eye on her and let me know if she moves?"

"Yes, no problem. I will ring you with any updates."

We say our goodbyes, and I slump in the seat and tap the phone on my knee as I stare morosely out the window. The storm hasn't abated, and it looks like it's going to be a rotten day.

I'll take the wind and rain. Heck, I'll even take another dip in the sea. At least out here, getting pushed about by the elements, I'm alive. I feel alive.

So my grandmother and the unicorns are involved, *shocker*. They are boundary stompers. When I try to remain in no contact, they keep butting into my life. Such small things like... I don't know, manipulating an angel to have me thrown into prison, and when I didn't scream for their help and I'm about to go into court, they club me on the back of the head and tie me to a chair just to invite me to Sunday dinner. Then there's this helping a missing angel that I've been accused of kidnapping.

Uh-huh. Unicorns are nuts.

Why though? That's what makes little sense. Why? I know they want me mated to a nice unicorn and popping out babies. I shudder. Even my dirty blood is good enough for that. But I can't do that from prison. I have the strength and power of four unicorns, generationally-passed-on magic. Does she want my power? Is that it? I understand they don't want me pining over an angel, so the motive for wrecking that relationship makes sense. But...

I'm missing something.

I grin as I tuck the phone away. At least I know where Robin is hiding, and she has handed me a piece of the puzzle. How kind. And instead of sneaking onto the gated estate in the middle of the night to bring Robin back into the angel's fold, I'm going to trot right in there wearing my Sunday best as I have an invitation.

CHAPTER
TWENTY NINE

I SHIFT into my unicorn form and clop into the middle of the field. I take in all the glorious grass—twenty-eight acres —and my eyes flick about in search of the perfect place to roll. There! I find the perfect spot. Cantering over, I check the ground with my hooves to make sure there are no hidden stones.

When I find the ground clear of anything that will ruin my long-overdue roll, I drop to my knees, flop onto my side, and with a grunt, I roll onto my back. My legs kick the air, and letting gravity take me, I roll onto my other side, scratching my spine, neck, and hindquarters as I go.

Oh, that's the spot.

Once satisfied, I stumble back to my feet and do a full-body shake. Much to my amusement, bits of mud that are stuck to my fur go flying.

Then, with a squeal, I'm off. I bolt across the field,

kicking my back legs behind me with delight. I do the wall of death around the perimeter, going as fast as I possibly can. Pieces of turf flip up behind me as my hooves thunder against the wet ground.

This is freedom.

I slide to a stop, leaving deep divots in the soil, and my nostrils flare as I snort. I snort again, clearing my nose, and then breathe deeply. The rich scent of churned grass, soil, and autumn fills my senses.

Satisfied I'm safe and the area is free from any predators that might be up for a unicorn snack, I drop my head and snatch a massive mouthful of grass. Little pieces spill from the sides of my mouth as the grassy flavour hits my palate. Yum, I'm in heaven. Granted, it's a little bit stalky now it's October, but it is full of fibre, and if I want to put weight on quickly, this is the best way to do it.

All we need now is a bit of frost. It stresses the grass, and it becomes sweeter. *Oh yes,* I think as I chew, *I'm a proper grass connoisseur.* I pluck another mouthful, and my ears swivel as my eyes flick about as I chew.

After dropping Robin's phone off, I went home, had breakfast with my family, and because of the bad weather, I took the kids to school and Story to work. She works at the same café I do—though I'm now only part-time—and unlike me, who serves tea and coffee, Story decorates wedding cakes. They are pretty—beautiful, in fact. She is incredibly talented and in high demand. I haven't gone to bed yet; even though I'm exhausted, my brain is too buzzy to sleep. Oh, a thistle! I nibble on the purple flower. It's late in the year, so it's a lucky find.

I also signed the final paperwork with our conveyancing

solicitors. Story transferred the full payment last week, and they were waiting for my signature to file everything with the Land Registry. I then moseyed my way to the estate agent to pick up the keys. I haven't been near the farmhouse. I lift my head and take the building in through the misty rain. Our new home is at the top of a small incline and overlooks the land. I'd like to step through the door with everyone first, and we won't be moving in for a while as it's knocking on the door of being derelict, and it isn't safe yet for tiny toes.

But I couldn't help myself. I had to come to the field. I shake my head in disbelief. Wow. This is so strange. It doesn't seem real. I can't believe we own all this land. My ears twitch. Part of me is waiting for someone to shout at me to get lost, that I'm trespassing.

Yeah, I needed time to eat, decompress, roll, run, and plan my next move. One thing I've come to realise is the raging anger I'm feeling is healthy. Anger is energy if I use it right. I just need to plan and take my time.

I ummed and ahhed about sending the Robin footage to Xander, but ultimately, I decided I couldn't trust him. He'd go in like a crazed bull, and in doing the *right* thing, he'd mess everything up. And Kleric? Well, I guess the demon is busy, and I'm very conscious of the fact that I've taken up way too much of his time. I also need to keep reminding myself the man is a stranger.

I find a blackberry bush creeping under the fence, and using my lips and tongue, I carefully pluck off the plump, juicy berries.

My sensitive ears hear a car coming down the drive, and my head snaps up to watch a strange car park with a squeak of breaks next to my Land Rover. I almost choke. What? What is he doing here? I narrow my eyes as I watch a familiar blue form unravel himself from behind the wheel.

I remember then I didn't let him know that I had arrived safely home. *Oops.*

Kleric's body shimmers with magic, and suddenly he's wearing a raincoat and Wellington boots. He opens the gate, closes it securely behind him, and with long confident strides, he heads towards me.

My eyes zone in on the paper bag that is rustling in his hands. Fancy carrots? Fae apples? *Ooh.* Now that there's an appropriate gift.

I am sorry I didn't tell you I got home safe. But what are you doing here? Is this demon my new stalker?

He tucks the paper bag under his arm and holds his hands up. "Hi, I didn't mean to intrude. Story told me where you were, and I wonder if you'll allow me to guard you... keep you safe while you graze."

What? Gah, what is she up to now? The shit-stirring pixie. *Why? Haven't you got anything better to do?* I toss my head and point my horn at him. A very sharp horn that is the rough length of a Katana sword, around twenty-four inches long. *I can keep myself safe.*

"Okay. Well, may I join you?" The demon looks sheepish.

What? Join me?

"Well, demons can shift." He tugs at his damp coat and rubs the back of his neck. "We can shift into anything."

Ah, yes, I forgot about that fact. That's another big reason other creatures don't like demons. They don't trust them as they can transform into anything they want, change their form to anything, another person, a mouse, a *unicorn*... I blink at him.

He tugs a carrot from the bag and offers it to me.

Of course I take the bribe. I lip it gently from his hand. *Thank you.* I've never had anyone shift with me before. In battle, sure, but never for fun. I awkwardly stand watching him as I crunch the carrot, and I'm suddenly a kid venturing into a playground for the very first time and unsure of what to do. I hope the thrum of excitement trickling through my blood will help. Make me less awkward. When I finish the yummy vegetable, I nod. *Okay.*

Kleric offers me another carrot and empties the goodies onto the floor, folding the empty bag and putting it into his inside coat pocket. I then watch, wide-eyed, as the demon shifts into a massive blue unicorn. I know he could have been any colour, but I love he has kept his beautiful skin tone.

My head tips back. That is a heck of a lot of blue fur. Yep, he's massive. Of course he is. And then he dares to ramble over to *my* rolling spot and gets down on his knees within the flattened muddy grass and rolls.

Like eating popcorn, I grab a purple fae apple, and its bitter taste fills my mouth as I crunch and watch him roll. He is rubbing his stinky demon scent all over mine. What a weirdo. *He's not even a real unicorn,* I think as I check out his huge horn. The little sun we have today battles through the clouds and the rain. The rays hit the tip of the horn, and it sparkles. I snort, turn my back to him and prance away.

With my back turned towards him, I don't even need to turn my head as my equine vision is epic, and I watch him get up, shake, and then slowly tiptoe towards me as if he's a big cat. Someone needs to tell him that his massive, dinner-plate-sized hooves aren't made for stealth. *Clip-clop* and wet grass *squelches*.

I squeal and bolt. He thunders behind me, right on my tail. I laugh uncontrollably. This is... this is so much fun! Even though with his long legs he could beat me in a race, he keeps behind me, a foot off my hindquarters. He keeps the same distance when I slow a little to test him.

I stop, spin on my back legs, and rear. He joins me, and our horns clash. I drop to all four hooves in shock and step back.

Wow!

Can we do that again? I ask him. Even my mental voice trembles with excitement. He nods, his dark blue mane whips around in the wind, and his black eyes sparkle with joy.

We can do anything you want, is his reply.

We square up to each other, and then we spar unicorn-style.

CHAPTER
THIRTY

SUNDAY COMES AROUND QUICKLY, and I feel more like myself every day. I still don't feel at ease surrounded by many people, and I won't be going to a concert anytime soon. Erm—not that I've ever gone to a concert, and I've always hated people, so that's not surprising or a significant loss. But I feel much better.

I have spent my time wisely grazing and training. There were a few hard-sparring sessions with my gargoyle friends —the work I did in prison has made my fighting style shine —and with all that going on, I've spent hours planning and now have several workable ideas floating around in my head on how to deal with the unicorns.

I also have Kleric, Forrest, and a tactical team on standby in case things go tits up... which, undoubtedly, they will as it's me.

Robin remains tucked up in the house that is in my

name, which riles me. My unicorn grandmother, I'm sure, is thrilled that she has got one over on me. How it must tickle her pink that she's using that house to hide an angel I went to prison for kidnapping. I know I shouldn't care what she thinks or what she does, but the entire angel thing is driving me nuts. And the pieces of the puzzle still do not quite add up.

Bad people don't have a reason to be dicks. I need to let the niggling feeling go and deal with the facts I have: all evidence points to my grandmother.

I brush my hands down the gorgeous dark blue knee-length dress. The material is spelled so I can carry some small weapons and defensive magic. For the final touch, I stuff an anti-magic band into the thin inside pocket at the hem.

The odd gold bracelets I'm wearing jingle as I smooth the dress back in place. I smirk. They aren't bracelets but special sneaky handcuffs. I hope I can change my outfit before I hunt for Robin, but I have backups to my backups just in case.

Yeah, as soon as I get my hands on her, I will have Robin trussed up like a turkey. *Let's see if she can run away this time.* No, she isn't getting away. I have zero intentions of letting that girl go until I hand her over, kicking and screaming, to Xander and, along with any or all of her accomplices, to the Grand Creature Council.

Unless they force me to kill them. Then instead, I'll drop off their severed heads. I'm done with playing games. Yep, I might be a tad pissed. I tuck my hair behind my ear. I'm still flashing the cash as I've used a potion to style my hair and makeup today. My multicoloured hair falls in beautiful shiny waves to my waist, and the spelled makeup means I can't rub it off if I touch my face. It will only disappear when I shift. I do love witch magic.

Silent, with her arms crossed and watching me with a wrinkle of worry between her brows, Story sits on the edge of the bed. We've been arguing for the past thirty minutes.

"Are you sure I can't come with you?" she whispers.

Gah, she won't get it in her head. I clench my jaw so hard my teeth ache. I don't even bother to answer, as I'm not repeating myself. There is no way I'm letting her fly into the unicorn's gated community. They would kill her without a second thought, and if anything happened to her... oh no... the thought of it knocks me sick. I would never *ever* forgive myself.

I draw in a breath, release it, and for our friendship, try again. "If I could, I'd take some micro-cameras so you could watch my back, but Ava said the wards won't allow them through. I can't even take my phone."

"But you're not a guest. You are technically a resident," she mumbles.

"Tell me something I don't know." I crouch down towards her so I'm at her eye level. "Please, Story, drop this." A knock on my door, and Justin pops his head in.

"Your demon is here."

Story scowls. Then a contemplative look sweeps across her face, and she visibly shakes off her worry and wiggles her eyebrows. "Kleric, eh?"

She adores Kleric.

I roll my eyes when she leaps to her feet and struts across my bed, singing, "Oh, Kleric. Oh, Kleric. Kisssss me."

Gosh, I'm so glad our argument has been forgotten. I

laugh as Story turns her back to me, crosses her arms and rubs herself and thrusts her hips as if she is in someone's arms. "Oh, Kleric," she wails in a high-pitched voice. "Oh, Tru," she says in a low gruff voice. And then she makes kissing, moaning sounds.

Mortified, I slap my head in my hands. She has the nerve to tell the kids off when she's just as bad. I shake my head. No, I take that back. She's worse!

"Shush, shush, you nitwit. He'll hear you." My arms flap about as I hush her.

She stops messing, and with a groan, she turns back to face me. Her grin fades, and her eyes go comically wide.

"He's standing right behind me, isn't he?" I ask.

She nods and then launches into the air. Giggling, she zips out of the room.

Horrified, I take a few seconds to build up the courage to move. *Great.* I oh so slowly turn around.

Kleric is leaning against the doorframe with a twinkle in his eye and a cheeky smile on his face.

I groan. He would see Story's antics as being hilarious.

"Get in here," I whisper yell, "and close the damn door." My face is no doubt glowing bright red. Hopefully, the makeup spell will help cover the worst of it up.

"You look beautiful." Kleric prowls towards me. His tail flicks behind him. It was his idea to donate his super-duper magical blood to power me up before I go deal with Robin and the unicorns.

Every little helps, right?

That is why he is here now. In my bedroom... I wasn't going to say no. If I'm honest, I've been craving his blood all week. "Thank you." I rock from foot to foot, and my bare toes dig into the carpet. I'm not that great with compliments. "Thanks for coming."

"Always." He strips off his coat and throws it on the chair by the window. His massive biceps bulge against his shirt as he undoes the top couple of buttons. "Come here and take what you need," he says gruffly.

I swallow the spit that is flooding my mouth and try to play it cool as my fangs snap down. I do my best not to flash them at him. With the door closed for privacy, he is all I can smell. The scent of him floods my bedroom, mingling with mine. Everything inside me screams that our combined scent is right. Perfect. I am safe, protected and lo—

Whoa there, steady on.

Yeah, eff that. My left eye twitches. I don't know this man, and thanks to his weird magic—we still need to talk about that—he might know me better, with me being in his head for weeks. But thanks to fate and Xander, I sure learned my lesson the first time I jumped into a non-relationship. I'm never doing that again. I'd rather be alone.

Xander never looked at you like that.

No, he didn't. I gulp.

Kleric's muscled arm wraps around my waist, and he tugs me towards him.

I let out a little squeak as we crash together, and I find myself pleasantly plastered against his bumpy abs and muscled chest. Even with our height difference, we fit together perfectly. I squeak again in fright as something tickles the back of my leg. I glance down, and it's his bloody tail! I didn't expect it to go rogue. The damn thing inches up my leg towards the hem of my dress, and with a scowl, I knock it away.

He drops his chin as he stares at me. His pretty black eyes are serious, and they dare to trace my face, my lips. He rolls his full bottom lip into his mouth with a flash of razer teeth.

My stomach dips. Crikey, that is so bloody sexy.

And...

I don't know what comes over me. It's like a switch is flicked. *Fuck it.* My body moves before my brain catches up. Like some freaky, out-of-body experience and of their own accord, my lips smack against his. At first, his mouth is stiff and unyielding, as it is stretched into a smug smile.

Dickhead. He better kiss me back.

Heck, if I'm doing this, I might as well go full hog. I kiss him harder, desperate, my lips impatient and a little bit mean. My left fang nips his bottom lip, and a bead of blood enters my mouth. I hum as his taste floods me, pulling a ragged sound from my chest, almost like a growl.

The realisation hits. He doesn't want to kiss me. I soften my lips, my heart hammers wildly, and my knees are moments away from buckling.

Oh no. I've made a horrible mistake.

Again.

There's a small pain-filled gasp of my breath, and I pull away. His hand wraps around my hair, and he tilts my head back. Growling deep in his chest, Kleric's mouth crashes down on mine... *then* he returns my kiss.

He kisses me back.

CHAPTER
THIRTY ONE

While I wait for the traffic lights to change, I rub my lips together, and my hand flutters up to trace them. Underneath my fingertips, my mouth feels puffy, and my lips tingle like mad from Kleric's kisses. I pluck at my bottom lip in an attempt to get rid of the goofy smile that is fixed on my face.

I'm smiling like a loon.

Not the best thing to do when rocking up to enemy territory. The demon kiss on my hand pulses along with my heartbeat, and, honest to fate, it feels like he's in the car with me. Add in Kleric's blood sloshing around in my system, and it's like I'm drunk.

Drunk on him.

I shuffle, rub my thighs together and adjust my seat belt.

It was just a kiss.

An epic, change-your-life kiss, but that's all it was, a

kiss. People kiss people all the time, right? It doesn't have to mean anything. I can find someone attractive, kiss them, and walk away. I don't have to do any magical bonding shenanigans.

Like I have ants in my pants, I shuffle again in the seat. *He likes me! He really likes me.* I grin and retrace my mouth.

At least this time, you got a kiss.

My crazy smile drops, and I let out a self-deprecating snort and wince. Yeah, if I remember rightly, I got a pat on the head from Xander once. I scowl as the traffic light changes. My heart then skips a beat, and my fingers tighten on the wheel as I enter unicorn territory.

Well, here we go.

I change gears and drive into the fancy residential street. Oh boy, look at that... Granny Ann has sure beefed up security since I was here last.

With my head swivelling like mad, I take in all the odd warning signs. They are scattered every twenty feet or so. All different variations with the same theme, telling people if they've not got permission to be here, they need to turn around and leave. Oh, and the big one with a colourful graphic of a human skull pierced by a unicorn's horn. So not ominous, no, not at all.

I drive towards a new parking area, and I can see the ward that Ava warned me about just ahead. It looks like the unicorns have set everything up so visitors must park and walk through the ward. From a security point of view, it's a good idea.

Though this extra security is all very strange. Thinking about strange... "What the heck is that?" I mumble. I squint and lean forward to peer out the windscreen as I catch sight of a clump of random magic that is floating smack-bang in the middle of the road. It's see-through and wavy. Perhaps a barrier or a magic scan?

The magic is so subtle, I don't think most people would see it. I cringe. I have to play this out like an idiot. I have no choice but to drive right into it.

So I take my foot off the accelerator.

Goosebumps erupt on my arms as I pass through, and... oops, the Land Rover's diesel engine coughs, splutters, and dies. The poor car shudders to a stop.

Oh, so that's what the magic does. Confused, I look at the visitor's car park, still a hundred feet away. Why bother?

Then half a dozen armed guards pop out of the ether. Huh. They must have hidden behind a Don't See Me Now spell.

I roll my eyes, pop the Defender in neutral, and turn the ignition off. Yes, yes, all very dramatic. I remember just in time to make a shocked Pikachu face, and I clutch my hands to my chest.

Smug—as my Defender hasn't got electric windows—I nudge the door lock down with my elbow and grab the window handle and crank it down an inch.

They've done all this to frighten me, and they want me out of the car, but I'll take my chance now to be a pain in the arse. After all, pissed-off creatures make mistakes.

The man in charge, a bear shifter, rocks up to my window. He leans against the roof and glares down at me. "Good afternoon, Miss Dennison. Will you step out of the vehicle and allow us to pat you down?" he asks.

I blink at him and, with utter fake confusion and a vapid smile, say, "Oh, can't I drive in?" I ignore his greeting and his jaw ticks. "I own a house around here somewhere." I wave my hands in the air and peek down at my notes. "Number se-seven," I stutter out the last word when I spot ginger fur.

Ginger fur? What the ever-loving f—

Hidden behind my seat, among all my work stuff, is the unwelcome sight of my cat. Dexter. I glare at him. "Sorry, just one second." I hold up a finger to the guard. "Something has just come up." I turn my full attention to my ginger stowaway.

"Mert," Dexter says as he licks his front paw. He spreads his toes and nibbles on a pink toe bean.

Arsehole, I mouth back at him. I lean between the seats and drop my voice to a bare angry whisper. "How the hell did you sneak in? Thanks, Dexter Dennison, but I don't need your help." I then spot... I groan, close my eyes and, with exasperation, boink my head against the headrest. "Why me?" I wail. *Story* is snuggled within the fur of Dexter's tail.

For eff's sake.

I open my eyes with the hope I'm seeing things, and nope. She is still there. Oh, and instead of her normal dress and bare feet, Story is wearing combats and boots. The pixie dares to shimmy, grin, and give me a little wave. I groan again. How the hell did I not notice the pair of them?

Kiss drunk.

Yep, that's why. I wrinkle my nose and give them the "wait till I get you home" deadly stare.

"I need to drop someone back at home," I say louder to the security guard, although my voice is a tad muffled as I have to push the words through gritted teeth.

I turn back to him just as he drops a spell to unlock the car door. The bear shifter rips the door open, and his pal *cuts* through the seat belt. Then the bear's grubby hands whip inside and grab hold of my arm, and he unceremoniously pulls me out.

My heels scrape against the tarmac. "What the hell." I whimper when the pieces of the original Land Rover 1989 seat belt clatter into the footwell. "Hey guy, you better pay for that." I point at the seat belt, and my lower lip wobbles. They aren't that expensive, but that's not the point. It was an original part.

"We don't want you to be late for dinner," the first guard growls, squeezing my arm and giving me a shake.

I'm an hour early. What a nobhead.

He drags me away from the car, and he yanks me up so I'm on my toes and unbalanced. "We can chuck some water in for your stowaway pet."

I look back at my friends and the abandoned Defender morosely. I should have known she was up to something when she dropped the subject of coming.

Ah, no. I wince. Her mate will kill me. I am a hundred per cent positive Ralph will wait until I'm fast asleep, and then he's going to stab me in the eye with his sword.

I watch, indignant. My nostrils flare as the seat belt cutter gets into my Land Rover and, *grinding the gears,* pulls it off the road and into the car park—good to know the wavy magic effect was only temporary, but I'm pissed that some random shifter is driving *my Defender.* Who taught that arsehole to drive?

Gosh, I hope Story knows what she's doing. *Please, fate, let them both be okay. I'll do anything.* I take a breath. No, they will be fine, and I'm not worried about Dexter. He can look after himself as he isn't an average cat. But Story... she should know better than to put herself in harm's way. *Don't you do that every day?* Yep, and now I am a hypocrite. I huff and shake my head as I'm tugged further and further away from my best friend.

My hands twitch with the need to smack these guys around. But I refrain as I have a plan, and with all the cat drama, they haven't yet checked me for weapons. Professionals, these guys aren't. So I let him shove me around without a peep of protest except for the occasional whimper.

I'm dragged down the road, and I'm manhandled through the ward. Ugh, that is highly unpleasant. It twists my insides. My hair feels like it is standing on end. Ava was right. If I were carrying any, this one would have killed all electronics.

"I knew your reputation was absolute bullshit. Rebel Leader," the bear shifter scoffs while giving my arm an extra painful twist and squeeze.

I play my part and whimper while, in my head, I stab him in the throat and skip over his bleeding corpse.

"She came to negotiate her freedom with a kitty cat," he tells the other guards, who all laugh along with him.

Negotiate my freedom, eh? As if.

"Did you read the Daily Shifter? They said she was in prison for murder. Bitch couldn't fight her way out of a paper bag..."

Most of my attention is still on the Land Rover. My shoulders sag, and I sigh when I see a flutter of wings and a flash of ginger fur as Dexter bolts from the open door and into some bushes as the seat belt–murdering guard gets out.

"... Shifter Assembly should give her to a strong mate. Not that anyone wants her dirty blood."

I turn my attention back to the guards. I'm surrounded. That's twenty-four guards in total.

Meh, that's doable.

The bear shifter lets go of my arm while he clutches his belly and laughs at something one of the other guards has said. He wipes tears from his eyes as they continue to pick my life apart.

I take in a shaky breath, and from a hidden pocket in my dress, I pull out a potion just in case what I'm about to do goes horribly wrong. They are all together in one controllable area, which is helpful.

The seat belt guard rocks up, flipping my car keys in his hand.

It's now or never. This should be easy for me. I rapidly blink, scratch the demon kiss on the back of my hand, and widen my stance.

Inside me, there is a caged, churning ball of power.

I close my eyes. I think happy, happy, happy thoughts as I metaphysically open the cage door and push the magic out. It trickles inside me, bubbles and then rips out of my chest and down my left arm. I hunch, grit my teeth and... *ouch, ouch, ouch.*

My eyes fly open as rainbow magic bursts from my left hand like a fountain. Whoa. The blast lasts for at least a minute, and at the end, it put-put-putters with a last puff of —I kid you not—*glitter.*

It stops.

The twenty-four guards stand motionless with their eyes glazed. I sag in relief. And then I lift my arm and stare at my shaking hand. My palm sparkles. "What the hell," I mumble. I laugh. It sounds a little manic. "What the eff was that?" Glitter really?

I may have put more spin on the magic than usual, as I'm still freaked out about my stowaways, and the stakes are higher now with them here. It also doesn't hurt that I'm full to the brim with demon power. I drop my hand and blink back at the motionless guards.

Wow, it really worked.

I gulp. Gosh, my mouth is dry as a bone, and my legs feel shaky. The kiss heats and pulses. He is concerned. *I'm fine*, I tell the nosy demon. *I will give you a shout if I'm not.*

The magic, my magic, has the power to either attract or repel, and the amount I blasted at them has left them inert... I scowl at their creepy expressions. My vampire compulsion used to be at a normal level until my unicorn powers kicked up a gear. Now I can do this...

I love-bombed them.

Uh-oh. This is on an entirely different level of wrong. I feel a bit sick. The magic is alien and strange. Before I gained control of it, it used to seep out of me and mess with people's heads. The bracelet Xander gave me helped me to control it. Over the years, I came to grips with the power until I didn't need the bracelet. Even so, this magic is my last resort, the shit-hit-the-fan option.

It frightens me. It frightens me so much I've locked it down so damn tight it is caged inside me. It is too danger-ous. I almost used it when Forrest and I were losing the fight in the warehouse before her dragon bit that massive chunk out of the building. And I am so glad he did, as it is not the kind of power I want to use in a fight. 'Cause if I make a teeny-tiny mistake, instead of love, I can make people rage or repel them to the point they run, which could get innocent people killed.

Love also isn't great. I stare at their creepy faces. Every time I move, they follow me with their eyes, like twenty-four loved-up zombies. Given the chance, they would rip me apart trying to *love me*. Hence the ward I have in my sweaty hand. I slide it back for safekeeping into its hidden pocket.

Everything so far is all right. I'd rather hack at creatures with my sword, and they can choose to hack at me back, rather than this—the guards watch me—take away their autonomy. Take away their free will. The power just feels extra wrong, immoral.

But sometimes—I lick my dry lips—it's the smartest choice as I want these guards to go home tonight to their families. They aren't bad people... They aren't all bad people. My top lip moves almost of its own accord to snarl at the bear shifter. I have bruises on my arm thanks to him. He deserves to get his head kicked in. He's a proper wanker. But the rest of them aren't trained to properly fight, and I don't want to kill people just doing their jobs.

Dexter struts down the road in a way only a cat can do. He weaves around the legs of the frozen guards, leaving his scent and smatter of orange hair—his calling card—all over their black trousers. Dexter and Story have built up an immunity to this magic. Not that they were near the blast radius, but if there's any lingering magic hanging around, I don't have to worry.

Story zooms towards me. "Nice glitter. You've never done that before."

"I know. It freaked me out. Shooting rainbows and glitter out of my hand has never happened before. Definitely a combination of worry, panic, and demon blood." I rub my sparkly palm on my bare leg and shudder.

The pixie plops herself on the bear shifter's head and swings her legs, bopping him in the middle of his forehead with the heel of her new boot. I smirk. "At least it came out of your hand and not your bum," Story says wisely. "You could have pooped glitter."

"Yeah... thank goodness." I narrow my eyes. "*Weirdo*, my bum, really? Pooped glitter?" I finish with a mumble and a shake of my head.

She grins at me.

Smart arse. I huff and rub my forehead. Story sure knows how to snap me out of shock. My lips twitch, and we both laugh.

I snatch my keys out of the seat belt murderer's hand and then poke, prod and guide the group of guards back into rough guarding positions. "Stay here, do your jobs, and act normal. Everything is normal. If anyone asks, I still haven't arrived. Do you understand?"

I shudder when they nod their heads creepily in sync. "Act normal," they say in zombie unison.

I blow out a breath. At least they aren't trying to touch me. That's something, I guess, a small mercy. "Wait for me. I will see you soon," I tell them. I then ask the remaining guards to come with me. They zombie shuffle behind me as we go through the ward. "Oh heck no." I run back to the Land Rover, and zombie guards run after me.

Story bounces on the bear shifter's head and giggles. This is too weird even for me. We are back down the road to where they first appeared.

"Wait for me here. Keep still and be quiet," I tell them. I get back the same creepy nods, this time without the unison chant. Thank goodness. "Oh no, not you two." I poke the bear shifter and the seat belt murderer out of the line-up. "Both of you stay over here. You're both coming with me." I separate those two from the zombie herd and then dig into my dress pocket, find and chuck my own Don't See Me Now spell at the group of guards. It covers the lot of them, and when they disappear, I feel like I can finally breathe.

"How long till they snap out of it?" Story asks. She is still perched on the bear's head. He has a little red spot from her kicking his forehead.

"I dunno." I pull a face. "I've never done it on a scale like this before. A few hours? When they snap out of it, they shouldn't remember a thing." I hope.

I point to the bear. "Did you, or anyone, inform the unicorns that I arrived?"

He shakes his head no.

Excellent, I thought not. "Okay, gentlemen, if you would follow me." It's time for us to go hunting.

CHAPTER
THIRTY TWO

I MARCH to the car and get the two love-bombed guards to turn their backs as I grab my work clothes. I've upgraded my combats to black ballistic fabric with a spell-repelling coating. The outfit looks like leather and cost me a pretty penny. Worth it, as I'm not about to mess this up—like I did last time. If Robin runs or starts something, I'm at least going to be prepared.

I shimmy into everything and stuff my feet into my boots. I plait my hair so it's out of the way and hang the dress up for later. With a last check of my spells and weapons, I'm ready to go.

I better make this fast. "Time check?" I ask Story.

"Fifty-two minutes till Sunday dinner." In a poor attempt to move the guard's head, Story tugs at his hair, and a clump comes out in her hand. She makes an oops face, lets it go, and the hair drifts to the floor.

Dexter gives it a sniff, then pounces onto the Defender's warm bonnet. He slumps against the windscreen to get a few sun rays.

"I know where your house is located," Story says.

I nod and shoot her a grateful smile. "Please show me the way."

"You still mad we came?" she asks in her singsong voice.

"Livid."

Story laughs, leaps from the bear's head, and zips away.

Leaving Dexter guarding the car and sunbathing, we all follow her at a jog. I hope the house is close. And it is. It's just down the road. Story hovers in front of a redbrick house which looks only a few decades old. On the right-hand side of the black door is a plaque. NUMBER 7.

Yep, home sweet home.

"Guards, watch the back door and stop anyone from leaving." They nod and move around to the back of the house. I twist the doorknob, and it turns. It is open. *Keep behind me*, I mouth to Story, and she nods.

"Hi, honey. I'm home," I singsong as I step inside.

Robin comes out of, I presume, the kitchen with a tea towel in her hand. We stare at each other. "You! What are you doing here?" she snarls.

I point my finger and circle it to encompass the house. "Back at you, angel cakes, this is *my* house."

She throws the tea towel to the floor. "You didn't drown. Pity." Her right hand touches the blade on her thigh. I'm thankful she has dropped the innocent act as it was nauseating.

"Yeah, thanks for that. I needed fresh air and a swim." I yawn and stretch. "It was so refreshing."

She drops her gaze to the demon kiss on my hand, and her baby-blue eyes narrow with pure rage. There is a *schwing* noise of a knife leaving its metal scabbard, and without missing a beat and with a strange war cry, Robin charges towards me, slashing the silver blade from left to right.

I grin.

Instead of reaching for a weapon, I twist to the side, and as she swings at my face, I catch her wrist and jerk her forward. With her arm extended, I snap my right fist onto her elbow joint. The arm crunches. *Oops.* Robin cries out, and the knife clatters to the floor. Broken, her right arm dangles. It flops uselessly at her side.

Ah, bless her. She looks a little pale.

With a scream of rage that pinks her cheeks, Robin aims her knee at my kidney, but I batter it away before it lands, and when she swings her left arm to hit me, I use her momentum against her, grab the flailing limb and tug it up behind her back.

I twist her away from me, kick the back of her knees, and flip her onto the floor. Both her arms are now pinned behind her.

Within two minutes of entering the house, she is restrained. A little anticlimactic, but I still have Granny Ann to deal with, so there is so much fun yet to be had.

"Get off me," Robin wails, flopping like a fish.

I sigh, and my eyes drift to the ceiling. "Give me strength," I mumble.

Why do I have to deal with this mess? I drop to the floor and place my knee on the small of her back. Gripping her good arm, I wrench it further up her back and give her elbow a little warning tap. "Tell me, Robin," I say, leaning forward so my words tickle against her ear. "Why me? What made you want to fuck me over?"

"Xander. He is mine."

"Oh really?" I chuckle. "No problem. Good luck with that. So what? You set me up for love as you wanted me out of the way?"

"The unicorn, Ann, told me that if I stayed away for a few weeks, she'd get the evidence to Xander that you took me. She told me he would go mad looking for me, realise that we are meant to be together, and that he'd see the truth."

The truth?

"You are nothing but dirt on the end of his shoe."

I shrug. Well, that is kind of what happened. He sees me as dirt. My grandmother's plan worked fine if she wanted us both to see the light.

"Okay? And?" I need her to hurry the eff along as I don't want to be late for Sunday dinner and the epic big reveal of my grandmother's master plan.

"And it worked too. The unicorn only wanted you at the Hunters Guild so she could bail you out and control you. Keep you apart from Xander. But my Xander missed *me* so much that he sent you to prison." She laughs, and my fangs snap down with my anger. She turns her head and flashes me a smug grin. "You ruined him by taking his blood. How dare you! He is an angel, and you're an abomination. But see, I ruined you right back." Robin laughs again. "It worked. It was working; why couldn't you just follow the plan?"

"The plan?" I tilt my head.

A tiny gasp escapes her lips, and she clamps her mouth closed.

"Oh no. Don't stop now, Robin. It was just getting good. Tell me." This time I tweak her broken arm, and she cries out in pain. "I'll heal your arm if you tell me, or I will use that big knife of yours to cut off a few of your fingers," I whisper.

Out the corner of my eye, I see Story shudder.

"She's going to convince you I will tell the Grand Creature Council that you kidnapped me and killed kids. She has more evidence you're a serial killer. Now heal my arm."

Fabricated evidence. Family, eh?

I nod. I believe her. What Robin said matches what Ava has found out. It's been a long game of Ann's, with whispers and rumours and obvious breadcrumbs she has been sprinkling around. Unfortunately for her, she miscalculated, and she tried to manipulate Xander.

The angel was too reactive. She wrongly assumed he would give me the benefit of the doubt. What with all our shared history, she thought he'd protect me. So did I. My index fingernail digs into my thumb's cuticle as I unconsciously pick at the skin.

But Ann was banking on him at least doing some poking around. So she could move me into a position to trap me? I still don't know... but Xander drop-kicked my arse like a hot potato, and like in good old Monopoly, I went straight to jail without passing go.

But now I'm back, out of prison, under the watch of the Grand Creature Council. Who are salty that they had to pay me off. I'm a known troublemaker with a sparkly reputation of being an unhinged hybrid according to a well-respected angel ambassador who went on record saying I'm a psychopath.

Shit, he's such a dickhead.

My unicorn grandmother thinks I'm broken, and no doubt she believes I will cave to her demands. Rightly so. I'll do anything to avoid going back to prison. With his rejection and our severed bond, Xander unintentionally softened me for my grandmother to give it another go. He is still her star-knight chess piece. And instead of changing the plan, when the court found me not guilty, she doubled down with this little stunt to seal my fate.

But a cornered creature doesn't necessarily do what it is told. While Granny Ann has been sprinkling the bread-crumbs, my team of misfits has been scooping them up and analysing them.

The question I keep asking myself is: what the hell does she want?

"Anything else?" Robin shakes her head. "Thank you. That wasn't so hard now, was it?" I give her broken arm a friendly pat, and she whimpers. It's music to my ears.

Grabbing a spare anti-magic band—the other is still tucked away in the dress's hem—I slap it onto her wrist. With a groan, poor little Robin is out like a light. I then tug her broken, rapidly swelling elbow straight, crunching the joint so it will set correct, and use a potion to heal it. I'm not a complete savage. And just in case she wakes up from the anti-magic effect, I spell her hands and feet together.

Breaking Robin's arm has made me feel so much better. It has also made me realise she's not worth my time. She's a pawn. And all I need to do is knock her off the board so she doesn't impede me anymore from dealing with my grandmother. Same with Xander—my grandmother's knight has got to go.

A messed-up little voice inside me is grateful this happened. Not for my stint in prison, but to be shown in no uncertain terms what the angel thinks of me. What I meant to him... I swallow. It's not nice to be shown the truth, but I'm glad it's sooner rather than later if sooner ended up being a waste of nine bloody years and not a hundred.

It's like a weight of fate and expectations have been lifted. There is something to be said for hitting rock bottom and having to claw your way out of the hole.

"You are so scary," Story mumbles from her perch on the hallway table.

Huh. I give her a toothy grin. I thought I was restrained.

"What was up with the creepy whisper?" I glance at her, and she pretends she said nothing.

Instead, she stands on her toes and looks about. "Do we... um... have time to look around?" Nosy pixie.

"No."

"Spoilsport."

All we get to see of this house is the hallway. If I took the time to poke about a bit, I wonder if I'd find eyeballs in jars and severed fingers. I hum underneath my breath. This house is way too much of a risk. The decision is made. Within the hour, it will be burned to the ground.

I call the guards inside. I give the seat belt murderer a handful of dangerous marble-sized orange potions and explicit instructions on how to clear the house and use them.

With a wave of my hand, the bear shifter scoops Robin up, and we jog back to the Land Rover, where I change back into my pretty dress.

"Will you watch over her while I drive?" I ask Story and Dexter, nodding in Robin's direction as the bear stuffs her in the back.

With a happy chirp, Dexter jumps in, and Story nods and flits inside. "We got this. Drive, we will be fine."

I slide my handcuff jewellery back into place and hand Story a potent sleeping spell. "In case Robin wakes. Be careful." I then turn to the bear shifter. "Wait here. Act normal. I will be right back."

"I love you more than life," the bear shifter moans.

Both Story and I stare at him with similar freaked-out expressions. "Yep, that is some creepy shit. Never, ever use that power around me again," she grumbles.

"Deal." I smirk at her and slam the back door shut. I hurry around to the driver's seat and undo my hair from its plait. The beauty spell from before makes the waves all perfect again. "Time check?"

"You have forty-six minutes."

Perfect. The time will be tight, but it is enough to drop off a package.

CHAPTER
THIRTY THREE

MY HANDS SHAKE as I drive to Xander's house. *I'm really doing this.* If I hadn't made a promise to myself, I might have wimped out and dropped her off at the Grand Creature Council building or at the Hunters Guild, but what are they going to do with her really?

I roll my eyes. She is the missing *victim*, after all.

I grip the wheel firmer to steady my hands. I will give Robin and Xander what they want, each other. The angel asked me to find her, and avoiding him and not dealing with his bullshit and this situation will make me feel like a coward. And my grandmother will win.

Nah, that will never happen. I promised myself that I'd bring her back to him, throw her at his feet, and she might not be at this very moment kicking and screaming... My lips twitch. But it will sure piss blondie off that Xander will see her tied up and snoring.

Yeah, in less than ten minutes, she will be Xander's problem, not mine. It's up to him what he does, whether he does his truth-telling thing to find out her role in this framing me debacle or not. It is out of my hands and up to him.

I don't expect an apology. A sorry-I-chucked-you-in-prison note. Yeah, shouldn't there be a fancy card for that? I snort. I expect nothing from that man. If Robin stays away from me, I won't kill her. If they both stay out of my life, I'm good.

"Everything okay back there?" I ask over my shoulder. It is worryingly quiet in the back, and gosh, it feels strange driving without a seat belt.

"Yeah, she's still out," Story yells.

I nod. "Great. Well, we are almost there." I hope Story doesn't pick a fight with Xander. It will be the first time she has seen him.

Have you got Xander's phone number? I haven't got my mobile on me. I throw my thoughts in Kleric's direction. The scar on my hand throbs. The clock inside my mind ticks down. I want to dump Robin at the angel's feet and run.

Are you okay? Do you finally have the pain-in-the-arse missing angel? His voice is a warm welcome inside my head, so different from the scratchy communication spells.

Yeah, and I am five minutes out from Xander's house. I don't even know if he's home.

I'll ring him.

Thanks, you are a star.

It isn't until I turn down Xander's street that the demon gets back to me. *He will meet you outside.* I sag in my seat. Here's hoping I don't even need to get out of the car. The less I see of Xander, the better.

Thank you, I tell Kleric as I shut our connection down the best I can. Clicking the indicator, I turn the wheel and drive through the angel's open gates and up to his massive, beautiful home.

Once upon a time, Story and I used to live here. My sensitive ears pick up the pixie's sharp intake of breath as I park. We both see Xander at the same time.

Dressed in grey jogging bottoms and a tight, long-sleeved top that clings to him, he leans against the front door with his arms across his chest. Butterflies tickle and batter against my insides. I wish I had claws like Forrest. If I did, I'd rip those bloody butterflies right out.

Instead, I dig my nails into my thigh.

Oh-uh, here we go.

Xander jogs down the three porch steps and heads towards the car.

I puff out a breath and open the car door, positioning myself so I'm halfway in and halfway out. Half-hidden, yeah, I am using the door as a shield.

"She's in the back. She has an anti-magic band on that knocked her out cold." My voice is professional. Clinical.

He nods, his gold eyes narrow as he prowls to the back of the vehicle and opens the back door. Story says nothing, even when Xander says a gruff, "Hello."

He even bows his head in respect to my fae monster cat, but Dexter turns his head and ignores him with a flick of his tail.

My heart hurts, and my soul cries when Xander pulls Robin ever so gently from the back of my car. Her head rests on his chest as he magically unbinds her hands and feet and removes the anti-magic band.

As he prowls towards me, his golden magic dances across her skin, checking to ensure she's okay. He hands over the anti-magic band.

I take it gingerly without touching him and flick it onto the passenger seat. I will put it away later with the rest of my kit.

"She is healthy. Her only injury is a recently broken elbow that was healed. Is that right?" he asks me.

I sigh and look away. I don't need a shouting match with him. I stick to honesty, and the rest is up to him. "She came at me with a knife. I broke her elbow to disarm her and then used a standard healing potion," I say in the same clinical tone.

His eyes trace over her inert form, and he takes in the empty scabbard on her leg with a nod. "Where did you find her?"

I frown. It takes a second to translate his words. The angel is asking me a normal question. Without the malice he usually throws at me. It's sad, after nine years of whatever we had, that I expected him to call me a liar.

I rub the back of my neck. "She was hiding out at the old cinema on Dickson Road. I have evidence to suggest that she had been staying there for seven of her missing weeks. She ran when I found her in the early hours of Tuesday morning. I will send you the footage. To get away, she booted me into the sea." I smile bitterly, reliving my mistake and the memory of the heavy weight of the waves as Mother Nature herself wanted to take my last breath. "From there, she went to the unicorns."

Xander nods. "Your grandmother?"

"I believe so, from what Robin has told me." I shake my head. "Anyway, there you go, one missing angel. I've got to go deal with the rest of this mess." My hair brushes against my cheek, and I batter it away.

It's through that movement that the angel seems to realise I'm in a dress. For a few seconds, he looks dumbfounded. His pupils dilate, and his mouth goes slack.

"Tru—"

"No," I snap. He can't look at me like that. "I've got to go." In quick clean movements, I slide back into the Land Rover and yank the door closed. I have the car in first gear, and I'm rolling down the drive before he can open his stupid mouth.

"Fuck off, fuck off, fuck off," I mumble under my breath.

I don't like how being around that man makes me feel. Like I'm back in the sea, and I'm drowning.

Story snorts and zips from the back. She lands on my shoulder, snuggles into my neck and pats my cheek. "Did you see his face? He was gobsmacked." She zooms to the back window, her nose pressed to the glass. "He's still watching!" she crows with glee.

The man is a total idiot. I hate him.

"I am dropping you both off at home."

"Nooooo—"

"No arguments. I need to do this alone. Can you please send all the footage and evidence we have on Robin to Xander?"

"Yeah," Story grumbles. "Everything?"

"Yes please. I don't expect him to believe us, but I said I

would." I pull up at our building, embarrassed at how close we live in proximity to him. At least the farmhouse is on the other side of town.

I open my door, and Dexter gives me a headbutt and kitty nudge and jumps over me and out.

Story follows him, her wings beating slowly and slightly drooping with her disappointment. "Have a nice *dinner*," she grumbles. "Time check. You are going to be late as you only have eight minutes."

"Thank you." Out of habit, I wait until they have both disappeared inside the building and then drive back to the unicorns.

To deal with my evil grandmother.

CHAPTER
THIRTY FOUR

MY UNICORN GRANDMOTHER sits in one of eight chairs at the head of her oak dining table. Dressed in a black skirt and a crisp white blouse, her body is at the perfect angle to emphasise her small waist, willowy frame, and long legs. Her orange, red, and yellow hair is secured in an elegant chignon bun. Like mini rainbows, her eyes shine with a multitude of colours, and a wicked, triumphant smile pulls at her blood-red painted lips. The scent of grass and wildflowers fills my nose. She tilts her head to look down her nose at me and, with a red nail, points at the chair opposite.

It's tough for me not to smirk. All she's missing is a cat, and then she'd be a perfect villain. I wonder if Dexter would help her out. No, he'd more than likely try to eat her face off.

I am not quick enough to sit as her henchman pokes me

in the back. He's not controlled by my love bomb. The twenty-four guards are still bumbling around outside. With a haughty expression, I take my time to brush my dress underneath me and take the offered seat.

With a wave from my grandmother, the unicorn henchman leaves the room.

"Grandmother, what is going on?" I say as I take in the empty table. "I thought I was coming to Sunday dinner?"

There is a flash of pity in her eyes. "At two o'clock, my solicitor is going to arrive with documents you will sign without a fuss," she says.

"Okay?"

"These documents will give me full legal power over you. We both know you are not well." One of her sky-high black heels rhythmically taps the floor as she adjusts her legs. Hands flat on the table, she leans forward, and with a sad smile, she makes her move. "If you don't sign, all the evidence of your nefarious deeds will see you back in prison, back to your little white cell."

I hiss. *And there it is. She plays her hand.*

I bite my lip and take a deep breath. I've only been here for a few minutes, and she's not messing around. "Nefarious deeds?" I whisper.

If I give her enough rope, she will hang herself. Right? What's it going to be? What does she want from me, children, a forced mate, my power? With anticipation, my heart picks up its beat.

"The angel, Robin, is here. I gave her shelter at your house."

I glance at the clock on the mantelpiece. Not my house

for much longer, as the seat belt guard should activate the orange spells right about now. Soon enough, the house will burn to a magically controlled crisp. Ann won't be able to use any fabricated evidence she has stashed there to control me.

"If you don't comply, I will hand over all the evidence I have, including her sworn statement that you kidnapped her."

So she's doing this, playing the serial killer narrative.

"Fabricated evidence," I growl.

Ann frowns at me and purses her red lips.

I can see from a mile off what she is doing without even having to say a word, but I'll play; if she expects me to throw a fit, she'll be waiting a hell of a long time. Thanks to Robin, I'm already three steps ahead, and with the house gone, Ann has got shit.

Everything she has now is just empty threats because she has no leverage. I lean forward, matching her body language. The table is cold underneath my palms. "And? The paperwork? What do you want, Grandmother?" I say *Grandmother* with a snarl. Every time I call her that, she winces. "What do you want me to sign? What are the terms of my surrender?"

"I want to make sure you can't hurt anyone again," she says boldly with narrowed eyes.

Er, what?

"Your father was not a well man." She sits back in her chair away from me and dips her chin. "Our family line is cursed with mental problems. The psychopathy missed me but affected your father. That is why I had no more children. I guess a mother knows deep down." She frowns, and her right hand flutters to her chest. "It was something I couldn't bear to see passed on, the cruel, evil streak. Your father, like you, could mirror people's behaviour and emotions, and although what he didn't hide was concerning, he was so charming." Ann smiles, and it looks so bitter.

So broken.

The life in her eyes pales as if, for a moment, she is stuck in a memory. She shakes her head, and her eyes shine with determination once again.

"He covered his tracks. I thought I had a tight enough leash on him. I didn't react quickly enough, and by the time I did, it was too late to save him. I failed. My love blinded me to him. It is so easy to allow love to convince you that everything is going to be okay. I had thought the problems had died with him. As you know, I didn't find out about you until you had grown. He took the secret of you and your poor mother's existence to his grave." She taps the table with her nail. "He should have never been allowed near her. He hurt you, a six-year-old child, and killed your mum because I didn't do my job as his mother. As your grandmother.

"I should have done more, kept a closer eye on him. It's my fault. I let you down. I had hoped..." She drops her eyes to the table as they fill with tears. "I had hoped you would be okay. You showed such strength, such empathy. But the unicorn power combined with the vampire side of you..." Her eyes snap up and meet mine with righteous determination swimming in their depths. "I will not stand by and let you hurt another person, Tru. This is an intervention. What you did to the poor angel is not okay."

My mouth is so wide my jaw is almost on the table.

It takes me a second to snap it closed. My brain is buzzing; it's going a hundred miles an hour as I contemplate her words. She thinks... Gah, I'm so confused. I scratch the back of my head.

"You will have access to the best doctors," she continues, "who will teach you to cope with your urges." She swallows and takes in a deep breath. "In time, I am sure, with the correct medication—"

I hold my hand up to stop her.

"This. Is. An. Intervention?" I ask. I say each word carefully as if my head is going to explode. She nods her head, and the pity is back.

Granny Ann thinks I'm off my rocker, just like my sperm donor.

I tilt my head to the side. "You think I... you think... me?" I huff, point to my chest, and chuckle under my breath. I slump, and my head rolls against the padding of the high-backed seat. My eyes trace the ceiling and the beautiful crystal chandelier overhead. The chuckle bubbles into a laugh that rips through my throat, and my arms have to come around to support hug my stomach. "You got the same made-up evidence Xander did," I hiss through my laughter.

Granny Ann is on the same game board as Xander. As me. She hasn't been the one playing us for fools. No, I've just found myself another pawn.

For eff's sake.

I don't know what the hell is going on, and... shit, I don't know where the chess analogies have come from. I've never even bloody played chess. I rub my mouth with the back of my hand, and I snort and shake my head.

My poor brain is fried.

My laughter dies as I stare at the ceiling and take deep, deliberate breaths. I need to lock myself away from people and let the world burn. But the desire to prove Xander wrong about me burns brighter.

I shake my head and sit up.

Ann has a face of thunder; I wouldn't be surprised if smoke billowed out of her ears. Oh dear. My laughing fit has not endeared me to her. I grab a white napkin from the pile at the end of the table and wave it. Her rainbow eyes narrow. She sure is not happy with my preverbal waving of the white flag. I drop the napkin on the table.

"I know this isn't a joke, and I appreciate the grandmotherly intervention, but you know I'm an assassin, right?"

She waves my profession away with a sweep of her hand. "I am not happy with that, but I can overlook it. I'm talking about you hurting an innocent."

"Okay. Let's get this straight. You didn't set me up? You didn't collaborate with Robin to drive a wedge between me and the angels' ambassador? You didn't fabricate evidence so Xander would lose his shit and send me to prison?"

"What? No, of course not," Ann splutters.

My eye twitches, and I rub a sore spot above my nose. "Why, then, did you instruct your men to assault me?"

Her eyes widen with disbelief.

"On Monday while I was in the Grand Creature Council's building, they knocked me out and tied me bleeding to a chair. Does that ring any bells? Ding, ding?

No? A unicorn called Hades gave me a threatening ultimatum to come to this Sunday dinner." I prod the table. "Or else."

"What? He would never." Indignant now, my grandmother gets to her feet. "Geoff!" she yells. "Please send Hades in here now!"

Within moments, dressed in a pristine suit, Hades struts into the room. "Ann, you wanted to speak to me?" He adjusts his cuffs and smirks at me.

He's an idiot and hasn't even bothered to read the room.

As if it's a throne and she is a queen, my unicorn grandmother takes her seat. She then, fingers digging into the wooden table so hard they turn white from the pressure, leans across and narrows her eyes. "Did your goons touch my granddaughter?" she says in a dangerous tone. It makes the tiny hairs on my neck rise.

Hades blinks at her. Ah, now he gets it. His face loses all its colour, and his cocky smirk falls. He submissively drops his eyes to the floor and nods.

"Did they knock her unconscious and tie her to a chair in my name?" Hades nods again. "Why? Why would you do that when I asked you to just pass on a simple invitation?"

He dares to give me a vicious glare.

Ooh, you are such a jumped-up little nobhead.

"I knew what she'd been doing, her blatant disrespect when you'd been so open and welcoming. You gave her a damn house, and she threw it back in your face. I wanted to give her payback, a taste of her own medicine," the unicorn mumbles.

"That wasn't for you to decide, and you stepped over

the line. You had my granddaughter attacked. You assaulted a female unicorn!" she yells.

"Well, she's not a proper unicorn. She is an abomination," he grumbles again in the direction of his feet.

"My grandchild!" she screams. "You little cretin—"

"Hey." I clap my hands, interrupting her tirade. I pin them both with a blistering glare. "If you can do this later, that will be great. However, I'd love to get to see him smashed on the back of his head if you need a punishment idea. We need to hurry this along. Just so it's clear, I haven't been murdering innocent creatures or kidnapping angels. This is all part of an elaborate setup. Here, give me your phone. Please? I need to make a call." I lift my chin and wiggle my fingers at my grandmother.

Without dropping her scowl at Hades, she shunts her phone across to me. It spins on the glossy wood, and I slap my hand down so it doesn't slide off the table.

I keep the phone on speaker as I dial Ava. "Hey, it's me. You are on the speaker. Can you send all the incriminating evidence you have gathered on my grandmother to her?" I lift my eyes from the handset to confirm with Ann. "Have you got a datapad?"

Ann nods and flicks her hand at Hades. "Go get it." He runs out of the room.

"Everything we have to her datapad please, Ava." I might as well share the information so she knows what a mess she is neck deep in.

"No problem. As soon as this call connected, it gave me access to everyone's devices. Sending all the information now," Ava says.

Ann scowls.

I smile at the phone. I'm glad the technomancy witch is on my side. "It wasn't my grandmother," I tell Ava, getting down to the nitty-gritty. "The evidence we followed was a setup from the beginning to send us all barking up the wrong tree." I rub my forehead. "Whoever is doing this is pitting us against each other."

"But..." Ava groans. "Yes, it was all a little bit convenient, wasn't it? It rubbed me the wrong way that everything was so sloppy but neat. I will backtrack and see what I can find." She hangs up.

Hades comes back into the room and hands Ann her datapad, and she immediately opens the first file.

Oh no, the house. I flick my fingers at Hades. "Oh, you might want to run to number seven. One of your guards is about to burn the place to the ground. Erm"—I glance at the clock and cringe—"any minute now. He's under a spell," I finish lamely. *Oops.*

"What!" Ann lowers the datapad and slaps it against the table. "You have spelled one of my guards to burn down your house?"

If we really want to get to the crux of the facts, I have spelled twenty-four of her guards. But who's counting, eh? I cough to clear my throat.

"What on earth? Tru, what were you thinking?" She shakes her head, and then horror blooms across her face. "Robin is inside!" she cries as she gets unsteadily to her feet.

I wave for her to sit down. "No, she's not. I dropped her off at the angel ambassador's house about thirty minutes ago."

"You abducted the poor girl again?"

I hold up a finger. "More like I relocated her. She was

lying about me and the"—I air quote the next word with an added eye roll—"kidnapping. Someone manipulated her to make that stuff up to convince you that I'm some serial killer, and you lapped that shit up..." My voice fades, and I grind my teeth. She wasn't the only one. I have been led by my nose, and it's kind of embarrassing.

Ann gives me an impatient get-on-with-it look.

"And they convinced me that you were fabricating evidence to control me. Good old Robin made it seem you had evidence against me in the house. Hence me burning it to the ground," I finish with a grumble. My bad.

With a groan, Ann drops back down in her seat, and without looking at him, she says, "Hades, deal with it, but come straight back. We haven't finished with our little chat."

Hades once again leaves, this time to go play fireman.

With a shake of her head, Ann grabs the datapad and again thumbs through the evidence. "I would still feel better if you spent quality time with the doctors. Burning down houses is not a normal pastime."

Ha, it is for me. I wisely keep my mouth shut.

As I watch her read, I mull over her words; she is far from magnanimous. She wants to save me? What a load of rubbish. *More like save me, save herself.* I'm twenty-six years old, and she's way too late. She is decades too late. My adoptive grandad already handled everything.

No, she just wants to use me.

"I can control myself. If I couldn't, many people would be dead," I tell her. "I might be far from human, far from a perfect unicorn, but I'm nothing like your son."

Any guilt she's feeling is not mine to bear. She has

known about me for over nine years and was happy to ignore my existence. We should go back to doing that again.

I should go home, but not before I fix this mess. It's clear we have an issue with communication, and I can't have someone use us like this again. My eyes narrow, and I tap my lips as I twist the patterns in my mind to make sense. The logical thing to do is to look at the outcome and infer the motivation. So...

They wanted to get me out of the way, but not just that. They used both the angel and my unicorn grand-mother to do it. Xander just got to me first. And he went scorched earth on my arse. He showed me who he was and what priority I was in his life. Xander might be a nice guy, the white-knight hero. But not to me.

I hum under my breath. I don't think it was ever about punishing me.

Otherwise, I would never have got out of prison, as they would have done a better job of framing me. They didn't. The evidence was full of obvious holes. It was laughably easy to pull apart.

Was the outcome to end my relationship so badly with Xander that it would never be repaired? To open my eyes to the truth of the man I loved, to see the real man I had bonded with?

Heck, it certainly did that. It was an outcome... but was it *the* outcome.

Nah, I don't think so. Who wins if I no longer love Xander? Or, more likely, who wins if I'm kept busy chasing my tail?

Arrah, I am too close to this. I'm too close to this to think clearly.

Okay, what was I doing before my life went to shit? Forrest and I were rescuing those kids. But... my eyes narrow. I'd started dismantling the blood trade, one baddie at a time. Was I getting too close? Who came into my life conveniently at the point everything went to hell?

Kleric.

Ding. Ding. Ding.

CHAPTER
THIRTY FIVE

NOW THAT MAKES SENSE. What do I know about him really? He was there in the warehouse, and I let him dazzle me with his smile, his muscles, and his luscious blue skin. His being there when everything kicked off was a tad convenient. With everything that happened afterwards, I never investigated the why.

I mean, who captures a demon prince?

"I need to go," I say to Ann as I scramble to my feet. "Are we good? Please tell me you don't have any more intervention plans. No more trying to get me committed or meddling with my life."

Her eyes lift from the datapad. "Well—"

"The answer is: we are good. You don't need to make an enemy out of me, Ann." I drop the grandmother shit as I only called her that to be petulant and to wind her up. She's far from a little old lady. She's a unicorn shifter in her prime. I keep my voice gentle, but my eyes I know are hard. I lock her with my dead-eyed gaze. "Please don't push me as you are never going to win. Ask yourself this: how did I stroll past twenty-four of your guards and remove an angel from your care? From under your protection, within the heart of your community. If I can do that and hurt no one, imagine what I can do if I'm really pissed."

For the first time, I see fear in her eyes. There, now she gets it. I'm not like her son... No, I'm worse.

"Oh, and get a grip on your people. I don't want to kill them, but I will if they come after me again. There are no more warnings. I'm done playing nice." I finish with a curling smile that tilts my lips up menacingly.

I leave it at that.

I strut out of the room. The dress swooshes against my legs, and the heels click against the wooden floors of my grandmother's mansion-style home.

What a waste of bloody time.

"Alright luv," says a voice with a heavy London accent. I tilt my head to see one of the thugs who knocked me out on Monday, and he is guarding the front door.

Oh hello.

I allow a little more sway in my gait, smile, and bat my eyelashes.

He raises his eyebrows and gives me a chin lift and a cheeky smile. Half-lidded with lust, his eyes run up and down my body. "You brush up alright," he rumbles.

Ew.

"Thanks." I get closer until we are scant inches apart, and I lick my lips.

His cheeky smile gets wider, and his pupils dilate.

266

My fist slams into his stomach, and with a groan, he flops forward from the impact. I hit him again as hard as I can in the face, aiming for the sweet spot on his jaw. He stumbles, and the front door rattles as he hits it. I step forward, palm his face, and crack the back of his skull not once but twice against the solid front door. With a moan at the back of his throat, he slumps unconscious to the floor.

"Alright, nobhead," I mutter.

As I open the door, I stand on his hand, and his body slumps and rolls—like the most inconvenient draught excluder. As I tug the door open, I crunch his arm. I make sure to knock his head again on the corner of the door.

The sun shines as I step outside with a massive smile on my face. See now. I feel so much better.

Perhaps I could come to Sunday dinner next week?

I take a deep breath in and taste utter chaos on my tongue. *I think I made my point.* My lips twitch as smoke blooms from the house down the street. The buzz of fire suppression magic tickles my skin, and shouts and screams rend the air. I never made myself out to be a saint. I rub my hands on my dress. Keeping your hands squeaky clean in this world is impossible. But I walk a line so I can still look at myself in the mirror and sleep at night.

I turn my head to watch the flames dance behind the trees. I hope the stupid house burns to the ground. It's my last connection to this place, to the unicorns.

My spikey heels crunch against the driveway stone and then click on the pavement. "Love you," is the moaning chorus as I pass some of the still love-bombed guards.

A few of the guards that I recognise were away from the epicentre of my love-bomb blast have woken up.

One guy is sitting on the kerb, rocking with his head in his hands. "I feel hungover, like I drank three bottles of fairy wine," he groans to his mate, who looks equally green.

"What the fuck is wrong with Bill?"

Bill—the bear shifter, opens my door with a dramatic bow.

"Thanks," I mumble as I scramble into my Land Rover. My leg jiggles as I drive away, nervous now as I know what I need to do. I need to speak to Robin. She was lying out of her arse about Ann's plans.

However, I don't know if I'll get the opportunity as Xander is very protective.

I groan as I stop at the traffic lights. I knew dropping her with Xander would bite me in the bum. I dropped her off like she was a live grenade and just ran.

First though, I need to deal with the demon. My hand burns. I make a fist and scowl down at the damn kiss. My silly, foolish heart flips. I don't want Kleric to be a bad guy, but I can't let my squishy side overrule all my common sense.

What do I know about him really? Nothing except for the taste of his blood and the feel of his mouth on mine. I rub my lips together and groan. I'm no good with people. I'm certainly not good with men.

Now the time has come the time to ask the hard questions.

I hate it.

I slide the car into its parking space and get out. I don't take the time to put away all my gear, I just grab everything, including the anti-magic band and Robin's silver knife I took as a souvenir, and with my bundle, I head inside.

I hurry up the stairs, bump the door of the flat closed with my bottom, and head to my bedroom, where I dump everything onto the floor to deal with later. I grab my phone, datapad, and a stick of white chalk, and stomp back into the living room.

Justin is sitting in his chair by the window; he looks up from his book. "Hi, how did it go?"

"Honestly? I don't know where to start." I rub my face as Story flutters into the room. "Where are the kids?" I ask her through my fingers.

"Ralph took them to see his parents. What happened?"

"Morris is at work?" Justin nods. I slump onto the sofa. "It wasn't her. Ann wasn't involved—well, beyond being lied to with phoney evidence like Xander." I laugh without any humour. I'm unwilling to go into the details of Ann's proposed joke of an intervention. "Kleric will come over soon. We need to prepare."

"What, dinner?" Justin asks.

"No." I hunch my shoulders and flick through the datapad, looking for... "This." I turn the datapad so it is resting on my knees and show them photos of the demon-killing circle I took at the warehouse.

Story and Justin both gasp.

"But... but I thought you liked him?" Story wails in an accusatory tone.

My shoulders slump further. "I do. I like him a lot, but that doesn't matter. Story, things with him do not add up. They haven't since I first met him in the warehouse and he gave me this." I flash the kiss on the back of my hand, and like they have done before, they both look at my hand blankly.

They can't see it; only demons and I can.

"I need answers, and he has them. I can't let him wiggle out of answering them. Hence trapping him in a circle." I'm going to have to deal with Kleric before this goes any further. Trap him so I can ask him questions, find out what the hell is going on and see if he's behind all this.

"He's not Xander." She's right. Kleric is as far away from Xander as you can get. He listens. "You'll hurt him doing this," Story whispers, her eyes swimming with the same conflict I feel inside.

I know. I roll the stick of chalk between my fingers and swallow. I nod at the datapad and wiggle the chalk at Story. She is, after all, the artist in the family. "Can you draw that?"

"Shit." We stare at each other, and she flies towards me and pulls the chalk out of my hand. With a grunt and a sprinkle of fairy dust, she throws it over her shoulder. "Okay. I hope you know what you're doing. I will need at least an hour."

We all stare down at our fluffy carpet.

Time to get to work, I guess.

CHAPTER
THIRTY SIX

GOOSEBUMPS SPREAD across my arms like a nasty rash, and heat prickles my neck. I feel sick, and my heart pounds so hard my entire chest aches. Kleric is downstairs, and I don't want to do this. I'm sitting in the corner of the room, in Justin's chair by the window, with a mug of hot tea in my favourite bee cup.

The steam tickles against my face, but inside I feel cold.

Everything inside me screams I'm making a mistake, but of course I power on anyway.

Justin left to take Morris, who will soon finish work, out to dinner to keep him out of the way while I interrogate a demon prince. I groan. Oh crumbs, it sounds even worse when I say it in my head that way.

There is a knock at the door, and wide-eyed, I look at Story. She shakes her head and glares back at me with a stubborn twist to her mouth. She thinks I'm making a mistake... but she helped me anyway.

"It's open!" I shout.

My chest rises and falls as my heart fights to remember its natural rhythm.

Kleric, dressed in tight-fitting combats, prowls into the room. He moves like a dream. "Tru, are you okay?" he asks as he takes in my slumped position on the chair and the shine of tears in my eyes.

No.

I almost hold my hand up to stop him from coming any further. His feet hit the carpet, and... and with a gulp, I lift my finger to signal Story.

She zips out from her hiding spot with the last of the chalk and flicks it across the pattern, completing the circle.

The demon trap seals, and with a whoosh and a blinding flash of white, it locks into place.

The magic crackles as Kleric freezes in the centre of the circle.

"I hope you know what you're doing," Story says as she flies past me, leaving us alone.

I hope I do too.

Kleric looks up, and his eyes trace the patterns of the circle adorning the ceiling with a slight nod. "The ceiling, smart. I wouldn't have thought to look up."

I cough to clear my throat. "I didn't want to rip up the carpet, and Story flies, so it made sense." I awkwardly shrug.

Kleric takes in a deep breath, and then the massive demon folds himself to sit on the floor. He is now in the same position as when I found him over six weeks ago. Chin resting on his knee, one leg bent and the other neatly folded underneath his upper thigh. This time though, his tail isn't flicking—oh, and he's fully clothed.

"Why?" he asks gently.

The breath I let out rattles at the end with the guilt that is strangling my throat. I can't meet his beautiful black eyes. I lick my dry lips. "Ann wasn't the one to set me up. She received information almost the same as what Xander had."

Kleric nods, his eyes intent on my face.

"I thought about who I met when things first went to shit. You. I don't..." My voice cracks. "I don't know anything about you, Kleric. Whenever I ask, you change the subject. You've told me nothing about how or why you were at that warehouse. I don't understand why you need to help me now unless you want to be on the inside, a front-row seat to manipulate me." My nails click against the mug as I grip it. "I'm sorry. I'm so sorry I trapped you in a circle, but I had no choice."

"Hush. It's okay. Your questions, ask away." The baritone in his voice sends a hot flush through my body. I close my eyes, just for the briefest of moments.

What am I doing?

"Why were you at the warehouse?"

He rubs his face. "If I may, can I start this tale further back?" I shrug.

The demon clears his throat, and a self-deprecating smile pulls at the corners of his full lips. "When I was twenty-one, I saw a girl working in a café, and I knew without even saying a word to her that she was my mate. There is only one perfect mate for a demon. To find a mate is rare. To find your mate so young is rarer still. I was ecstatic. But the girl was bonded to another."

My heart misses a beat.

"To spend the rest of my immortal existence watching over her would have been enough, worth it just to be in her presence. Even if we never said a word to each other." He sighs and carefully watches the varied emotions that no doubt play across my face.

"I told no one, but I got a position at the Demon Embassy to be close. I watched and waited, helped in the shadows when I could until I heard she was rescuing some children and was going to walk into a nightmare. So I slipped inside the warehouse, rescued the kids, opened a portal to the Sanctuary, and cast a spell to vaporise all the creatures that wanted to do her harm. Keeping her as safe as I possibly could. I then stepped inside a circle and spelled it so no one could see."

Kleric looks up at the ceiling. Again with that soft smile, his black eyes sparkle. "But my mate is powerful, and she broke down the magic of the circle, and for the first time, we were face-to-face." His smile of joy is so beautiful. "The royal line marks our mates with a kiss." He drops his gaze to my hand, then drags his serrated teeth over his bottom lip.

A tear rolls down my cheek.

"An instinct I could not fight. A kiss to connect. So a humble prince is able to protect his mate and show a public claim, a warning to any demon on what hell will come for them if they harm even a hair on her head."

"We are mates?" I rasp as my head spins.

Whoa.

Remember what it is like to have your heart ripped out. To be rejected. I remember. Fate, how I remember, and I'd never ever do that to another person. I can never do that to Kleric. I'd never be so cruel.

Kleric is my mate, and... and he sent all the evidence. My tentative joy grinds to a halt, and I forget to breathe. Kleric did it. He set me up. He set me up to... save me?

Fuck.

I gasp. His plan resulted in me going to a new kind of hell. He fought for me and was genuinely horrified when Xander lobbed me into an off-world prison instead of taking me to the Hunters Guild, which is the correct procedure.

And... and I'm messed up in the head because I understand why he did it. If the boot was on the other foot, could I watch him be in love with someone else, or worse, in love with an arrogant angel who didn't reciprocate? That's a special kind of torture. Could I watch as he was starved of blood and affection? Used and made to feel so small...

Me. Xander did that to me, and I let him.

And Kleric saw all that happen. He said he was twenty-one, four years older than me, so I was seventeen. It must have been just after I met Xander. Nine years he has been waiting. While I was waiting for Xander to notice me, Kleric was waiting for me. What a pair we are.

My stomach dips. No, I couldn't watch that. I'd fight for him and show him sneakily the truth as he had to come to the conclusion by himself.

I'd have done the same.

Bloody hell, we are made for each other.

I can't even tell him not to do that again because I know it would never happen again. The demon was desperate to save me.

Wow.

Story has been telling me for years, and I didn't listen. So the only way to get through my stubbornness was for him to pull something like this. It just went a bit tits up as Xander, being Xander, is unpredictable. Of course the dickhead angel gets the blame, my one-sided bond goes up in flames, and Granny Ann sees a way to manipulate me as the three plans end up crossing and, boom. Fate effs me over.

I nod. It all makes sense.

"So you sent the evidence to Xander and my grandmother to open my eyes?"

Kleric blinks at me in confusion. "Evidence? I didn't send the evidence. Tru, I left the warehouse with the henchman dead and knowing your bonded was on his way. I didn't know about the backup. I would never have left you if I'd known what you'd face."

Uh-oh.

"You didn't set me up? Plant the evidence?"

Kleric steps through the glowing circle and kneels in front of the chair.

My mouth flops open like a fish. Whoa, now I feel stupid. A demon trap, my arse. The circle was a duff one.

It's a magic replenishing circle, not a demon trap. He cups my face in his big palm, and his thumb brushes my cheekbone. "No I didn't set you up. I would have waited a lifetime for you. I would have never touched the soul bond you'd formed with Xander. Listen to me, just so we are clear: I will never, ever put your life or happiness below my own. You will always come first."

Whoa, now I feel bloody selfish.

He is a better person than me, a better person than I

deserve. I would have gone all Rambo on his arse if he had a bond with another woman. No way I'd be so patient, and no way I would share.

Well, that's two for two. I'm no Sherlock Holmes.

That white collar must have zapped away all my brain cells. Mistakes happen in threes, so perhaps I need to be extra careful with any new theories knocking around in my skull. I'm glad I didn't voice all my thoughts out loud.

I can't believe he thinks we are mates. A demon mate. My fae assassin grandad would have laughed himself sick. Gosh, I wish they could have met each other.

"We are mates," he grumbles.

Yep, he heard me, and he hasn't yet run away. It clicks then about what he said about our connection with the demon kiss.

"You knew all along what I was doing with the circle?" I point a shaky finger at the ceiling.

Crap. Of course, he did. He knew, and he came here anyway. Gah, in my panic I forgot he can listen to every thought that rattles around in my head.

"I felt your pain, and you projected your dastardly plan into my head the entire time." His hand finds my wrist, stopping my heart for a beat and all my racing thoughts in their tracks. Kleric pulls my hand up between us and his fingers trail across his kiss, leaving little shivers of fire in their wake.

"Yet you came anyway," I rasp.

"Of course. Always."

"I don't know what I am doing," I whine. He kisses my forehead. "I don't know what to do with a mate. I tried the bonding thing with Xander, and look at the mess that turned out." A mate! Bloody meddling magic and fate. It's like the universe thought, "I know we can't trust Tru to get it right, so we will do it for her." Oh no, this is destined to go tits up.

"Can we take things slowly? You know, like, go on a date?" I blink up at him—even kneeling, he's massive. Silence, like a living thing, stretches between us.

"I've never been on a date before," I mumble.

"A date?" his voice catches. "I'd love that." He would? Get in! We are going on a date. We both grin at each other.

"Baby steps?"

"Yeah, we will take things slow." Kleric's eyes drift to my lips. There's a small gasp of my breath before his hot mouth crashes down on mine.

Slow.

CHAPTER
THIRTY SEVEN

I RUB my swollen lips together and secretly duck my head down so I can poorly hide my loopy-looking grin. I really do enjoy kissing him.

Story, sitting on the arm of the sofa, mouths the word *mate* and wiggles her eyebrows.

I can't help grinning back at her. So much for her giving us privacy. Nosy pixie. I can't even be mad. I slide my favourite twin swords into their crossbody scabbards. We are getting ready to paint the town red.

Well, not the entire town. Hopefully, just Robin's face.

"You still aren't coming," I growl at her.

"Why? Why do I have to stay home? I know you'll be taking Dexter."

"Dexter?" Kleric asks, his black eyes sliding away from my bottom. Huh. I think he likes my fancy new combat leather-look trousers. "You're taking your cat to war with the angels?"

"War," I scoff. "We aren't going to war. We just need to ask Robin some questions. Oh." I gasp and clap my hands with excitement. I love he is young and not an old know-it-all. It's so nice he doesn't know *everything*. "Dexter isn't a normal cat; he's a beithíoch."

"A beithíoch? Aren't they huge fae monster cats, furless horrible eat-your-face-off things?"

"Purrrt," Dexter says, his timing impeccable as he struts towards us.

"He has all his fur," I mumble.

"Huh. A monster cat." My demon eyes my fat ginger cat with a disbelieving shake of his head.

The datapad pings with more files from Ava. I hum as I grab it. I pull up the files. Ava has done another deep dive on Robin. A new photo flashes up on the screen. My top lip curls into a snarl. Xander with a group of what I presume are angels. With a familiar girl resting her curly blonde head on his arm, beaming a smile at the camera. Seeing her makes me cringe.

Robin. Fate, I hate her.

"What are you up to?" I grumble at her photo likeness. "Are you really an evil mastermind?" I tilt the datapad at a different angle. The group of angels are all dressed in Earth fashion. Robin has a gorgeous brown autumn coat on, and the shiny red shoes she's wearing are on point.

I use my fingers to zoom in on the red shoes.

Something about them tickles my brain. I frown and shake my head. They are nice shoes but have no idea why they have got my attention.

"Can I use your bathroom?" Kleric asks.

"Sure," I mumble with a wave of my hand. "Use the one in my bedroom." My eyes fixate back on those glossy red shoes. I shake my head and drop the datapad on the arm of the chair. Yep, I'm going mad.

"Tru, can you come here a sec?" Kleric calls from my bedroom.

"Yeah." I wander over, and when I open the door, he's standing by the equipment and clothing I dumped on the floor earlier. My cheeks heat. "I'm not usually such a slob," I mumble.

Wow, this is awkward.

"I didn't want to dig about," he says. His voice sounds odd. Kleric points at the pile. "I can feel the magic. Tru, why do you have a demon blade?"

"What? The silver blade?" He nods, and I poke the hilt with my toe. "That's the blade that Robin tried to stab me with. Well, more like she did this slash, slash, slashing in my face." I wave my hand to imitate the motion and roll my eyes. "I disarmed her by breaking her elbow, and I took the knife as a souvenir."

"Angels don't carry demon blades."

"Well, it's hers. She had it strapped to her thigh. When she clocked the demon kiss on my hand, she ran at me—" My words grind to a halt, and my eyes widen. We look at each other.

Oh, bloody hell. Robin looked directly at the demon kiss on my hand, and she has a demon blade.

"Robin is a demon," I say in a strangled whisper. I wobble a little as my head swims. "If that Robin is a demon, where is the Robin in the photo?" *The real Robin.*

I rush back into the living room with Kleric hot on my heels.

I grab the datapad and pull up the photo to show him, and it all *clicks* in my head. My knees give way, and my weapons click as I sink into the chair.

I don't even have to pull up the footage of the warehouse that day as it is embedded in my mind. The people, the pile of dead creatures behind the ward in the warehouse's backroom. I do it anyway. My fingers flick across the screen of their own accord, pulling up the footage.

"Robin is a demon," I mutter to Story as she perches on my shoulder. "The real Robin is dead." I hit play, and with a flick of my fingers, the screen of the datapad projects onto the living room wall. Kleric and Story watch the footage intently, and while I watch, I get swept back into the memory.

The smell of ozone makes my sensitive nose itch. Inside the room is the heavy magic buzz of an active ward.

The ward, an opaque dome, blocks me from entering as it fills the entire room. Cautiously, I give the ward a poke with my blade and meet no resistance as the tip of my sword disappears. Huh. This ward isn't meant to keep people out. It's more to stop sounds and smells from escaping.

I lay my palm millimetres above the buzzing surface, and the magic nips at my hand. With a swirl, like the parting of clouds, the opaqueness obediently falls away.

For the second time tonight, my mind struggles to make sense of what I'm seeing. Coloured rags. Someone has haphazardly piled lumps of multicoloured clothing and... It is like an optical illusion, one of those ambiguous images.

I tilt my head—

Then I see it. A random shoe. My head snaps back as if I have taken a punch to the face. The shoe is a glossy red, and it is falling off a foot. The rest of the body becomes apparent. It is trapped underneath a dozen other bodies.

Not rags. People.

My rapid breaths fog the dome. They have dumped people inside the ward. Each body left in an undignified heap, as if whoever they were in life didn't matter. Stomach acid burns up my oesophagus. Only lots of swallowing keeps it down. Something deep inside me whimpers and withdraws to rock in a corner, but I can't allow myself to physically follow up on that instinct.

"Mother Nature," *Story whispers in horror.*

I allow my mental voice to be laced with vampire compulsion when I tell her, "Don't look, Story. Please don't look." *She needs no more nightmares. I force myself to look, to count, as I take in the horror. I need to know what I'm dealing with.*

I gulp and shove away the guilt that rattles me to the very core. I couldn't have done anything about this. I know that logically. From the state of their remains, these people were long dead before I even knew of this warehouse's existence. This wasn't my fault. No, it was them.

In my mind's eye, I see the puddles of blood on the concrete floor, and my top lip twitches with a snarl. I'm then immensely grateful to whoever vaporised those bastards in the main warehouse and to whoever saved those kids from this awful fate.

I need to take down the ward and allow the cameras to get DNA samples of the bodies, but rightly or wrongly, I can't do it. I can't seem to make myself. To do it feels wrong, sacrilegious. So with a heavy heart, I turn away and, reaching for the door, close it behind me with as much care and reverence as I can muster.

The dead woman with the glossy red shoes was Robin.

Bile burns a path up my throat, and this time I can't swallow it down.

Story flits from my shoulder as I jump to my feet and stumble into the kitchen to spit the vile mouthful down the sink. "Sorry, I know that was gross." Kleric fills a glass with water and rubs the back of my neck.

I rinse my mouth out and go so far as to run the water and squirt a little bleach down the sink. "She was dead before I even stepped inside the warehouse. A demon has been wearing her face," I mumble to Kleric. "I just know it."

I push the glass onto the counter, drop my chin to my chest, and lean against the sink. The dregs of bleach down the plughole sting my nose as I take some big steadying breaths.

When I'm steady enough to move, I will ring Ava and tell her what I think I know. I can't make a mistake on this.

"Kleric," I whisper. He rubs the base of my spine and kisses the top of my head. "Who the hell did I drop off with Xander?"

CHAPTER
THIRTY EIGHT

RAIN SPLATTERS against the passenger-side window as we drive. The interior of the car is built for the giant of a man who is driving. Elegant, with all sophisticated lines, and incredibly roomy. I guess it'd have to be for Kleric to drive without shifting down to an average size. The flicking lights from the oncoming traffic and streetlights highlight his beautiful face.

Before we left, and not wanting to make yet another mistake, Ava confirmed everything. Robin's remains were now at a specialist lab awaiting family collection.

I ask myself, how could this be missed? Too many dead bodies, and no one cares enough to push them through the system to give their relatives closure. I care. I rest my forehead against the cold glass.

I should have cared more at the time while in the warehouse. I should have listened to my instincts, forcibly removed the ward and let the micro-cameras scan for DNA. If I had, we'd have discovered Robin's death seven weeks ago, and we wouldn't be in this mess.

And maybe... maybe this entire shit show would have been worse.

I don't know what Xander would have done if he'd found me in the warehouse with a dead angel. He wouldn't have taken me to prison, that's for sure. No, he would have killed me. I sigh, and my stupid, still-healing soul hurts.

Now I feel like I'm going to war.

I have to deal with the bloody angel again, and this twisting, horrible feeling in my gut, a churning mix of guilt and fear, is playing havoc with my stomach. I puff out my cheeks and blow. My hot breath leaves a foggy patch on the cold glass.

"Maybe things will be amicable," I mumble. The glass squeaks as I draw a little demon.

"Maybe."

"When we get to his house"—I sit up straight—"I will say, 'Xander, Robin isn't the angel you knew. She is, in fact, a demon.' And of course, shocked"—my hand flies to my chest, and I clear my throat and prepare to lower my voice to a perfect rendition of him—"Xander will say, 'A demon, you say? Oh, I believe you as she didn't have sugar in her tea. Let's ask her some questions, find out who she is, and then you can take her away. Thank you for bringing this to my attention.'" I turn to eye Kleric, and he winces. I slump into the seat and stare back out the window. "Yeah, I thought not." I swipe away the rapidly fading demon.

We are Xander's unwanted cavalry, and this is going to be a nightmare.

The streets are almost empty, with people not wanting to brave the sideways rain. It is another horrible night. My leg jiggles, so I force my thigh into the leather seat to stop it. The more I think, the sicker I feel. It's already been six hours. How many other angels are compromised? Is it just Robin or a small minority? What if they are all demons, and we've stumbled into an incursion?

Shaking my head, I recheck my magic supplies to make sure I haven't overlooked anything. I scowl when my hand lands on the pile of anti-magic bands. Useless things. I wish the one I'd used on fake Robin could have peeled the demon disguise away. Unfortunately, there are limitations to all magic. Demon's magic isn't an illusion; they change shape—just like shifters—on a cellular level, so there isn't any magic to peel away.

We pull up outside Xander's sprawling house with its fancy horseshoe driveway, and I open the passenger door. Fur tickles against the back of my hand as Dexter jumps out and leaps over the nearby fence. I then release hundreds of micro-cameras programmed to record the area around Xander's house. I doubt very much I will get a single one past the angel's ward.

Cameras are a go, I inform Story, using the freshly laid communication spell.

"Will your cat be okay?" Kleric asks, his worried gaze fixed on the direction Dexter's ginger butt went.

"He'll be fine." The door thunks closed, and I pull out a necklace.

I wrap the black cord a few times around my hand and dangle the black stone so it catches the light. The purple veins running through it sparkle and shine.

"This is a bloodstone. Jodie, the owner of Tinctures 'n Tonics, says it will work as demon radar. I presume the demon or demons involved are masking their magical signatures, as the Robin I met felt like an angel. The stone needs priming with a couple of drops of demon blood, and once activated, it will last a few hours. Any demon will have to be close to the stone, within about ten feet. That means you can't be near, or the bloodstone will only pick you up. I know it's not ideal." I lick my lips.

"You need my blood?"

"Yes please." I hand him a sealed finger-prick lancet.

"And you are telling me you want to go in there alone?" Kleric rubs his face, and his worried eyes crinkle at the corners. "I don't like it."

"I know." I reach over and squeeze his hand.

He flips it and cradles my hand, stroking the demon kiss with his fingertips. I'd also hate being left behind. If this were a hit, I'd jump the back wall, use magic to slice my way through the ward, and slit demon Robin's throat. Job done.

But I can't do that, what with my shiny new job. Oh, I accepted the job offer from the Grand Creature Council. So I can't sneak inside like an assassin anymore. I must knock on the front door like a professional.

This is a hell of a first shift, with no training, I might add, but Kleric and Mr Brown, the barrister, can be very convincing, and the powers that be let me do this as a signing-on bonus.

Yeah, great. I think I missed a trick and should have asked for money.

I electronically signed the contract and waved goodbye to the simple life I envisioned of spending my days hiding away, fixing the farmhouse, and eating grass. Maybe I can do that in a few years? Well, if I don't get myself killed first.

"I have Dexter. I won't be technically alone."

I hand him the necklace, and Kleric breaks the seal of the lancet and pokes the tip of his index finger and gives the digit a good old squeeze. A drop of blood bubbles up, and he slathers it onto the stone. Another drop follows, and with a magic hum, the stone begins to glow. It glows green. He hands the necklace back to me, and we get out of the car.

The rainwater splashes against my calves as we leave Kleric's car and hurry up the driveway towards the house. Two armed angels in wet weather gear block the way. That is new. Kleric keeps back as I check the angels with the bloodstone. It remains black. *The guards are clear.* The angels stiffen as Kleric comes to stand by my side, using his massive frame to shield me from the worst of the weather.

"We've come to speak to Xander," I tell him.

"The ambassador is busy."

I keep it short and sweet. "It's an emergency."

Underneath his dripping hat, the guard on the right scowls. He turns and raps his knuckles on the door and then opens it a crack. "Sir, we have a woman here to see you." He cocks his eyebrow, and I narrow my eyes.

"Tell him it's Kleric and Tru."

Xander's voice comes from inside. "Let her in. He stays out. I will not have that demon in my house." I snort. I can't help it. The angel might have more demons in there than he knows.

"Weapons off," barks the other guard.

"No." Hell no. No way I'm going into the house unarmed.

"You need to remove your weapons." He then makes a mistake: he attempts to grab me.

There is the potent scent of sulphur, and the guard is suddenly flopping on the ground. His heels beat against the driveway, and foam froths from between his lips.

"What the hell?" the other guard says as he takes a swing.

I snap a kick into his side, right against his liver. He loses his balance, and with a pain-filled groan, he stumbles back.

Dexter drops from the porch and lands on him.

Crunch.

The giant cat sits on the unconscious guard. Dexter batters his head with a massive paw.

Kleric makes a strange gurgling sound in the back of his throat as the monster cat blinks back at us. "Beithíoch," he murmurs.

Dexter opens his mouth, and his teeth close around the guard's head. Dexter can chew through bone.

"Dexter," I say in a warning tone. "No."

His eyes go cross-eyed as he looks down at the guard, I tap my foot, and his pink tongue reluctantly pushes the guard's head out of his maw. "Breow" is his pitiful reply.

"What a good boy." A sneaky claw pricks against the guard's stomach. "Gentle Dex, you can't play with him, and remember, you can only eat the demons." I reach over and gently stroke his giant head.

"Not this demon," Kleric mumbles.

Dexter sighs.

"Come on, up." The three-hundred-kilogram cat gets off the squished guard. I shake my head. I then glance back down at the foamy guard. At least the rain is cleaning his face. "What did you do?"

"I shocked him with my magic. He'll be fine."

"What is the holdup?" Xander shouts from inside the house.

"The girl won't remove her weapons." Kleric fires back with a perfect imitation of the first guard's voice.

My mouth pops open, and he winks at me.

"It's fine," Xander growls back. Softer, he says, "She can't use them properly anyway."

Dickhead. I don't care what he thinks anymore.

"Here." I hand Kleric two healing potions and two anti-magic bands. "Can you deal with that?" I frown at the squished guard. Kleric smiles and takes the potions. The rain drips off his nose. It takes some gall to leave a demon prince out in the rain.

I don't like this. Kleric's worried voice fills my head.

I know. I'm sorry, but I've taken the job now, and this is something I must do. I've dealt with insurmountable odds, and this is nothing. Just a house call.

It sure isn't the time to break out the emergency dragon.

You don't need Forrest's dragon. I will rip this house apart if you need me to.

With our connection, at least he knows what is happening. I will need to learn to keep him out of my head. But not today. I rise up on my toes and kiss him. His mouth is hot and perfect. The taste of him fills my mouth, and all I want to do is stand out here in the rain with him.

Reluctantly I pull away. Then with a normal-sized Dexter, I push open the front door, and we step through Xander's ward.

A whoosh of warm magic wind whips away any drops of rain that dare to cling. The door closes behind me. I pull out the datapad chock full of evidence and roll my shoulders.

It's showtime.

CHAPTER
THIRTY NINE

I HOLD out the datapad with all the evidence. The angel viciously knocks it out of my hand, and the datapad lands on the orangery's tiled floor with a plastic crack.

"Well," I huff as I rub my stinging hand. "That wasn't very nice. Come on, Xander. Please, at least listen to what I've got to say before throwing a hissy fit. I'm happy to beg. I will get on my knees if I must."

Xander drags his hand through his hair, exasperated. "I've known Robin since she was born. I would know her anywhere." With that comment, jaw steeled, signalling like a child that our conversation is over, Xander folds his arms across his chest, a stubborn expression on his face. He stares straight ahead out the window to the pretty cottage-style walled garden at the back of the house.

I shake my head, and I stifle a sigh. I don't yet want to

play the new job card. Arrah, he's so frustrating. Why will this man never listen?

"Think." I reach out and flick him on the forehead. I smirk when he can't hide his shock. "Think about what you are doing. It's not Robin. I am so sorry, Xander, but the angel you knew as Robin is dead." I point at her. "That is a demon wearing her face."

"Liar!" Xander snarls.

Shocker.

"Why did you let her inside? You know she broke my arm," Robin wails.

I eye fake Robin, the *demon*, who is currently hiding and trembling in the corner behind two other angels. If I roll my eyes now, I worry they will get stuck in the back of my eye socket, and I will have to whack the back of my head to unstick them. "Why don't you just shut up," I snap back.

Not Robin puts her hands on her hips. "Xander. She tortured me for information, held me captive for weeks, and you just let her waltz in here, in my safe space." Her voice goes higher and higher in pitch.

So much so that Dexter, who prowls closer to her and the two other angels, lets out a hiss.

Anger flashes in the cold depths of Xander's honey eyes, and... Uh-oh, the hero complex is activated. Alert-alert.

Smoky white magic with little gold flakes bleeds out of Xander's hands, and then he is holding a gigantic sword. It's bigger than a longsword. Double-edged, with a straight blade.

It's his angel blade.

With no posturing and with a twist of his wrist, he swings the sword at my neck!

Shocked, I lean back and sidestep. The huge sword whooshes past. Whoa. The bloody thing missed me by a fraction of an inch. "Dickhead!" I shout. "So it's like that, is it? I like my head on my neck, thanks very much. Trying to chop my head off while I'm unarmed," I mumble. "That's a new low even for you."

Fine, I gave him a chance to end this peacefully. Whatever happens now is on him. Blood rushes through my veins, and I can hear my heartbeat. The familiar taste of adrenaline coats my tongue as the trickle in my system turns into a flood as I get ready to hand this man his arse.

Let's show him how I use my swords. Fate only knows he has had this coming for *years*.

Like a dancer, I twirl around Xander, giving myself some much-needed space, and the muscles on his back and shoulders bulge as he spins to face me.

The angel rotates his sword.

I unsheathe both of mine and grin.

"Why did I bring her back to you if I wanted to hurt her? If you can just look at the evidence—"

"Because you are mad. Robin is right there!" he yells. "She is not dead." The muscles on his forearm flex as he sweeps the sword in to knock my leading leg aside. I dance out of the way.

"Yeah? Well, I would rather be mad than downright delusional." I dash towards him and slice straight down with the right blade. I put all my power into the swing. He blocks. "Just a tip," I say through gritted teeth as our swords clang. "You really need to brush up on your listening skills." As I speak, my left sword is already moving. It sweeps sideways right to left across his stomach, and a fine mist of gold blood rents the air.

He grunts.

"And your sword skills. First blood to me." I grin, duck under his next swing and, using the pommel, hammer a short, brutal blow to the weeping cut on his stomach. Then I strike with the other sword.

Xander staggers back, shaking his head. An imprint of the flat of my blade is a red mark on his cheek. He rubs the welt on his face, and his liquid-honey eyes glow. He is livid.

I flash my fangs at him.

Xander blocks my next swing, knocking my arm aside before his fancy angel sword bursts into white flames.

Uh-oh.

I blink white dots from my vision as Xander slashes his fiery blade towards my face. I scramble away just as the hot blade brushes across my collarbone. It takes a few seconds for the pain to register. My nerves scream more so when I'm hit with the smell of my own burned skin. *Ouch.* Weirdly, my blood feels like it's on fire.

I use the pain and roll to the ground, avoiding another flaming swipe, and spring back up to raise my sword to block the next strike. His sword cuts through mine like butter.

Fuck.

Now in two pieces, the top part clatters to the floor. I shrug and jab him in the shoulder with the molten-hot, broken blade and follow through with my other sword, slicing his right sword arm and severing the muscles and the tendon at the radius.

The angel grunts.

I kick him in the chest and reverse the broken blade, driving the pommel into his face. Xander's head snaps to the side, but he doesn't go down. Utter shock flashes across his face. *Surprise.* Who says I can't bloody fight? He then wipes his mouth on his forearm and smiles.

Um. Okay.

The angel transfers the sword to his left hand.

I shiver.

He's testing me, and he is like the bloody Terminator. I've cut him to ribbons, and he isn't even wobbly! "I could do this all night," I taunt him. *Yeah right.*

Dexter lets out a warning meow as one of the angels peels out of their huddle and tries to rush me.

Oh no you don't.

The primed bloodstone which I've wrapped around my right wrist glows green. Ah, a demon masquerading as an angel. He does an oh-so-scary war cry.

I laugh.

"Worried you're going to lose your meal ticket?" I ask the demon as I spin on my toes to greet his blade. "Excuse me, Xander," I yell over my shoulder. I drop the broken sword and kick it out of the way. I hold nothing back. I have my orders, and these demons do not have permission to be on Earth. They are illegal invaders.

My sword sings as it slices the air. It slides through his neck, and his head slides off with a wet thunk to the floor.

"What are you waiting for? Deal with her!" Fake Robin cries, pushing the other angel at her side towards me.

The angel pulls out her sword and charges. The bloodstone glows green. I spin and slide the blade up neatly through her ribs, and I bury the blade in the heart of the second confirmed demon. I give the sword a good twist so the organ is shredded. She crumples to the floor.

I flick chunks of flesh and the green demon blood off my blade into a stunned Xander's face.

"Not Robin!" I bellow.

She scowls and narrows her baby-blue eyes. "Xander, why are you just standing there? Protect me!" she yells.

Xander remains frozen. Golden blood runs down his arm and drip, drop, drips from his loosely curled fist.

I made a mess of his arm.

The scent of his blood mixes with the demons'. His sole focus is on the green blood pooling around the bodies of his so-called friends.

I wonder if he's getting it yet.

The power within his sword winks out, and the white flames die. The orangery instantly cools.

"Come on, fake Robin. Let's see what you've got." With a cocky grin, I hold my arms out wide in invitation. It's enough to make her react.

She stomps past Xander towards me. "You are pathetic," she snaps at him as she rips the angel blade out of his inert hand. It's a little long for her, but whatever.

The bloodstone glows green as she leaps in the air and strikes from above. The swords clang as I catch the now cold angel blade with mine. *At least she doesn't have any angel ability to light the thing up.* I can't kill her yet. All I have to do is make her bleed. Splash a bit of green. She can't explain away that.

She lunges at me; her strike is fast like a snake.

Strike. Block. Strike. Block. Strike.

She's good, well trained, but I'm better. I just have to be

careful as I don't want to kill her. I move my balance to the left, and when I catch the sword with her next hammer-like strike, I knee her in the kidney. I dance away to do a beautiful close-quarters spinning kick, one I perfected in prison —seems kind of apt. My foot hits her in the clavicle, and underneath my boot, the collarbone cracks.

As she rocks back, I smash her in the nose with the heel of my hand. Her nose crunches. *Ew.* It is gross and wet underneath my palm. I step back, wipe my hand on my trousers and grin toothily as green blood gushes down her face.

And there we go.

As she blinks away tears from her broken nose. I point at her face and say, "Oops. You have a little something... right there on your face. Are you bleeding, fake Robin? Xander, you better heal your poor demon's nose."

Xander lifts his eyes from the floor to Robin's now not-so-pretty face.

Everything in the room stands still as we are sucked into a vortex of volatile angel magic and pain. "Who are you?" he says in a deadly whisper. "You are not my sister." The livid, agonised expression on his face is so bad that I take a shuffling step back.

Sister?

Ah, shit. No.

CHAPTER FORTY

I RUB the back of my neck, slouch, deflated, and the burn on my collarbone stings as my heart takes a nosedive into my boots.

Xander ever so slowly prowls towards his fake sister and grabs hold of his blade—from the pointy end. I wince as the double-edged sword slices into his palm and fingers as he uses it to drag the frightened demon towards him.

Her impractical shoes can't get traction as she slides through the blood on the floor.

"Who are you!" he roars.

When she doesn't answer fast enough, he slaps her across her face. With a cry, she lets go of the sword and Xander flips it. His bleeding hand is now wrapped securely around the grip.

His golden magic flashes up his body, healing all his wounds instantly, and he presses the angel blade underneath her chin. "Shift into your natural form. Now!" he bellows.

Robin jumps with fright, and there is a rush of liquid as urine runs down her legs.

Oh. Oh heck.

I have a real issue with always rooting for the underdog, and when a creature pees from fright, it makes me feel bad.

I don't want to feel sorry for her. I need to remind myself of what she has done to me and to others, especially now that I know she's wearing Xander's sister's face.

No, not just her face; she's a perfect carbon copy.

The magic on the house wavers. Xander is changing something. Dexter butts against my calf, and then the kiss on my hand heats as Kleric strolls into the room.

"Demon Prince, is this one of yours?" Xander snarls.

"Well, contrary to popular belief, Xander, I don't know every demon from my world. I can tell her magical signature is masked, and she reads as an angel. But with the green blood dripping down her face and the glowing bloodstone. I'm positive she is a demon. I can force her to change. But it will be painful for the both of us."

His black eyes soften as he turns to me. *Are you okay? I felt the burn. Will you allow me to heal you?* Kleric carefully brushes the wispy loose strands of my hair out of the way so he can see. He sucks in a breath. My demon has a healing potion in his hand, ready to go. The viscous silver liquid sloshes against the vial as he holds it up for me to see.

I'm fine, soon. I can't let him kill her without getting the answers we came for. I step over the puddle of urine and make my way closer. *I feel shitty. Kleric, Robin was his sister. No wonder he was unwilling to listen. I was subtle as a sledge-*

301

hammer. A demon is wearing your little sister's face... nice one.

You didn't say it like that, and it's not your fault it wasn't in the files. He must have done that to protect her.

Yeah. I guess. How did I not know he had a sister? I slide next to Xander. "Did I tell you about my new job?"

Xander's blade wobbles as he turns his head to look at me. The sword nicks the trembling demon's neck. "What?" He narrows his eyes at me and then turns back to stare at Not Robin and her green blood.

"My new job. I'm the new executioner." With a fingertip, I lean over and push the angel blade away from her throat. "I'm going to find everyone who is involved with this debacle, and I'm going to make sure they are appropriately punished. You have my word."

"You're an executioner?" He laughs under his breath. Xander's angel blade disappears in a puff of white smoke. "You outrank me."

"Yeah, so they have led me to believe."

Hunters capture, assassins kill, and then there are the executioners. Executioners have the power to kill anybody, and so high up on the chain of command they are a law unto themselves.

"I scored high on tests, and with my skills and the way I handled myself in prison, I've been told that I'm a perfect fit." More like no one is daft enough to take the job. But whatever.

He washes his hand across his face. "When you arrived, why didn't you start with that?"

"I wanted to see how things would play out without throwing my weight around. I have a training course to do,

302

lots of rules to memorise. But for this case, they made an exception."

"I can read between the lines. You refused the job the first time they asked and then took it so you could deal with this and save me."

I hum with amusement. What the eff. If only I were so altruistic. The angel exalts himself. *Save him.* As if.

No, this is pure revenge on my part. I notice the stubborn angel still doesn't say thank you. I shrug. Then wince as the burn on my chest stings.

Kleric reaches over and hands me the opened healing potion. *Thank you.* I tip the vial onto my sizzling skin. Instant relief. The burning sensation cools. Inwardly, I groan.

Gosh, I didn't realise how much pain I was masking until it was gone. Xander's sword is horrible.

"We are fortunate this is a demon problem, and we have a demon prince willing to monitor my work so that I wouldn't cause a massive incident. Anyway, that's the background and the crux of the situation. I wanted to let you know so we are not fighting over her. I will deal with this." I nod at the demon, and when I get no further objections, I turn my full attention onto her. "Now please shift back into your original form."

"But if I do, he will kill me," she says in a nasal voice caused by her crushed nose.

You idiot, I'll kill you. I rub my temple.

Or the angel will.

If she doesn't drop the identity of Xander's sister, I think any minute now he is going to rip off her head with his bare hands.

Her eyes are still streaming with tears. I don't know if it's from the broken nose or from getting caught. I don't really care.

I shoot a warning glance at Xander. The last thing I need is for him to react to what I'm going to say next. "I will make you a promise. If you change back without Prince Kleric forcing you, I will make you a promise not to kill you. You will live a long life. But you must turn back, and you must not lie about anything else going forward. I need the truth. Give me the truth, and I promise to keep you alive."

While she mulls that over, I glance back to check on Xander. "Will you help me with your lie-detection skills?"

The angel stiffly nods. I don't have to tell him that potentially hearing about his sister's death is going to be painful, but I hope he can keep it together long enough so we can find out the truth.

"Okay. So do we have a deal?" I ask her.

"You promise you won't kill me? Do you promise you won't allow anybody else to kill me?"

"I promise." With a worried twist of her lips, the air changes around her, and her form dissipates. It isn't fast like a shifter, and it's not effortless like Kleric's shape changes.

She's a low-level demon, Kleric explains in my head.

Ah, okay. So being a low-level demon, is it hard to change shape?

It should be impossible.

Her form shimmers back into existence with an almost gag-inducing, smack-you-in-the-face stench of sulphur. The blonde curly hair and the baby-blue eyes are gone, and in Robin's place is a pale, sickly grey demon.

304

She stands at least a foot shorter, and the clothing that she was wearing as Robin now hangs off her thin frame. She steps out of the ill-fitting shoes, dropping three more inches, and kicks the discarded shoes out of the way. She has sharp cheekbones, her now-healed nose is almost flat, and she has no hair and no eyebrows. Her black demon eyes are overly large, and her mouth is tiny. Interestingly, she has almost no neck, and her grey stick-thin arms are oddly long.

I clear my throat and rapidly blink. Her smell is making my eyes water. "Thank you for turning back. What is your name?" I rasp.

"Cynthia. I didn't kill anyone."

"Lie," Xander says in a dull tone.

She jumps and covers her mouth; her enormous eyes go impossibly wide.

I give her an incredulous stare.

"Okay, okay. I did, I did! But they killed Robin and the other angels." Her bony grey finger points to the dead demons on the floor.

I nod. Okay. "How did you get to Earth? How did you get past all our checks?"

"A portal. An illegal secret portal. We arrived here six months ago, just the three of us."

Ah. That's really bad. I puff out my cheeks, and I search the floor for the dented datapad. It must have got kicked in a corner during the fights. I retrieve it and pull up a map of the city.

"You came through a secret portal? Can you show me on this map where it is?"

She takes the datapad out of my hands and studies the map. She points at an area. "Here. It is here, on this street."

I mark the street and send the details to Ava and Story. I will have to hunt down anyone who has snuck in using that portal. For that, I'll need a gateway witch. A witch should be able to tell me how long the portal has been activated and deactivate it.

I will contact the Grand Creature Council with an urgent request for a witch, Story says in my head.

Thank you. I lower the datapad and turn my attention back to Cynthia. "Just the three of you?"

"Yes."

"And who planned everything?" Her finger snaps out, and she points at the male demon. I shake my head. "Use your words, Cynthia. Who planned everything?"

She swallows, stares at the two dead demons and then whispers, "I did."

"Who killed the three angels?"

"They did." She fidgets. "But it was all my idea. We have been here for six months, jumping bodies and making money with the illegal blood trade. Vampires have a lot of money." Her upper body moves as she nods, and a slimy grey tongue flicks out to wet her thin, puckered lips and the tip of her nose. "We specialised in children and rare species."

Xander steps forward, and Kleric, who at some point has moved to stand behind him, reaches over and squeezes his shoulder. The angel closes his eyes and, with a sigh that seems to rattle in his chest, he steps back.

Cynthia doesn't notice what is going on behind her and continues. "The angels came sniffing around the warehouse one day. We didn't go after them on purpose. They came to us. Angel blood goes for an extortionate amount of

306

money. It's so powerful, so rare. So we drained them." She shrugs.

"Why did you assume Robin's likeness?"

"At first, we wanted to make sure nothing led back to us at the warehouse. I used to do it all the time, take on someone's body, take them for a spin. It is fun. Draining their blood and bank accounts goes hand in hand." She smiles.

"I make sure the cameras see me out and about before I make them disappear. Just so nobody knows what happened to them, you know? I used the cinema that time with Robin. I like the building, and it has a powerful ward. For some reason, they keyed it to demons. So it makes a great safe house."

Huh. That might have been the reason I didn't get fried by the ward that night, because of Kleric's blood being in my system.

"So after the angels were dead. I walked in wearing Robin and left by the back door." She grins, flashing pointed black teeth. "I turned into a seagull and flew away. Then I went back to work."

"So draining the blood of kids, innocent creatures, and stealing their money. Got it." I'm getting a pounding headache, and with each word out of her mouth, I'm finding it harder and harder to stay neutral.

"Yes. Oh, we also harvest organs." She says this smugly, in the same tone as I'd say we make ice cream.

I swallow. I don't look at Kleric or Xander as she tells me oh so casually about her thriving business of exsanguination and organ procurement.

She shrugs. "No one was bothered. They were all expendable until Aspin took the wrong type of kids, and you started sniffing around." Her grey face scrunches up. "Killing the locals, riling them up, frightening them, and making it impossible to trade. We'd get one good contact, and you would kill them." She throws her long arms up. "And then we'd have to deal with another idiot. How can we work like that? It became time-consuming, and it was bad for business. So we dug up information about you, and we found him." She nods to Xander. Her grey bony finger scratches her ear. "I remembered the angels, and as he's their ambassador, it gave us the perfect weapon to get you out of the way. I sent him things to implicate you in Robin's disappearance."

"Ah, smart."

Cynthia preens and licks the earwax from her finger.

Ew.

The same digit then somehow disappears up her flat, squished grey nose. She has a good root around. "It worked like a charm. We sent the same things to your relative. She was very vocal about wanting to end you. The unicorn really wants you dead. You should have killed her." She licks the snot from her finger and adjusts her dress.

"When you got out of prison, I knew you wouldn't leave well enough alone, and you'd come sniffing around to the last place Robin was seen. I was right. But you didn't follow me straightaway. I led you to the unicorns, and you still didn't come, and for over five days I had to wait around. And when you did, you broke my elbow, swallowed what I told you about your evil grandmother, and then you brought me back to the ambassador. It worked. I was positive the unicorns had killed you. When I woke up from the null band, Xander made me dinner." She grins and I glare at her.

"Why aren't you dead? I handed you everything on a plate. But you didn't... You didn't take the bait. If you just did what we wanted you to do, the problem would have gone away. Our business was booming while you were in prison. It could be again."

They must have another location, another warehouse.

"Why are they here?" I nod at the two demons.

"Why should I take all the risks?" she whines. "I needed help. They had to take on the dead angel bodies to help me get under his skin." She points back at Xander. "He was so easy to manipulate the first time around. Everyone hates you, and no wonder. You dig your heels in deeper by coming back here with evidence, and you dare to bring the prince! We didn't know about Prince Kleric's interest in you." She eyes the kiss on my hand with a flicker of disgust.

Her black eyes go to Kleric, her tone cajoling. "We would have moved our operation down south if we did. I didn't know about the kiss until after she took me from the unicorns this afternoon." Her eyes snap back to mine. "When we fought, and I tried to drown you, you had gloves on. I did not know." She growls. "That's your fault. We had to point the blame for your death on the angel. It would have worked too. He would have killed you. The plan was perfect. Prince Kleric wouldn't have known if you had just come here alone. My logic was sound."

I feel so tired, and so sick.

Do you have questions? I ask Kleric. He tells me, and I relay them. "The demons, your accomplices, were they like you? Lower demons?"

"Yes."

"How do you change shape?"

She scowls and angrily flashes her shocking black teeth. "We use demon magic, a potion. I can share all the details."

Oh, she will share everything. Every victim, every person who has dared to buy from them. I will not rest until families have closure and revenge. Yeah, by the time I've finished, even taking willing blood vampires will need a contract because they will be so frightened of any mistake they make.

"Okay. Anything else that you want to add?"

Cynthia shakes her head.

"We will go into more detail later."

I lift my eyes to Xander. His honey eyes are full of anger, sorrow, and resentment. "She wasn't lying."

"Okay. Thank you."

"So are you letting me go now? Yes?"

"No."

"But you said you said I could go home. You promised," she whines.

I pull out some restraints and an anti-magic band. "I never said you could go home. I promised I wouldn't kill you. Cynthia, you are smarter than that, and when you wake up, we are going to have a lovely long chat." I give her an evil smirk, twist her away and grab hold of her wrist.

I have a massive urge to bag her hands so that any residual snot, spit, or earwax doesn't rub off on me. I avoid her fingers as best I can and slap the anti-magic band on her wrist. She slumps unconscious to the floor.

"But you are going to wish I did. Every day, every minute of your long, long, miserable life. You're going to wish that I had killed you this night. Once I have rung every single drop of information out of you. I have the perfect place for you to go."

I have the perfect white cell.

With no more preamble, I drag Cynthia off the floor, and with an unladylike grunt, I unceremoniously throw her over my shoulder. Kleric steps up to help, and with a smile, I wave him away. *I am good.* With Dexter licking his lips at the demon over my shoulder, we head towards the front door.

Xander clears his throat. "You fought valiantly, and even though we have had our differences, you risked your life to show me the truth."

What. A. Dickhead. My lip twitches with disgust.

You know that's not true, I say to Kleric.

I know.

I sigh as I remind myself to be nice. To be kind. The angel is grieving for his sister.

"You have really grown into a beautiful and strong woman, Tru," Xander says, following us out of the orangery and into the hall.

I grind my teeth. *He can stuff his words up his arse.* The angel is seven weeks and a prison stay too late. I pick up the pace to the front door.

"We are bonded, after all."

I stumble and turn so fast—oops; Cynthia's head bounces off the wall—I stare at the determined angel with exasperation.

Gorgeous honey eyes with their sprinkles of gold framed with thick, black lashes look into me like he is reading my soul. He smiles at me, and with the hallway light shining behind him, he looks like a golden god.

My eyes flick to the massive blue demon who stands watching me with his gentle, kind eyes. Kleric nods, opens the door, and steps into the rain.

Dexter runs out after him.

The demon kiss pulses on my hand.

I huff, turn and continue walking down the hall, and with a wave of my hand, I say, "Sorry, Xander. I'm way too busy. I have a prisoner to interrogate and a portal to close. Demons to hunt." I click my fingers. "Oh, and please forget about the silly adolescent bond. Kleric is my mate." I grin and step into the rain.

Xander's honey eyes narrow with utter confusion as the door slams closed in his face.

THE END

Dear Reader,

Thank you for taking a chance on my book. This is my fifth-ever book! Wow, I did it again. I hope you enjoyed it. If you did, and if you have time, I would be *very* grateful if you could write a review.

Every review makes a *huge* difference to an author—especially me as a brand-new shiny one—and your review might help other readers discover my book. I would appreciate it so much, and it might help me keep writing.

Thanks a million!

Oh, and there is a chance that I might even choose your review to feature in my marketing campaign. Could you imagine? So exciting!

Love,
Brogan x

P.S. DON'T FORGET! Sign up on my VIP email list! You will get early access to all sorts of goodies, including: signed copies, private giveaways, advance notice of future projects and free stuff! The link is on my website at **www.brogan-thomas.com** your email will be kept 100% private, and you can unsubscribe at any time, with zero spam.

P.P.S. I would love to hear from you, I try to respond to all messages, so don't hesitate to drop me a line at: brogan@ broganthomas.com

About the Author

Brogan lives in Ireland with her husband and their eleven furry children: five furry minions of darkness (aka the cats), four hellhounds (the dogs), and two traditional unicorns (fat, hairy Irish cobs).

In 2019 she decided to embrace her craziness by writing about the imaginary people that live in her head. Her first love is her husband and number-one favourite furry child Bob the cob, then reading. When not reading or writing, she can be found knee-deep in horse poo and fur while blissfully ignoring all adult responsibilities.

facebook.com/BroganThomasBooks

instagram.com/broganthomasbooks

goodreads.com/Brogan_Thomas

bookbub.com/authors/brogan-thomas

youtube.com/@broganthomasbooks

Also By
Brogan Thomas

Creatures of the Otherworld series

Cursed Wolf

Cursed Demon

Cursed Vampire

Cursed Witch

Rebel of the Otherworld series

Rebel Unicorn

Rebel Vampire

Printed in Great Britain
by Amazon

44165054R00189